What Readers Are Saying

"A dead body. A Mexican cartel. Organ trafficking. Ayahuasca. Gilly and his friends are on another adventure, with danger and romance on every page. *Crushing Cabo*, Larry Mollin's captivating sequel to *The Pool Guy's Kid*, is another story that's tough to put down."

—Ken Shickler

"Picking up where *The Pool Guy's Kid* left off, this young adult novel with Gilly Montrose and gang will get your attention on page one. From the complicated relationship with his father, Duke, to the close-knit group of friends searching for one of their own, *Crushing Cabo* brings suspense, love, and comradery to every page. Larry Mollin is the leading voice of a generation, and this book will delight readers of all ages."

—Pam Putney

"In *Crushing Cabo*, the second book in The Pool Guy's Kid Series, Larry Mollin again brings intrigue, danger, and passion to every turn, through the eyes of protagonist Gilly Montrose. And did I mention it's funny, too? Gilly and the gang will need all their wits and luck to survive this unplanned adventure in a foreign land to find their friend. *Crushing Cabo* is a compelling read from start to finish."

—Fran Irving

"Gilly Montrose and gang are in the midst of an adventure in *Crushing Cabo* that will test their friendship, loyalty, and resilience. In this sequel to *The Pool Guy's Kid*, Larry Mollin once again brings together a novel filled with mystery, romance, and suspense with Gilly Montrose and company."

—ANGELA CORSO

"Larry Mollin has done it again with *Crushing Cabo*—the second book in The Pool Guy's Kid Series. It's a most enjoyable ride up the whole Baja Peninsula. Filled with mystery, danger, and lots of young love from the very first page, this is a must read by the definitive voice of a generation."

—ERIC PARSONS

CRUSHING CABO

A Shadelandhouse Modern Press book
Crushing Cabo
a novel

Crushing Cabo is a work of fiction. Characters, incidents, names, and places are
used fictitiously or are products of the author's imagination. Any resemblance
to actual events, locales, organizations, or persons, living or dead, is entirely
coincidental. Any references to real places are used fictitiously. To the extent
any trademarks, service marks, product names, or named features are used
in this work of fiction, all are assumed to be the property of their respective
owners and are used only for reference. Use of these terms does not imply
endorsement.

Published in the United States of America by:
Shadelandhouse Modern Press, LLC
Lexington, Kentucky
smpbooks.com

First edition 2025

Shadelandhouse, Shadelandhouse Modern Press,
and the logo are trademarks of Shadelandhouse Modern Press, LLC.

ISBN: 978-1-945049-61-3 (paperback)
ISBN: 978-1-945049-62-0 (epub)
Library of Congress Control Number: pending

Cover and book design: iota books
Illustrations created using AI-assisted tools
Author photo: Jackson Mollin

LARRY MOLLIN

CRUSHING CABO

A NOVEL

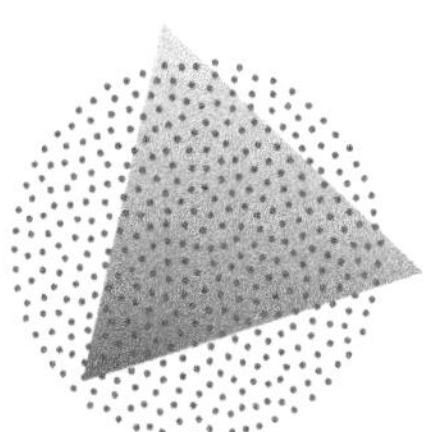

book two of

the pool guy's kid series

Shadelandhouse
MODERN PRESS

Lexington, Kentucky

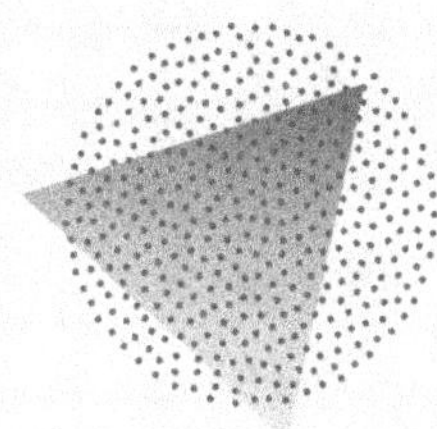

MARLENA

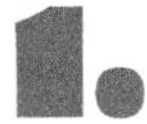

right Now

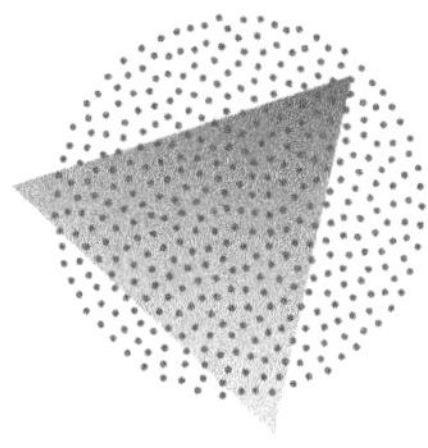

this is Not the way i eNvisioNed My first vacay iN
cabo. My father, the legendary Beverly Hills pool swab, Duke
Montrose, would go on ad nauseam about the wonders of Cabo
San Lucas, the jewel at the tip of Mexico's Baja Peninsula, the
sunnier playpen of sunny California. Dad's stories after he and
my mom split were invariably about out-of-body drunkfests and
free-spending divorcées on hotel lobby prowl, or rock stars and
models behaving badly on the beach. Credit Duke's obligatory
single-parent warning for me, his kid Gilly, to always do what he

says, never what he does. Good a reason as any why the hedonistic paradise's allure never moved the needle for me. My Chilean-born mother, to the day she died, would shake her head at the thought of the place. Not her style. Not a library in sight.

As a West LA homeboy, I knew that someday, perhaps when I had stupid money to blow, I'd get to experience it myself. Until then, Mexico for me was TJ—Tijuana—the border city with San Diego and a convenient place to still get a car reupholstered cheaply, buy cool knives and cooler fireworks. Cabo, it is not. Cabo is rarefied, its coastline lined with luxury resorts. Not that I'm luxuriating. It's long after midnight, and I'm hiding for my life in this moldy wooden closet in the cabin of an antique cabin cruiser that's been cruising north from the city's marina for a good hour.

If VJ, my best friend, hadn't failed to show at our much-anticipated reunion back in the U.S. of A., my old gf, Leticia—now *his* gf—wouldn't have rallied us to find him. By us, I mean the Beverly Hills Five, the high school kids who brought down the Jacuzzi murderers' crypto play. You know, me and Fern, Leticia, Aeura, and VJ. All of us but one returned a year later to Fern's father's estate outside Palm Springs to catch up as planned. VJ never made it. Leticia was worried and it was contagious. VJ's folks were unaware, off on a Scandinavian cruise, which made Leticia feel more pressure to locate him. She believed that VJ was lost somewhere in Baja after attending a yoga weekend in Todos Santos, a surfing town north of Cabo. He was due back a day before our get-together, and it wasn't like him to ghost us. VJ is wireless AF, an IT guy—a Japanese-American computer maven who found yoga to release the stress of coding at Stanford, where he's a sophomore. I want to make clear, his sudden disappearance isn't an excuse for me putting myself in danger. It's the Wounded Bird Syndrome I can't shake that's to blame. Yes, Marlena—sad, broken, beautiful bird—you know who you are. And I know where you are.

You're so close to the cabin's closet that I can whisper to you if I dare. Peeking through the crack in the louvered door, I can see one of the OG hard guys who dragged you down below, gagged your mouth, and tied you to the metal chair. His slick, black hair is streaked purple, and he sports a death's-head earring. He sits before you stone-faced, cleaning a nasty-looking pistol. I'm convinced that they don't know you were meeting someone here tonight or I wouldn't have had the time to hide. They would have at least searched the boat for me before it took off. I'm safe as long as I stay quiet. But where are they taking you?

An older, tattooed Mexican badass comes down the ladder from the deck, and the two talk in Spanish, while you, Marlena, squirm mutely trying to interrupt. I understand their every word. One is impatient and wants to get it over with it. The other cools him. You kick at your chair with your cowboy boots, frilled-edged short white shorts riding higher on your struggling, tanned thighs. As you garble a desperate plea, your flowing red ringlets shake in distress. The older of the two slaps your face, stifling you. I feel the sting. They're following orders, and the older one tells his cousin to trust El Chino (translation—The Chinaman). The tough guy yawns and heads up to the deck with a prolonged glance at you, Marlena.

What a waste.

He says that in English for you to hear and tremble. In my cramped space, I clench tighter, fighting the urge to charge out. Time may not be on my side, but it's all I have. I steady and wait.

It's impossible to avoid flashing back a few years to LA when I was holding up in a junked propane tank with hired killers on my tail. That worked out. This is worse. Way.

If my girlfriend, Fern, hadn't been so jealous of you, Marlena, I wouldn't be here by myself, with none of my friends knowing I ditched the comfort of Cabo's elite Palmilla Hotel. No one believed your obvious lies about VJ. Why did you tell me the truth? Gratitude for my challenging your abusive boyfriend? Guilt for luring VJ into God knows what? What? You were going to tell all tonight, Marlena. It can't be a coincidence that you're now in this predicament that I'm in, too, though the word *predicament* sounds too proper for the raw reality of the deep shit that threatens to smother us. Daddy Dukester would say, *Gilly, don't make the same mistake over and over like me.*

Too late. The boat powers onward, and its speed increases to full throttle. The inboard twin engines vibrate violently, screeching in angry protest. How did I end up here? Let me rewind.

2.

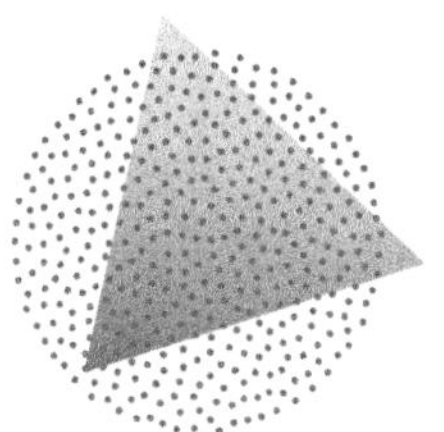

tHree days ago

-He's big-timing us?

--What happened, Leticia?

Leticia took the heat, repeating the same story about our friend's disappearance, as each of us stepped into the big Jacuzzi at Fern Fifer's father's mid-century estate in La Quinta, the uber-desert oasis southeast of Palm Springs. I'd arrived the night before, so Fern, my gf from the exalted Hills of Beverly, and I could have some time alone. We needed it. With me away, a sophomore at UC Riverside, and her doing a semester abroad in Paris, our relationship was suffering from more than distance. Fern said it needed raison d'être. I overreacted, made fun of her Parisian pretentiousness, and said things I shouldn't have. It ruined our night and most of the next day. We were both relieved when Leticia arrived and we could focus on someone besides ourselves.

Leticia looked like she hadn't slept for days but was still as naturally stunning as ever. We embraced upon welcome, and she kissed me. Yes, it lingered too long. At least that's what I imagined Fern thinking. Next, Aeura, our free-spirited Korean-American friend arrived alone. No accompanying Nigerian princess. Aeura was by herself and as content as I'd ever seen her. She was tanned and it suited her. The second I complimented her, I realized that Fern wouldn't take it well. Too late. Aeura and I have a special bond, and Fern knows it. I tried to keep our greeting warm and casual. I tried, but Aeura was so excited to see me, she pulled me in tight.

I learned to surf in Goa on the Indian Ocean, Gilly. I'm a goofy foot.
-Of course you are.

Fern, bless her heart, hugged her way into the embrace, and Leticia followed in a group grope. There was a lot of love between us all. We'd been through tough times together, and nothing could have felt better than to be with friends. Minus one. We couldn't ignore the elephant in the Jacuzzi.

Where's VJ? He RSVP'd the evite!
-With many happy emojis. That was last month.
--It's beyond rude. Do I take it personally?
---Fern, not everything is about Fern.

----There's no way VJ would let himself miss this.

Leticia filled Aeura in, just as she had with Fern and me. I didn't mind hearing the story again. VJ had finished a Kriya Yoga retreat in Todos Santos and had a few days to explore before his plane back to LA from Cabo. Leticia repeated their last phone call. He'd run into someone he knew from hiking Joshua Tree last fall. A Marlena something, of Marlena and Beau, a couple who lived in a 1950s trailer in the Yucca Valley. Marlena was a travel nurse. Beau, older, was a local, a bartender/bouncer in a Pioneertown saloon, a hipster watering hole near Joshua Tree. Aeura and Fern had never heard of Pioneertown. I'd been there. It's an off-the-grid, vintage Western movie set town, complete with the best little music venue in rock and roll, Pappy & Harriet's.

Duke has a prized P & H sweatshirt signed by Keith Richards from when he jammed there.

-How's Duke?

Aeura, thanks for asking. Answer—as usual, beyond help.

It really was true. My dad was going through some tough medical issues. His liver was failing. Fern knew, but the others didn't need to. Not now. I steered us back to VJ. Usually, Leticia would keep us on point, but she was clearly not herself. She second-guessed her best guess that VJ might be staying with this Marlena outside Cabo.

Might be?

-VJ said she invited him. To a ceremony, ayahuasca, you know.

--What!? VJ? Mind-expanding woo-woo? Mr. Digital Data, our VR-gaming wonder boy?

-I pushed him to become more spiritual. I was concerned with his wellness.

Leticia had recommended that he try Kriya. It's known to work for the mind and soul, not just the body. After some crushing LA Rams losses, I'd FaceTimed with VJ and he'd gone on and on about this particular yoga discipline. I'd never heard him talk about tripping.

VJ did tell me he wanted to understand himself more.

-Nothing weird in that. That's why I travel.

--That's why I have a therapist.

--VJ loved doing this yoga camp. Experienced people, healers. I encouraged him to go. I booked the flights. He never got on the one home.

Aeura and Fern held on to Leticia with unconditional support.

It was working for him.

-Not your fault he's missing.

--Or is he?

I had to bring up the fact that he could be purposefully staying away. Maybe working off the effects of the experience. I'd never had ayahuasca or any mind-altering drugs, but I'd seen other kids on mushroom trips, good and bad, and the often bizarre aftermaths. Leticia was adamant.

What's the diff?! He needs our help. We have to find him.

And then there was VJ's last cryptic communication to his lady love. Leticia showed us the text message. It had no words, only a yellow biohazard emoji and a ha-ha face.

That was three days ago.

3.

right NOW

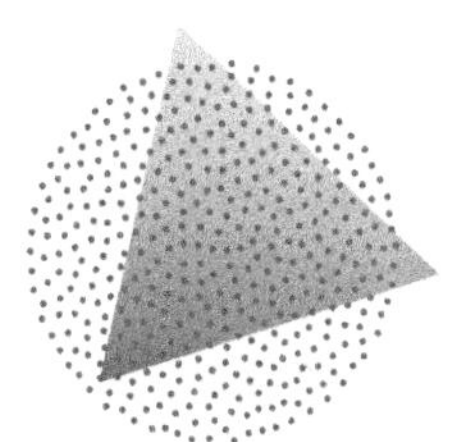

I can feel it rocking at the mercy of the waves. We're still in open water, and that's not a good thought. From the deck, I hear the older man yell in Spanish to the younger. *Drop the anchor.* Staring through the crack in the cabin's closet door, I see Marlena's young, purple-haired guard make for the ladder to the deck. The engines shut down, and it's quiet enough to hear the activity above. The boat steadies, anchored. Vintage hydraulics whir. A launch lowers, creaking into position. I take my chance. Out of the closet, I can smell the fear from Marlena. She turns and sees me as I free her gagged mouth. Her parched, bruised lips mouth my name.

Gilly! Hurry!

I do not need the reminder. I work the fat, blue knot of synthetic marine rope that binds her hands behind her back. My fingers are numb from hiding and can't work as nimbly as I want them to. A drop of sweat from my forehead makes the line slippery. I feel her frustration and double down. It loosens. Her hands wiggle out, joining mine now in attacking the ties on her feet. We work as one, with *alacrity*—one of the Duke's favorite big words, often used with *f-ing*, to add to the urgency. The stinging smell of gasoline being splashed on to the deck above us clarifies their intention.

Marlena is to die. Panicked, the hippie nurse who lured VJ into who knows what bolts for the ladder. I hold her back and keep her below. We cannot let them see us. She shrinks into my chest, my heart pounding more than hers. She's older than me and has a beauty that glows. She's grateful and surprises me with a kiss of thanks. I pull out of it to listen. Their rubber dinghy hits the water. Its small engine catches and revs. They're moving away.

Go!

We race up the ladder with f-ing alacrity. A gunshot cracks! We hit the deck. The red glow of a flare gun's charge lights up the boat in a sickening hue. The gasoline-soaked deck ignites with a frightening whoosh in the strong ocean breeze. It's an inferno around us, with only one way out—up! I grab Marlena's hand and pull her atop the canopy roof over the deck. There's fire all around us and no time to hesitate. We have to jump. Shaking, undone, Marlena beats on my chest. The flames—howling white heat—are on us.

I can't—

-What?

I can't swim.

I push her off anyway and leap into the dark Pacific.

4.

two days ago, morning

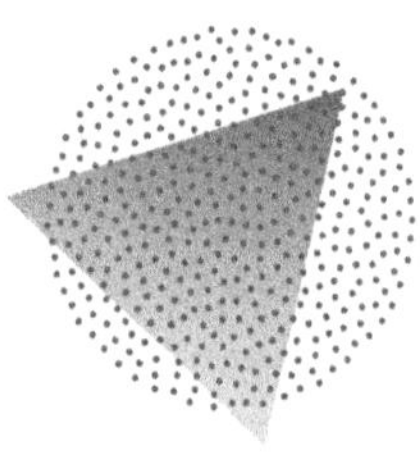

to Leticia's chagrin, i totally missed the turnoff to pioneertown and we ended up on the twenty-nine palms highway in joshua tree, ten miles east, twenty minutes later. That was fine with Aeura, who wanted to at least drive through the famous state park since we were already there. Fern, riding shotgun next to me, still half asleep on the early morning road trip, didn't have an opinion. We were four, in my very used Toyota SUV, a gift from dear Dad for my graduation. Leticia was not having it.

Turn around and go back. Use the damn GPS! We're wasting time.

-Leticia. Take a moment. Let's at least drive through the park. I've never been. It's amazing.

I had to agree with Aeura.

--Feast your eyes. California dreaming.

Duke had me out here camping as a kid, and the magic always returns. The red and yellow mystic rock formations and mysterious cacti reaching for the sky were the headliners of the Joshua Tree landscape show. I slowed the car to sightseeing cruise speed, and it was all awesomeness around us. We'd spent the night at Fern's dad's place, resolved to head into the high desert's Yucca Valley in hopes of getting a lead on Marlena from this Beau in Pioneertown. Leticia was convinced that it was our best and quickest route to get more information on VJ's whereabouts. Aeura wanted to keep driving ahead.

And, like Gilly said, maybe you're overreacting. VJ may not want to be found.

-Aeura! I never said Leticia was overreacting.

I could feel daggers from Leticia, embarrassed eyes from Aeura. I really missed having VJ along to help me navigate these moments with three amazing—though sometimes strong-minded—women, each of whom at various times I'd had a thing for. It was très awkward, especially since Fern and I were not on solid ground. The fact that Aeura was once again solo and available to me only made it worse.

Leticia's right. Turn around, Gilly. Now!

And there you have it, boys. Failure to launch. I turned around.

***

Pioneertown lays at the top of Pioneertown Road, an eleven-mile, two-lane stretch of curving mountain blacktop. One way in and one way out, it winds uphill through crazy colorful rocks as spectacular as the ones in Joshua Tree. It's an exhilarating stairway to heaven, despite the occasional roadside marker to commemorate a traffic fatality. It was as clear a day as you're going to get, and no one in the car spoke a word. There was hushed silence for which I was relieved.

The final approach into the little Western town is unpaved and dusty. Rows of old-timey, nineteenth-century storefronts line two streets. Blacksmith shop, telegraph office, undertaker's, sheriff—it was designed for the camera. Other than two Wild-West–themed vintage saloons, Pappy & Harriet's music hall, and a period motel, it's mostly two-sided facades, flats built for the filming of 1940s B-movie Westerns. As an industry worksite, it died out when the Westerns did and went all to shit, or so Duke tells it. Sometime, twenty years back, it was resurrected by artists and outcasts looking for cheap, remote housing and freedom away from the established binds of civilization. Creativity ruled and the word spread. What was secret and a sanctuary slowly slipped away and took on a more commercial life. Pioneertown became what it is today—a mountaintop, seven-day-a-week business. It's a destination location, an endless artisan flea market of hippie offerings and kitsch, with food, drink, and psychedelic drugs that cater to the Joshua Tree hipsters and tourists who want something different, something wilder.

Pioneertown buzzes with those in the know. The saloons are the real deal, with swinging doors and Mexican food as authentic as the tequila-soaked floors. Music playing over the speakers is always biker bar rock, and there's dancing and hooting it up from early morning to early morning.

We parked in the gravel lot and headed for the Red Dog first.

We should definitely order up some lunch here. Believe me, VJ would approve.

-Gilly! Let me talk to the bartender first.

Of course.

Leticia bellied up to the bar with Fern right behind her for support. It was almost noon and already raucous. The bartender was a woman with that weathered desert rat look, bandana around her head and a neck tattoo of scorpions mating. As I watched, Leticia put on her most persuasive smile and got right to it in a loud, clear voice. Channeling her Canadian cousin, she first apologized.

I'm sorry. Is Beau around?

-ID please.

What?

-Are you twenty-one?

No, pardon me. I'm not asking for a drink. Beau? Is he—

-No Beau here.

The barkeep looked left, looked right to prove her point and then moved on to another customer. Not one to be bullied, Leticia stayed in place. She wasn't giving up. Neither was I. Off I went and joined the food line to order. Don't think I was slacking on my buddy. Before driving us up here, I spent the early morning hours calling every hospital in the Cabo San Lucas area. My Spanish is solid, and so were the answers—*no patient like VJ.* Same with the police stations. I spoke to every one of them, including an officer in Todos Santos who said what I was thinking.

Tal vez se enamoró.

Maybe he fell in love? I mean, he was tripping. Could VJ have met someone and connected with them, you know, spontaneously, randomly, madly? People do. My 'rents did. It doesn't mean the relationship's going to last—only that you become obsessed with each other, so nothing else matters. Temporary insanity, lust, love, that's how Duke once explained it to me. Leticia was also wondering this about VJ. I knew one thing. If we seriously thought he was in trouble, we were going to have to get our asses down to Cabo to see for ourselves. That kind of road trip required air miles or real money. Next in line to order, I watched Aeura across the room shimmying her way through the rollicking dancers. Not a care in the world. I put in for three brisket tacos, two mushroom asada ones, nachos, and two large Diet Cokes we could share.

Working the food pickup area was a ratty local kid who had to be a tweaker. He offered me a choice of weed, speed, or psilocybin pills. While considering/not considering a buy, I gave it a shot.

So you know the bartender Beau, right?

-Duh.

Ya, I'll take a sativa pre-roll. Is Beau working here today?

-Uh, maybe.

With that, he cackled at some joke only he understood and flashed his meth-eroded teeth. I paid ten bucks for my pre-roll and was feeling that I'd earned the right to ask him about Marlena, when Aeura joined and pulled me away to whisper.

Marlena Raskin, travel nurse and Healer, with a capital H.

-Sounds right. Who told you?

No one. She posted a business card on the lobby bulletin board, with her WhatsApp number and a thumbnail pic. She's hot.

Aeura showed me Marlena's business card. She was a red-headed vision in the hippie mode. I could tell Aeura, who played for both teams, was attracted. Was VJ? Aeura and I held that thought between us.

Ready to show Leticia?

-Definitely. Right after you get our food.

There's always something about Aeura that I love. Fern is right to be jealous.

right Now

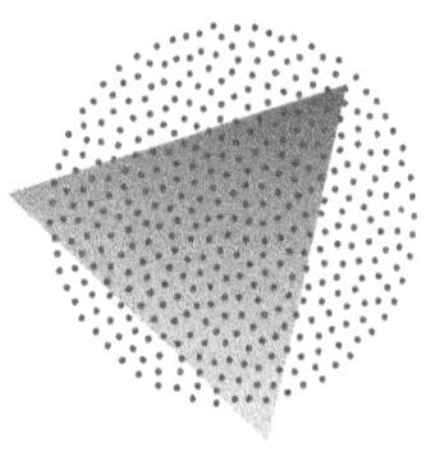

Hitting the water, i can feel the ocean's salty smack. It's warmer than I expected, and I'm thankful. I stop my descent and pinwheel my feet into reverse. My arms are strong and attack the water, pushing it below in healthy heaps, propelling me upward. The water is too dark to see anything of Marlena. I break the surface as the boat explodes in a freaking fireball of murderous intent. Flaming debris showers down, lighting up the night like the Fourth of July in Marina del Rey. I must submerge again to dodge it, my ears ringing with echoes of the blast.

Holding my breath, I feel Marlena thrashing nearby and go for her. Her right arm flails with desperation and strikes against my forehead. We're close, face to face. Her eyes are luminous, green, and alluring, filling with hope. I grab her beneath the armpits and bring her up, our heads bobbing above the waterline.

The acrid air of destruction surrounds us. She convulses with new breath as a wake wave from the explosion crashes down on us. I grab at a section of smoking teak deck flooring that's floating by and shove it under Marlena's thin frame. Buoyancy takes over. She steadies, bobbing above the water, her life force rising. She nods, and I hold on to the wood spar to catch a breath. With a moment to think, I'm convinced that the boat had to have been anchored close to shore. The men fled in a dinghy—a rubber launch not meant for distance. In this moonless, cloudy night, there's still one problem. Not meaning to, I say it out loud.

I don't know which way is land.

Marlena answers, her voice like honey.

Whichever way you choose will be right.

Corny as that sounds, it bolsters me. Her Healer career, capital H, may be for real. Is this what VJ saw in her? Without hesitation, I go with my gut. I'm not a surfer like Duke. Never got stoked, to his disappointment, but I'm a good swimmer and put in my hours in the raging blue off Venice Beach, watching Duke rip. I follow the sound of breakers in the stillness and set our course. Adding some kick to it, pulling Marlena along, I start us off at a measured pace. It's as good a time as any to ask.

What were you going to tell me about VJ?

-There's still time.

For what?

-To save your friend's life.

The roar of the sea drowns out the impact of her words. I see what I fear.

Marlena, hold your breath!

Before she can react, it hits. A rolling, rogue, mother of an angry swell overwhelms us, plunging Marlena and me deep into the liquid abyss. We tumble out of control underwater, trapped in an infernal washing machine of doom.

6.

two days ago, morning

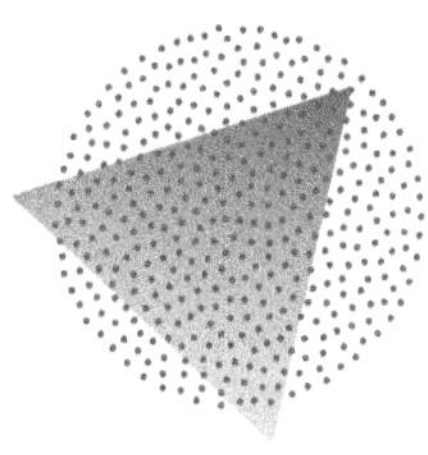

Leticia relaxed and savored the red dog's tacos with approval. Fern, too, was over the moon about the mushroom one. Passing the Diet Cokes among us, we all agreed on the food. The touch of Tex-Mex added to the flavor of the outlaw-themed saloon. Leticia and Fern had joined Aeura and me, empty-handed, at a table to the side of the dance floor. They had nothing on Beau that I didn't already know. We let Aeura's big score percolate but only for a few bites. Leticia's torment was too real.

What do we do now? I'm out of ideas, guys.

-Aeura?

--Well, we could call Marlena.

Aeura tossed that out as nonchalantly as she could. Leticia and Fern's reaction was priceless. Both went from incredulous to OMG in a heartbeat. Aeura glowed and showed off Marlena's business card. Leticia and Fern's whoops were hardly registered above the whooping it up of the Red Dog crowd. Leticia gave Aeura a big hug. Fern kissed me, for real. I held her close, surprised by her sudden affection. She nibbled my ear.

I don't want to fight.

-Me neither. Or feel jealous.

I kissed her back. I knew what a treasure I had in Fern. I have to be more careful around Aeura. Leticia stood and swayed to the rhythm of the music—her inner debate club captain returned.

Aeura, give me her WhatsApp number. I'll make the call.

-Maybe Gilly should. A guy—not competition—you know?

No I don't.

--Did you see her picture? VJ may—

Got it! OK. OK.

I finished a taco, with Fern's help, wiped off the crumbs on my face, put the phone on speaker, and hit up the internet video mobile number for Marlena Raskin, Travel Nurse and Healer. With my iPhone propped up on a Diet Coke cup, we huddled close. I really didn't think anyone would answer. It didn't have to ring for long.

Hello from sunny Todos Santos. I'm an RN available to provide services.

And there she was on a video call, in the middle of our table, in the middle of the Red Dog Saloon, in the middle of Pioneertown. Marlena, red-haired earth mother goddess, accessible to all for hire. She smiled and I smiled back. I could feel the pull. She was an enchantress, for sure.

Hi, Marlena. This is Gilly Montrose from West LA. How are you doing today?

-Fine, busy. What's this about?

Leticia couldn't help herself. She jumped into the call, moving me over.

We're looking for a missing friend, VJ. I believe you know him.

-VJ?

Asian American, 19, good-looking, ayahuasca seeker?

Marlena wasn't smiling anymore. She took a pause to pretend to try and recall the name. It was painful to watch. She wasn't good at deception.

Doesn't ring a bell, sorry. You have the wrong Marlena, perhaps.

-Marlena!

Beau?!

We turned and, behind my shoulder, eavesdropping, was Beau, her significant other. The off-duty bartender with long hair, a rough beard, and a prickly attitude hijacked our call and took my phone, going off on Marlena.

We need to talk, M! Seriously. And you need to not talk.

-We are done, Beau. D-O-N-E!

Irked, Beau's bushy eyebrows furrowed tight into an angry V.

You bitch!

-You soulless excuse for a human being!

You don't know what you're getting into, you dumb twat!

--Oh, OK, mister. That's rude. Please make your own call.

I tried to be polite and snatched my phone away, with Marlena still cursing at him on the screen. That didn't go over well with the snarling Beau. He came at me hard. With a push to my chest, I went flying backward into a dancing patron—a neatly bearded, unhappy hipster, as I remember, looking up while upside down. Before I could gather up the phone from the floor and get to my feet, Aeura coiled and launched herself at Beau to push him in the chest. It might as well have been a brick wall. All it did was make him grunt and shove Aeura back into the table with Leticia and Fern and what was left of our lunch. Fern grabbed a jumbo Diet Coke cup before it tipped over and tossed the carbonated pop right at the enraged Beau, splashing it over his pressed white T-shirt.

Not to be outdone, Leticia grabbed the Sriracha sauce dispenser, aimed, and hard-squeezed a stream of the hot sauce at Beau's eyes. Bull's-eye. He screamed in pain and charged. A guy the size of a refrigerator, wearing a Raiders jacket, tried to cool things. A wild swing from Beau missed the peacemaker and hit his wife square in the jaw. That tore it. Chaos followed and, with it, what will be remembered fs as the best bar fight in Pioneertown all year.

I grabbed my three angels. With commotion raging, we snaked our way out the swinging doors. I couldn't believe that the WhatsApp call was still active.

Hello? Marlena?

-I'm here. Thanks for standing up to him, Gilly.

Right. What about VJ!?

-Who?

--You know who. I'm his girlfriend. Did he forget to mention me?

I'd seen this aggressive side of Leticia before. She was a competitor and wasn't giving an inch. Marlena was more passive-aggressive. She canceled the call. My phone went back to my lock screen photo of me and Fern kissing at the Grand Canyon. My Beverly Hills gf cooed.

I love that photo.

-Focus, Fern. Marlena's lying. VJ's with her.

--Leticia, that's a guess. We don't know that.

-Yes, Gilly, so I'm going to Cabo to find out. Who's going with me?

---How are we going to all get there? It'll cost a fortune.

I have an idea, peeps.

And Fern did. She also had a father back in Beverly Hills with a private jet.

7.

right Now

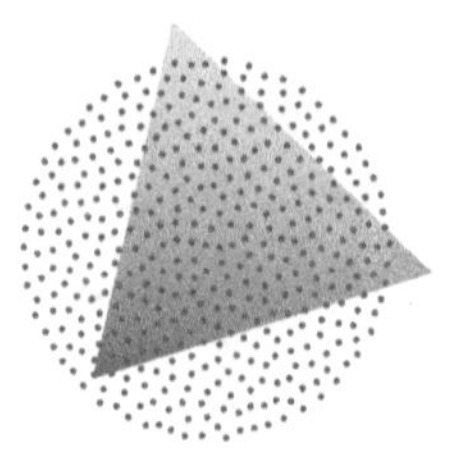

the sun cracks the horizon. I can feel it on my eyelids. Salt blinds my eyes, and I must strain to open them. The sea is finally calm, and the dawn's early light reaffirms what I've sensed for a few hours. We're out much farther in open water, farther away from the shore. I'm too weak to correct my mistake. After we survived the damn wave, I must have gotten disoriented and, in the blackness, headed us the wrong way, out to sea. I'm sick with the thought. A waterman like Duke wouldn't understand such a blunder and would be all over me. I'd take that heat gladly now.

My lips are too dry to part. My spirit too low to beat myself up. When I change position on the small wooden spar that buoys us, my muscles cramp. I try to curse and nothing comes out. Marlena is lying, stomach flat, on this wooden shard of what's left of a boat explosion in which she was supposed to die. I hear a labored gasp and know she's alive. Parched, our thirst will only get more intense, more maddening with the rising sun. So much pain to look forward to in this endless ocean drift. Marlena stirs. I want to apologize, but the effort seems too great. She feels me and utters first.

Thank you.

-No. No, we're lost. Done.

She shakes her head, not accepting the reality of my fatal mistake. She actually smiles. I'm forgiven but feel no solace. I'm nineteen years old and this is it. This is all. Oh, me of little faith.

A horn blast vibrates through my body with a clarion affirmation of life. I see a fishing boat nearing. It cuts through the morning mist, gleaming like a ship of shining armor. How could Marlena have known? With a hand steadied on the spar, I stretch up my body and wave to the boat.

Ayudar! Help!

They blow their horn twice. Heavenly music to our waterlogged ears. The happiest lyrics reverberate in my brain. They're from a rousing old gospel song that Duke would blast on the truck stereo at the end of our Friday jobs. We'd thump palms on the dashboard to the beat, singing along and singing loud.

Saved! We are saved! Glory hallelujah, Kingdom come! We are saved!

8.

two days ago, Late afternoon

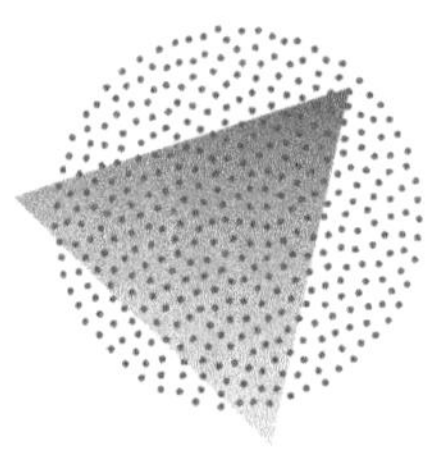

VJ AND AYAHUASCA? *What am i missing?*

-Maybe a girl.

Oh boy! He's in trouble.

The first thing I did when we drove back to Los Angeles from the Yucca Valley was find the Duke. I was happy I could help him finish a modern, water–feature–loaded pool, high up in the Trousdale Estates. The winter sun was setting over the coast and, from our vantage point in the 90210, you could see the properties below, each with its pool sparkling in the last light of day. This was

Duke's turf—a surefire trigger for him to tell endless celebrity pool stories, but not today, not with his body betraying him. It was hard watching Dad hunched over, compensating, adjusting, pretending. He was in pain and didn't want me to see it. His liver disease had progressed, according to the email I got from Abby Jo. He held a hand up to stifle any comment from me about his condition. I respected that, and we carried the gear back to the truck in silence till he shared a general observation of the geography.

Take away the surfers, and Todos Santos is all seekers, fakers, and thieves. Abby Jo knows.

***

Abby Jo, my dad's old girlfriend, was his current housemate. The chain-smoking, gray-Afroed, unemployable investigative journalist was there to greet us. I was back in the Bentley Street apartment in the shadow of the 405. Home sweet home, West LA. I'm sure that when Duke invited Abby Jo to move in with him after I went off to college, she didn't think he meant to be his caretaker. But that was what she was, and she never complained. She had a colorful vegetarian dinner ready, low in phosphorus and calcium, she pointed out. She was doing her best to keep him alive, and I know he loved her for that. I told them that Fern, Aeura, Leticia, and I were flying down to Cabo in the morning on a Fifer Lear jet to track down VJ—last known whereabouts, Todos Santos. Abby Jo took a few moments, trying to swallow a medley of carrots, and then expounded.

I had a friend of a friend who went for a yoga retreat and came back with a boob job and two husbands. It's wild.

Abby Jo hadn't been to Todos Santos since she took part in a naked bicycle ride to celebrate the millennium.

It was very liberating, though, as uncomfortable as it sounds.

She figured the hippie wellness culture had expanded. After yoga retreats and quack surgery centers, ayahuasca tourism seemed a natural. Dad hadn't said much during the meal, eating peacefully, exhausted. When he did speak, he let out more than he intended.

I read on Reddit, Mexico's a hub for organ trafficking.

Duke took my hand and, half in jest, told me that if I happen to see an O negative liver lying around, he could use it. He's near the bottom of the Medicaid list for organ recipients. It was a sobering reality for Duke. He and Abby Jo vented in outraged harmony.

Was it because of my DUI or that tax evasion mess? No. It was because of my unresolved federal marijuana bust at a Bill for President rally in 1992!

-Bureaucratic pigs! Luckily, people are dying all the time.

But only 13 percent of all people have my blood type, Gilly. I'm special.

-It's going to happen, honey! I'm writing scorching emails. They can't take the heat or the hate.

Clinton was cool, but not for stoners.

I love my dad.

***

Leticia had brought Aeura back to her place in Westwood to spend the night. Her mom, a UCLA professor and micromanager, was beside herself that Leticia was going to Cabo just like that.

Aeura provided good support, bolstering the strong defense that Leticia presented. It had been four days since anyone had heard from VJ. His own folks had no clue what was going on. In the only communication that Leticia had with them during their fjord tour in Norway, they'd asked her to pick VJ up at the airport.

As if he was on the plane. He's nowhere. Or somewhere and he's doing it again.

-What? Doing what?

This tidbit caught Aeura off guard. She stepped back, eyes on her friend, as interested as Leticia's mom in hearing an explanation. Leticia took a swig of red wine and sighed.

Last summer, he cheated on me with his lab partner.

-Ooo...

He confessed. I forgave him.

--That was a mistake. VJ's officially dead to me.

A loser at the relationship game herself, Leticia's mom cracked with unbridled bitterness. Aeura doubled down supporting her friend.

Doesn't matter if he did or did not. He blew off our reunion, and that's not like VJ. Something's wrong, and it started in Todos Santos.

-I thought you were going to Cabo. Where's Todos Santos?

Leticia was prepared, as always, and schooled her mom with an AI capsule she'd downloaded. She hit play.

"Todos Santos, seventy-five miles north of Cabo San Lucas, was founded as a mission in 1723 and eventually became known for sugarcane production. Over the decades, the dusty dirt roads that led to this town on the Pacific attracted bohemians and backpackers, artists, and wellness lovers."

That's what drew VJ. Then this Marlena witch...

Leticia couldn't speak. She lost it, quaking with emotion. Her mother rose from the table with disgust and bused the dishes, trolling.

He's not worth it. And you should know better!

On her way to the kitchen, Leticia's mom didn't have to look back to know that her daughter threw her a middle finger. Aeura, who had no winner for a mom either, gave Leticia comfort and understanding that was genuine and appreciated. Leticia had only known the globe-trotting Korean American for just over a year, but they'd been through hell together, helping to solve the murders of Aeura's father and stepmother. She knew that Aeura Kim was a beacon of resiliency. Leticia had only lost a boyfriend.

I just thought VJ and I had something special.

-Boys at nineteen don't get fidelity. Of course, girls aren't much better.

Oh? What happened to your Nigerian princess?

-She pulled a VJ! Stop!

That had Leticia laughing through her tears. She kissed Aeura's cheek in gratitude.

I'm lucky to have real friends like you, Gilly, and Fern.

-We're lucky to have you, and so is VJ. Fern said to bring a valid passport and pack light.

Yeah, so there's more room for her luggage.

True dat!

***

In the magnificent flats of Beverly Hills, behind the sturdy walls of Fifer, three pieces of matching Louis Vuitton luggage were already placed by the front door in anticipation of the 7 a.m. pickup. In the Ashe/Leandro designed dining room, Fern sat finishing a Door-Dash-delivered dinner with her live-in therapist, the octogenarian Dr. Guttenberg. He'd been giving some possible scenarios to explain VJ's disappearance. Notwithstanding accidents or being a victim of foul play, the psychiatrist felt that the ayahuasca journey could cause profound change. Guttenberg cautioned Fern not to indulge in any psychedelics there.

You don't know what they're giving you. VJ may have had a bad reaction.

-Why wouldn't Marlena have just said that?

There could be many reasons. Will you be in danger, Fern?

Like a local, Fern gobbled up the rest of her massive Nate'n Al's pastrami sandwich, rye crust and all. The thought of danger hadn't crossed her mind, and she really needed to talk to me.

Please tell my father, we'll be at the Palmilla. I'll be by the pool. I don't expect to budge far.

-You think VJ is with this Marlena?

Leticia does, Gilly does, Aeura does. It won't take a team effort to find that out.

-Then enjoy. I'll explain to your father why you needed a mental health break. And a plane!

Since he's sailing off St. Bart's with a woman half his age, I'm sure it won't even register.

Her phone chimed. It was me. We were in sync. Fern took the call in the pantry.

Sleep here tonight, Gilly. Come around the back.

-I thought you'd never ask.

Did you try to call Marlena again?

-Over and over, like a Russian hot bot. She won't answer.

Leticia's going to be crushed if he's with her.

I didn't expand on that. I believe in aiming high, and Marlena qualified. She was maybe five years older, so there was that. The good and the bad of an older woman. VJ was always a player with the ladies before being in a committed relationship with Leticia. As much as I'd once obsessed on Leticia in high school, I knew that the debate club beauty's need for control at times could get old. VJ was down in Mexico to experiment, experience, push the boundaries to know himself better. Marlena felt like someone rare that, given the chance, you'd want to be with. A teacher, a fantasy, a Healer, with a capital H. *Oh, those green eyes.* I made it a point not to mention those eyes to Fern. The last thought I had before I slipped out of Duke's apartment was that if VJ was with Marlena, at least he was alive. Because another solid reason for ghosting us was that VJ was already dead. When my phone's ringtone sounded with the piano coda of Eric Clapton's "Layla" (blame Duke for my classic taste in music), I assumed it was Fern wondering why I was taking so long. I was wrong. It was Marlena asking for my help.

I listened as I drove to Fern's. In a bit of a bind, Marlena didn't have much time to explain. I detected a bit of an English accent as her stress level rose. She had information to trade.

Do you do Venmo, Gilly?

-Maybe. How much?

Can you do a grand?

-Uh, no. Maybe my girlfriend can.

You have a girlfriend, too.

-So you do know VJ. Is he OK?

Angel, he's fine. Get the money. Call me right back at this number.

That was the idea. Posthaste, I talked a dubious Fern into staking the $1,000 Venmo to Marlena for a VJ update. It was a wasted effort. Marlena flaked and didn't answer the return call, no matter how many times I tried. After that, it went sour between Fern and me. She lit me up and I didn't take it well. We shared her bed and not much more. Back to back, I couldn't fall asleep. After an eternity, I whispered.

Are you sleeping?

-No.

Are you thinking what I'm thinking?

-Make-up sex?

Yes!

-No. Not thinking that.

I was bummed, resigned to be alone with the terror of my battered feelings till Fern's body shook with laughter. She turned to me, arms pulling me closer than close.

Gotcha!

Afterward, we shuttled off to dreamland, sailing as one love, deep into the wee hours before dawn.

9.

right now

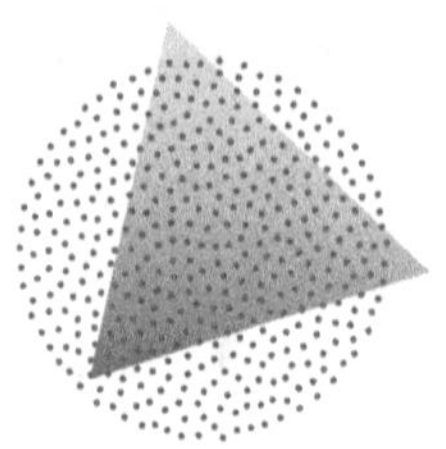

the crew of the fishing trawler *Magdalena ii out of el pescadores*, a village south of La Paz, is headed for the Cabo San Lucas marina with a hold filled to capacity with grouper, yellow fin, and sea bass. A good mood abounds as we chug south. They're happy to help Marlena and me and have made us more than comfortable with wool blankets, rice and beans, and strong black coffee. We're grateful for these local fishermen, and it doesn't hurt that Marlena has made them all smile a little brighter. Fortune is with them on the trip. The conversation we overhear is only about spending their bonuses back home when they get paid. Warming in the morning sun on the open deck by the wheelhouse, our backs are against giant coils of netting, Marlena looks at me with her green eyes.

I should be dead.

-Twice.

I need to stay dead.

I question this. It seems to me that the first thing to do when we get on dry land is notify the police. Marlena finds this comical and makes me feel like a clueless ten-year-old.

They own the police.

-Who?

I ask, though I guess it. Mexican gangsters? Of course. The mainland Mexico City cartel stretching its influence into "BCS," as Marlena calls it. Baja California South. It's a thing.

It's not just Cabo. They're into everything in Todos Santos. I mean, everything.

-And what does this have to do with VJ missing?

Before she can reply, a crew member interrupts to take our plates and empty cups. It seems to take forever for him to move away and for her to answer. When she does, she asks me to understand that she didn't know what they were doing with the information.

I was an intake nurse part time at the ayahuasca camp and did VJ's physical. It got flagged.

-For what?

Blood type. He's being prepped for organ removal surgery Sunday— tomorrow.

I didn't see that coming. Holy shit. Marlena is telling the truth, which is why they want to kill her.

And what now? If we can't go to the police, where can we go? Who helps us help VJ? I'm having the same uncomfortable feelings I'd had two years before—nearly to the day. The slender thread of mortality dangling in my gut, the urgent call to uncertain action. That experience in Los Angeles has marked me and my friends, *mi compañeros de armas*. I think of Fern, Letica, and Aeura waking up this morning in the sweet luxury of their Palmilla Hotel suite, with no idea what they're getting into—only that they're mad at VJ and angry with me for trusting you, Marlena. Like VJ trusted you. I have a million questions before we dock, and you have nothing else to do but answer.

10.

Yesterday

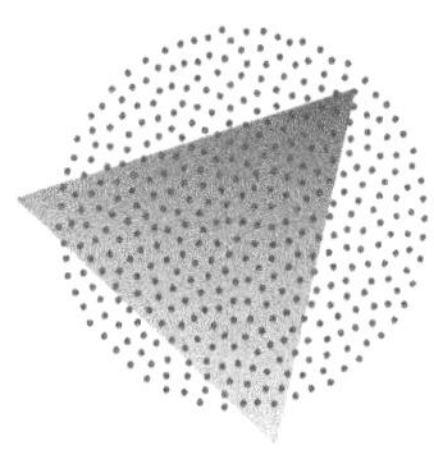

 Fern woke
up at the first sound of her vintage Hello Kitty bedside alarm
clock. I didn't move till she shook me hard, out of a dream that
was filled with suck. Lost somewhere, I can't get to school to
take a final exam for a class I barely attended. Struggling to
move, it's like I'm walking through mud. You know the dream.
So lame. And there was Marlena, slogging along with me,
encouraging me.

WTF!? I was exhausted trying to figure out the Marlena call and then the no call. She'd seemed desperate. She needed help, our help. Fern didn't want to hear it—she'd moved on. She'd come to an obvious conclusion. To her, Marlena was a hippie con grifter, and VJ was shacked up with her, boffing his brains out.

I mean, she said VJ was fine, didn't she? Fine.

-Fern, you think she's a liar.

He's doing her. Hormones gone wild. Men are repeat offenders. Ask my mom.

-What? This is VJ we're talking about.

Fern had promised Leticia that she'd keep the secret. Burst my bubble, will you. It seems I was the last to know that my buddy VJ had cheated on Leticia just three months before.

Never told me. #surprised

-#notsurprised. Tell me you don't find Marlena sexy.

Loaded question that I should have answered with a lie. I didn't. It was like Fern wanted to get mad at me by asking. Crazy, I wasn't the cheater but was taking the blame. Back to me again, we finished dressing. Fern declared that she'd done her part. She'd booked a three-bedroom suite at Cabo's Palmilla Hotel and arranged for our transportation. She intended to use the search mission as a vacation. And she didn't want to be there when Leticia confirmed the truth about VJ and Marlena.

I couldn't help myself.

Well, that's a good justification for being selfish.

-Did I tell him to go to a yoga retreat, take ayahuasca, and get sexually healed?

Sexually healed?

-Leticia said they've been in an intimacy rut. Like we are!

What?! We weren't last night. Wait! You and Leticia discussed our...?

-Of course.

I tried to reel in my emotions and keep my mouth shut. It's a lesson I never seem to learn. This time, I was lucky and didn't have the will to challenge her. I said no more.

* * *

It was still dark when we got into a limo to take us to Van Nuys Airport for the early morning flight. I put my earbuds in, played a *Lonely Planet* podcast about Todos Santos that Leticia had emailed me, and tried to find some peace. By the time we caught up with Leticia and Aeura, the day was already a fail. The plane was a King Air NetJet—not Fifer's personal plane, which was being serviced— and Fern was as outraged as a Karen. I was embarrassed for her. We took seats on the lounge chairs as far away from each other as we could get, and a tired flight attendant gave us breakfast boxes. That was good. Croissants, butter, and loquat jam. Having to explain to Leticia and Aeura about the Marlena call, less good. No matter how I played devil's advocate, arguing the opposite, Leticia was convinced, like Fern, that Marlena and VJ were lovers.

She said he was fine, and that's not fine with me!

-More time for snorkeling. The Palmilla has it all. Did anyone else pack a bathing suit?

Aeura added this brightly, going through the luxury hotel's website on her phone. She didn't see the withering look that Leticia gave her. Fern and I did. It kept getting tenser. We sat on the tarmac for almost three hours, while they figured out a mechanical issue with the air filtration system. I ate, I slept, I ate some more. It was not a happy time. When we finally got airborne, we were ordered right back down by the tower, before reaching altitude, and directed to land immediately at John Wayne Airport in Orange County on a TSA matter. There, in a sealed-off area, it took forever to clear Miss Aeura Kim. She was suspected of previously traveling with a known cocaine runner from Nigeria. Only after Aeura's persistent pleas of innocence and TSA's painstakingly sorting through our luggage were we finally released and our flight to Cabo was allowed to continue. In flight, south of the border, the claws came out and with them, the mean girl in each of them.

Leticia and Fern were all over Aeura for causing the delay.

Your girlfriend smuggled cocaine?!

-You wasted important time!

Not giving advance notice about her passport problem was a problem for them. They ganged up on Aeura without mercy. Defensive and challenged, Aeura was all about whataboutism. Wasting time? What about Fern and Leticia's own self-centered BS that Aeura has had to endure? Both friends have had her captive on video calls or IG, whining on and on about whether Fern should get plastic surgery or why the editor of the *Daily Californian* had it in for Leticia.

I can't get those hours back! They were trashed!

-Don't expect any more calls from me!

--Or me!

Thank you!

It ramped up and then ran out of emotion. Each welcomed the silence, when it finally descended. I stayed out of it all and slept with noise-canceling earbuds in. Aeura, Leticia, and Fern—I knew the best that was in each of them. This was not a shining moment.

***

By the time we got through Cabo customs and made it to the Palmilla Hotel, it was after 9 p.m. It had been a fourteen-hour travel day, and the girls weren't moving. Room service to the suite and then sleep was their only desire. I couldn't relax, kissed Fern good night without much passion, and went down to the café to clear my head. If I hadn't, I wouldn't have tried Marlena's phone number one more time. I was shocked when she answered. She sounded frantic.

Gilly! I can't talk. They're on to me. Beau told them!

-Told them what? Is VJ with you?

Meet me as soon as you can at Marina Cabo San Lucas, slip 258. Goodbye.

Great. Call over. That's all I got from her. So...do I stay or do I go? I could hear Duke humming that song by The Clash with those words, taunting me. What would you have done? Same as me. I hustled my butt out of the hotel and took off for the Marina, thanks to the only Uber driver still working the late shift.

***

Marina Cabo San Lucas is where the Pacific Ocean meets the Gulf of Mexico. It's at the southern edge of the city, which is packed with hotels, restaurants, and bars. At this hour, all the boats were in for the night and it was ghostly, walking through the silent slips of high-end yachts and more yachts. Raised by the water, I knew my way around marinas and found the locals' docks and slip 258. The boat was an old cabin cruiser. No one was on deck. I stepped aboard and knocked at the closed wooden hatch door to the cabin below. No one answered. I tried the latch and it was unlocked, so I went in to peek around. It was the right boat. Above the bed was a photo of Beau and Marlena that did her justice. I was cropping him out in my mind, admiring her image, when I heard a commotion outside. A muffled female voice struggling, legs kicking, men cursing and coming on board. I was trapped below and hid in the cabinet, hoping for the best.

You know how that turned out.

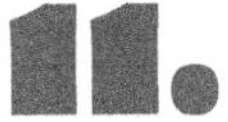

11.

right NOW

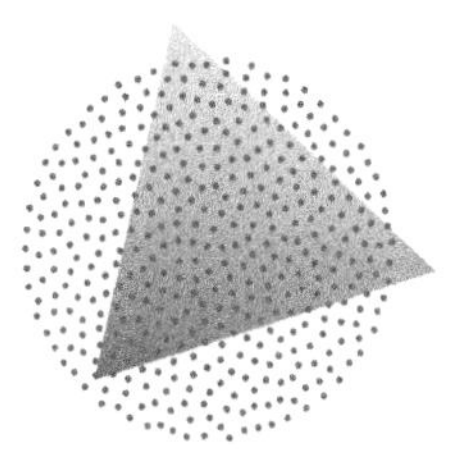

Los Arcos is a set of mammoth rocks rising out of the water, formed with natural arches in the middle. An iconic monument of the region, it welcomes boats that are making their turn from the gulf to the ocean. It's majestic and eye-catching, and I've only seen it before in photos. I stand and salute it, though I'm not sure why. Marlena laughs at the gesture and also stands to salute. We're anxious to feel the stability of solid ground again. The captain of the *Magdalena II* cuts the engines and leaves no wake, guiding the fishing trawler into the jetty toward the commercial dock.

The sun has been up for a few hours, and I'd say it's maybe 8 a.m. on Saturday. Somewhere north of Cabo, in a back bush medical facility, VJ's under sedation, waiting for a surgery that takes place in 24 hours—a surgery that he won't survive. His organs will be removed and sold. Marlena has told me all she knows about the cartel's operation. I'm now in as much danger as she is—in as much danger as VJ is. I lost my phone and wallet in the ocean ordeal. I have to hope I can talk a cabdriver into taking us to the Palmilla Hotel, where I can get some money from one of my friends to pay for the ride—assuming they're still there. Marlena has agreed to help as much as she can.

The trawler's crew knows the drill, and they dock with precision and pride. With the boat now tied up, Marlena and I return our blankets and await permission to disembark. The captain is a religious man and, with the entire crew, holds hands on deck and says a prayer of thanks for the good fortune. There is a fish broker waiting to come aboard and calculate the haul, along with another man who looks more like a bodyguard than a dockworker. He's wide as he is tall and wears a black leather overcoat, though the day is warm. We shake hands with the crew and the captain, who wishes us luck. I hold on to Marlena, and together we climb onto the wooden pier, which meets our wobbly legs, still rocking. I steady Marlena and she steadies me. She is close and kisses under my ear. It gives me chills.

What's that for?

-Miracles.

For VJ, too?

She doesn't answer. Instead, her fingers dig into my back. We pass the fish broker going aboard. Marlena's eyes are on the other man—the squat man in the black leather overcoat who is talking on a cell phone. She ducks her head into me to cover her face.

I think he works for El Chino, the new boss.

-What's he doing here?

The cartel controls the local fishing fleet. Just how it is.

-Would he recognize you?

I don't know. I don't think so. As a nurse, I'm always masked.

-Keep walking.

We hit the street that lines the wharf, and I sneak a glance back. The big man is talking to the trawler boat captain who points our way.

He's looking at us.

-No.

Yes.

-Gilly, leave me. Go. Or they'll be after you, too.

I don't listen and signal to an idling taxi. The yellow car rumbles our way, and I usher Marlena into the back seat with me.

Palmilla Hotel, por favor...

12.

saturday morning

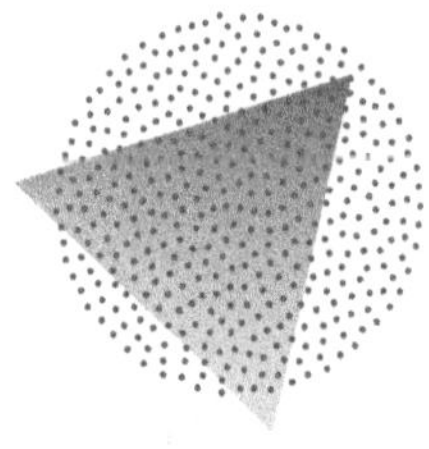

HAVING A CONTINENTAL breakfast ON THE POOL deck above the glistening azure water of the Gulf of Mexico is as dank as you can get. Real rock star accommodations at the Palmilla, where suites start at $3,000 a night. The mood beyond our table was joyous, with hotel guests starting their day in paradise. At our table, the sumptuous breakfast treats lay uneaten. Fern, Aeura, and Leticia sat in stony silence, jaws tight, lips dry, digesting Marlena's story. I'd been lucky to catch them before Leticia and Aeura took a bus for Todos Santos in search of Marlena, who now sat before them telling all. They learned as much as I did about VJ's situation. It was a lot to take in, and it was scary. We were in a foreign country, seemingly powerless, yet our next move could determine his fate. Leticia broke the silence with tears and self-recrimination. She was angry with herself for thinking he was cheating on her.

He really wasn't?

-He wanted to expand his mind. Not his body.

Marlena assured her. She was contrite. She got a commission for steering seekers to the ayahuasca center where she was a nurse. It was and is legit. It had a shaman and everything and was geared for weekenders who didn't want to spend a full week in preparation for imbibing the brew. It was considered by aficionados as *ayahuasca* light. Most initiates had rewarding trips. But with VJ's rare blood type of B positive, he was kidnapped by the cartel to fill a custom order.

This all was feeling close to home. I felt oddly relieved that VJ was not Duke's blood type and chilled that the order would be filled from a living donor. Marlena had only learned about the organ trafficking from her ex-boyfriend. Beau had been an occasional drug mule between Mexico and the United States for the cartel overlord. But this was different. Marlena had broken up with Beau over this insidious new business, and he'd turned El Chino against her.

The police protect the cartel? For sure?

-And the church protects them, too. They're very generous.

Do you know where VJ's being held?

-Yes. A little hospital outside Todos Santos. Inland, remote.

Marlena had worked there on plastic surgery operations as an anesthetic nurse. Never this. They'd tried to kill her, which was proof enough for the girls that Marlena was leveling. Without police, who could they turn to? Aeura was the one with the most practical path—for the most Aeura of reasons.

As someone who's been in jams on a few continents, my first call is always to the U.S. Consulate.

-You really think there's one here?

Aeura did. She was surfing the web and found a U.S. Consular Agency, the smallest outpost of the foreign service in Cabo.

You'll never guess where it's located.

-*At the hotel bar?*

Close. Across the highway in the Shoppes at Palmilla mall!

Unbelievable. You can't make this stuff up. Aeura held out her phone so we could see the coincidence for ourselves.

Yelp says it's open at 10 a.m.

It was nine thirty. We made plans to go there. Marlena, it was agreed, would stay out of sight at the hotel.

***

Fern and I walked Marlena into the fabulous three-bedroom suite. Fern was more gracious than I'd ever seen her.

Take a shower. If you need some clothes, you're welcome to my closet.

-*Thank you, Fern!*

Marlena hugged her and then hugged me while Fern looked on. *Thank you, Gilly.*

The enchantress goddess queen dug her fingernails deep into my back again, which I hoped Fern didn't notice. Marlena excused herself and hit the head. I could understand how VJ got suckered by her. She was the real deal, an ideal, though with questionable judgment. I was glad she'd blown off Beau, who seemed unworthy. These thoughts were swirling as I quickly changed into my Hecho en Venice board shorts and UC Riverside T-shirt. Then we were off for the lobby. Once we were out of the room, Fern was not so gracious.

You were with her all night?

-Did you miss the part where we were clinging to a sliver of boat for hours?

You find her more irresistible or less, now that you've bonded?

-Fern, we're trying to save VJ. This is serious.

Yes. Then why aren't you kissing me and telling me you love me?

There was an open maid's supply closet next to the elevator. I pulled Fern inside.

What are you doing? Leticia and Aeura are wait—

She didn't get to finish. In the dark of the soapy-smelling closet, I kissed her with all the longing I'd built up at sea. Fern met the intensity with longing of her own. A kiss to remove all the jealousy from her. When we stepped out, my legs felt as wobbly as they had when I stepped off the boat. Fern was the real thing, too. She squeezed my hand and said it first.

I love you, Gilly Montrose.

-I love you, Fern.

That wasn't so hard.

****

On the second floor of the Shoppes at Palmilla, between a trendy designer swimwear boutique and a condo time-share shop, was an agency of the U.S. Consulate. It was manned by a local secretary and mother of five, Carmela, and an intern fresh out of George-town University School of Foreign Service, Foster "Flip" Marks. He was taller than me and bronzed. Leticia, Aeura, Fern, and I had all entered the agency together. Leticia felt that a critical mass would get the fastest response, and she was correct. Flip came right out to greet us as US citizens.

Welcome to the U.S. of A. Passport problem? We can help. I'm Flip Marks.

Flip had a casual European style going on and a slight accent. We would learn that he was an American raised in Chile, of all places, and he was schooled in Switzerland and in the United States. Our Chile connection helped to get the ball rolling and the small talk out of the way. We all introduced ourselves. He shook our hands and made sure to make eye contact with each of us. He wasn't much older than us and had the right smooth stuff to go far in the diplomat biz. We asked to speak to him in private and crowded into his inner office, which was smaller than our hotel bathrooms. He beamed an uncertain smile.

So, this is not a passport problem?

-This is life and death.

Leticia got his attention. He closed the door to the office. It was hard to ignore the antique cartoonish Uncle Sam clock on the wall. We didn't have much time. Less than twenty-four hours. But we had Marlena, and Flip was all ears.

When we stepped out of his office ten minutes later, Flip was white-faced. With the real foreign service officer on vacation in New Zealand, this was Flip's responsibility—a chance to make a difference, to be a hero, or the chance to get involved in something he shouldn't and be a zero. Warned by us against involving the local compromised authorities, Flip, the grandson of an ambassador, reached back into his very being and, like a tower of jelly, said sorry, he couldn't help.

What!!!

The girls exchanged the same look of quiet outrage and triple-teamed his sorry ass.

Flip, I'm an Instagram influencer. Are you prepared for me to light you up?

-But I'm not qualified, Aeura.

--Car, Flip!

-Leticia, please. Can't this wait till tomorrow? Consul Craig will be back.

---Concentrate. Car. And a spare US Marine, if you have one.

Fern added that smart ask, and Flip buckled under the power of the three. In Spanish with a Chilean accent, he asked his secretary to order up the consulate staff car for him to use and said that he'd be out on business for the day. He gave my three angels his most BMOC smile.

I guess I'm the closest thing to a Marine. ROTC at Georgetown. Come on.

We followed Flip down an elevator to the garage, feeling more positive than we deserved to. Waiting for us was a mammoth, white Kia Telluride, with U.S. Consulate shield logos on both front doors. I jumped into the front seat.

Swing by the hotel and we can get Marlena. She knows the hospital's location.

-Need that. Everyone comfy?

He looked back at the girls. They were spread out in the two back seats. Aeura waved, eyes twinkling.

Thank you.

He blushed and accelerated out of the garage. If I wasn't mistaken, Flip was flipping for Aeura.

13.

rigHt NOW

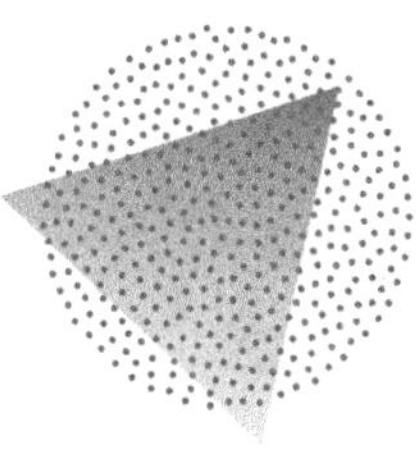

fLip driver. i play navigator, though he knows the area better than me. The girls are in the back seat dishing on Marlena's looks. Aeura thinks her oh-so-red hair is colored. Fern thinks her boobs are fake. Leticia thinks she has green contact lenses. The closer we get to the Palmilla Hotel's grand entrance, the more my stomach tightens. I see one police car parked in front, then two, an ambulance, an EMT van, and several milling hotel guests, hushed and looking in, beyond the open-air lobby of the luxury resort.

Let me out!

Before Flip slows down to deal with the besieged valet, I bound out of the car and into the rubbernecking throng. Their faces are grim, and they talk in whispers about a dead girl. I hear someone say that she fell from the hotel's highest tower.

Not a guest.

A diminutive bellman feels the need to point that out. I'm thinking the worst and push closer to see the EMTs kneeling over a sheeted body that has landed in the tiled courtyard. The splatter adds a garish hue to the terra cotta. A gurney moves through, and the uniformed EMTs lift the body onto it. A lock of red hair flops out from beneath the sheet. Oh, Marlena. Suicide? No way, José. Cartel found you. Cartel killed you.

In the open lobby, I scan the crowd, backtracking to Flip and the girls parked outside. I pass two *federales* huddled with a hotel manager and the man with the leather coat. The manager keeps nodding, and I wonder what he's agreeing to. If he's confirming suicide, the fix is in and VJ is screwed.

Gilly! Fern yells. The girls and Flip are hurrying my way. Leticia cannot contain herself.

Hotel security saw a red-headed lady jump off the roof and kill herself.

VJ's screwed.

UNIVERSITY
LeticiA

saturday, before NOON

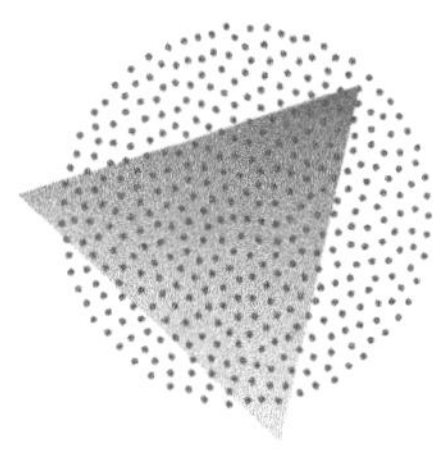

VJ WAS IN A GOLDEN HAZE. He'd been in and out of consciousness for days, it seemed. It wasn't unpleasant. It was, however, confusing. Sunlight brightened the white, sterile hospital room out in the boonies of Todos Santos. The West LA born and bred achiever, now a sophomore at Stanford in computer engineering, had an IV drip in his right arm. His left arm was connected to monitoring devices. Sedated, he was floating on a comfortable cloud. His body was belted into the bed with restraints, and he couldn't move his arms to scratch his nose, which needed serious scratching. No matter how hard he tried to concentrate, he couldn't. He was certain that he hadn't been given ayahuasca, but what that meant, he couldn't figure. He'd wanted to expand his mind to grow and push boundaries. The goddess he'd confided in with his deepest secrets had encouraged him to try it. She was a nurse and said it was safe. She promised to be his lifeguard. She had green eyes and flame-colored hair, and he wanted her approval. Was that wrong? Leticia would understand and forgive. Where was this lifeguard who could enrich his life? What was her name? He strained to remember. Marlena! It burst out loud from his lips.

Alerted, the surgeon himself, Dr. Ricardo Foo, known in the cartel as El Chino, entered the room to check out his patient. In an old-school physician's lab coat, with a bedside manner that didn't include courtesy, he regarded VJ as if he were already dead. Foo was once highly regarded in his field and in China had held the government contract for harvesting the organs of executed prisoners. He supplied the very lucrative organ trade for most of the 1990s—his peak years. If he hadn't run afoul of the politics back in the capital, he'd still have that legal supply. Out on his own, his income depressed, he was unfairly arrested in Beijing as an enemy of the state. It took almost all his money, but he was able to escape to Mexico. With a decade in hiding, a bad drug problem, two bad marriages, and a covered-up murder, he landed in the clutches of the cartel. They protected and rehabilitated him. El Chino became their doctor. Within a few years, demonstrating his gifts for refining torture and dealing death, Foo's status rose to that of a regional capo. In Baja South, his appointed turf, he used his skill set to expand the smuggling and extortion businesses. On the dark web, the disgraced sixty-year-old surgeon had developed a new network of black-market organ buyers that was unmatched. So were the prices he demanded, with the collection clout of the cartel. As of late, El Chino was searching for living donors like VJ with rarer blood types.

Foo pulled back the sheet and gelled up VJ's chest. With an ultrasound device, he ran a digital scan and, on VJ's bare skin, he made notations around the gelled area with a black Magic Marker. VJ watched him watching the scan monitor. The near–twenty-year-old tried to speak. In response, El Chino increased his sedation level. Before VJ drifted back inside the cloud, he saw dotted lines drawn on his chest. WTF?!

***

Beau, the bartender from Pioneertown, was pouring coffee for himself in the back bush medical facility's break room. He was still sleepy from the flight south and was ultra-nervous. He looked up with an apologetic smile as Dr. Ricardo Foo joined him.

I got here fast as I could. I'll get Marlena in line.

-It's been taken care of. You'll need a new boat.

Beau hadn't expected this. He understood what was implied and didn't inquire further, though his insides were twisting for a woman he once loved. There would be time for him to mourn later. He needed to reinforce his loyalty to the cartel or like Marlena, he was doomed. El Chino grabbed Beau by the shoulders and told him that he was needed to clean up the weekend's surgeries and then, on Sunday night, to accompany some precious cargo from Cabo to Houston. Eyes, kidneys, liver, and heart were the big casino of organ harvesting. As unhappy as El Chino was with Beau for trusting Marlena, delivering the goods of an O negative donor was jackpot.

You're getting a second chance.

-Thank you.

Beau had been in the doghouse with the cartel before El Chino. He'd once dumped a shipment of cocaine when he erroneously thought he was being busted. He'd been working off the debt ever since. The post-op cleanups involved the nearby wild cougar preserve. The predators were always hungry for flesh. No human evidence left behind and a good accompanying story had been Beau's idea. They'd used the preserve a month earlier and planted the deceased donor's ripped clothes there. The police had concluded that a foolish ayahuasca tripper had entered the cougar preserve and suffered the consequences. No muss, no fuss, no one the wiser. El Chino rewarded Beau for that. His mistake was sharing all this with the more scrupulous Marlena. When she found out what she was actually complicit in, she was out on Beau, way out. Along with a piece of his soul. The cartel henchman in the leather coat joined them and poured coffee, with a nod of recognition to Beau. El Chino's eyes stayed on Beau.

Diego, you saw Marlena with an American boy.

-Yes. Gilly Montrose. He's registered with three others at the hotel. Nowhere around.

They'll be back. Beau, Palmilla, go. Find out if he's a threat.

2.

riqHt NOW

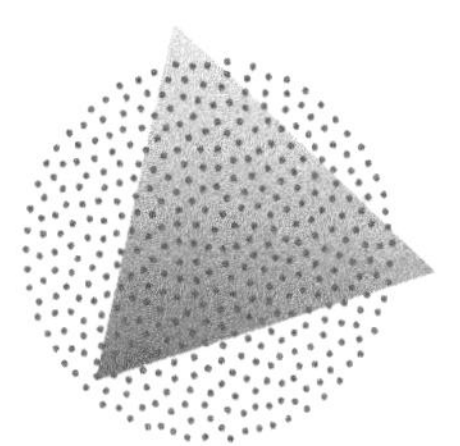

MArLeNA's deAtH HANqs HeAvY WItH Hurt over the rooM, especially in my heart. I risked my life to save hers, only for her to lose it trying to help us. The amount of suck that represents is unfathomable. Spirit soar, Healer! She promised to lead us to the facility where VJ's being kept. Without her, we have to adjust our plan. We're in retreat, seeking sanctuary in Flip's time-share condo on the hillside outside the Cabo business district. The consulate intern is a stand-up guy to do this, a brave guy. If we move forward, we know there's danger, but we have no choice. Flip serves us iced tea, and I see him linger with Aeura and share a smile. She doesn't seem to mind. Leticia has been browsing on her phone.

There are only three medical facilities listed in the vicinity of Todos Santos.

-We can split up. Gilly and Flip are fluent in Spanish. I can get by, too. In high school, I did an immersion semester in Barcelona.

Fern rolls the r to show off. She has given up her resort vacay and switched to warrior mode. She's all in and I'm glad. I give her a squeeze of affirmation, our bodies close and trembling—not from being turned on but for the anxiety inside us. Aeura's ready to get going.

What about the yoga and ayahuasca camps? I'll take those, Gilly.

-Ya, good. There could be something there. He was at both.

Adding to the degree of difficulty, the facility where VJ's a prisoner may not be publicly listed. Marlena said it was private, way out in the bush. There will be a time crunch, too. Flip says the drive to Todos Santos should take an hour but never does.

You get behind farm vehicles and it seems like forever.

-We'll deal with it. Do you have a gun, Flip?

I do.

-Bring it.

Leticia knows best. Fern insists on going back to the hotel first to grab a jacket for later and a cheaper purse.

I'll stand out with a Dior bag.

The hotel idea takes hold. Flip, like me, thinks it's a terrible idea and vetoes it. I shrug my shoulders.

Hey, Flip's driving.

It's always a relief not to be the bad guy, especially when Fern and I are finally getting along so well. We're all set to go, when Aeura beseeches our driver.

My Nikon is at the Palmilla. Please, let me grab it.

Flip folds like a 1990s mobile phone.

I ask Flip to park on the highway. No sense in our being visible at the valet drop-off, in case señor leather coat is lurking. Aeura hops out of the consulate car to head for the hotel entrance, with Fern right behind her. I watch them disappear and turn to Leticia next to me in the back seat.

How are you holding up, Tish?

Leticia, my longtime high school crush, melts into me in a tsunami of emotion.

I feel so helpless.

-Hey, you got the A-Team with you. We took out the Armenian mob, we can do this. VJ's going be in your arms tonight.

Leticia kisses my cheek and steadies. Flip throws his weight in.

The minute we locate him, I'll go all ugly American. I can be an official pain in the ass.

-Thanks, Flip. Will the consulate notify Marlena's next of kin?

--If that's her real name.

If it is, Marlena Raskin didn't show up as a US citizen.

I'm not surprised. Out of the window, I see an open Jeep pass us. I grab Leticia and pull her down with me to the car floor, out of view.

Gilly!

-That's Beau, Marlena's ex, in the Jeep!

--He turned into the Palmilla driveway. Does he know Aeura and Fern?

Unless he's brain-dead, Beau would recognize them from our bar fight at the Red Dog Saloon. That's enough for Flip. He springs out of the car to warn them. Man, what would we do without

Flip? Alone with Leticia, I give her my bravest smile. She squeaks, breaking again.

Do you think VJ slept with Marlena?

-No, you heard her. It was a mind trip—not about sex.

I've been really hard on him. Not loving enough. VJ shouldn't be here.

I hold her again and don't care who sees it. Fern and Aeura, camera around her neck, are shepherded by Flip. He hustles them to the car. I open the rear door for Fern. Flip gets the front for Aeura. Fern sees my arm around Leticia and understands. She looks smart and sexy in her most conservative resort attire. I put my other arm around her, pulling Fern in with Leticia and me. Flip puts the car in gear. Just to be safe, we duck low as we pull by the Palmilla. Once on the main road, we feel comfortable enough to breathe.

The Beau guy didn't see them. He went straight to the front desk and the hotel manager.

-You think Beau's looking for Marlena?

--I don't think he's come to grieve.

As I say this, I know the answer could also be that he's looking for me, since I was spotted with her. I don't share that tidbit with the others. Aeura is all cat-ate-the-canary smile and dangles a hotel notepad for Flip's benefit and ours. Fern nudges her.

Just tell them, Aeura. We got a lead!

-Marlena used the hotel phone and left us a number.

3.

saturday afternoon

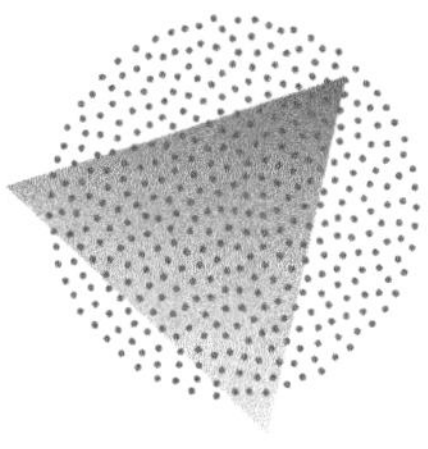

 Juana
Toro, was biting her nails down to the stubs. Processing the
personal and payment information on a completed application
of a sixty-nine-year-old male, she was having trouble focusing.
Juana hadn't been herself since Marlena had called. The client,
an experience-seeking American senior, looked forever hip,
sitting in the underlit, minimalist-designed reception area,
trying to complete a cell phone call about a music gig in LA in

spite of the bad cellular signal. Bunky Green was his name, and it sounded familiar to Juana. She'd google him later, when she was off her shift.

Please come with me, Mr. Green. I need to take your vitals.
-Solid.

Bunky, a journeyman 1970s drummer and a legend in his own mind, followed Juana as instructed, eyeing her swaying rear. Juana was a divorcée from Mexico City. She got recruited for this by a travel nurse she met on a MedFlight to Phoenix. Marlena was her age and said an English- speaking RN could double her salary and live by the beach in Todos Santos as an anesthesia assistant in plastic surgery. Juana didn't need any more encouragement. She wanted a life change and moved to Baja California Sud.

When the Palmilla Hotel ID came up on her phone earlier, she was uncertain and let it go to voicemail. She hadn't expected the message to be from Marlena. It was a warning for Juana to get away while she still can. *Now she tells me.* Juana had just agreed to work the weekend on two hush-hush surgeries with a Dr. Foo at Athena, the now-defunct private plastic surgery center. She had to work the yoga camp and ayahuasca retreat to make ends meet since the plastic surgery center went bankrupt. The young RN had been thrilled to hear Marlena talk about it reopening and, with it, the sweet paydays. This weekend was going to cover a better rental for Juana, putting her toes firmly in the sand. Her ex would eat his heart out for something like that. She finished Bunky's exam and excused him. He put back on his rhinestone-studded cowboy shirt and gave Juana his most earnest look.

Sure you don't want me to pull down my pants? You did say "vitals."
-We have what we need. Thank you.

She was good at suffering fools, if the price was right. Ever the professional, she smiled brightly at Bunky. She was due at surgery and kept it brief.

El curandero will prepare you for tomorrow's ritual. There's a bench outside where you can wait.

-Can I blow some vape there? Last chance to get toxic before the cleansing.

If you'd like.

Bunky took her permission as flirting. She was zoftig and cute, and after a few down decades, he was here with his son to repair their relationship and to rejuvenate his own spirit. The old rocker gave his hat a jaunty tilt and winked at Juana on the way out. Juana had been with an older man once before and enjoyed the experience. It was a one-night fling that she couldn't forget. The sudden flashback had delightfully driven the strange Marlena voicemail back into the distant reaches of her mind, when her cell rang with a local Cabo number. This time Juana answered.

Hola.

* * *

Hola! Hi. Mi nombre Fern. Habla English?

-Yes.

The only paved road up the peninsula to Todos Santos was Los Cabos 19. The five of us—me, Fern, Leticia, Aeura, and Flip—bumped along at a good clip in the consulate Kia, listening intently to Fern's cell phone on speaker. The choice of Fern to call the number that Marlena had left on the pad was much more contentious than I thought when I suggested it. Flip agreed that a woman's voice would be preferable, and I felt that Spanish-challenged Leticia might be ineffective and too emotional. Fern would be a better way to go. Leticia seethed and cursed at me. I let it go. Then Aeura went all cranky that she wasn't even considered. She was the one who found the lead, and she asked for us to reconsider her. Even when Flip flopped and backed Aeura, I persevered. I felt that strongly. Leticia and Aeura reluctantly agreed, and Fern made the call. The Beverly Hills Barbie was as cool and calculated as I knew she could be.

Thank you. I'm a friend of Marlena. You know her, yes?

-She's no longer here. Sorry.

Don't hang up, please. I'm coming to Todos Santos. She asked if I could grab a few things she forgot at...the workplace.

-The workplace?

Si. Me das direccions, por favor.

The pause on the other end of the line stretched beyond pregnant. No answer was forthcoming.

Hello?... Hola?

Nothing. Leticia couldn't control herself.

Please! A boy named VJ is due to have surgery tomorrow. Help us find—

Juana Toro hung up and turned her phone off. In our car, the temperature boiled over. Fern was livid.

You dunce! You scared her off! That just totally doomed your boyfriend!

-Me? You were losing her, Fern! Everyone could tell. Gilly, you know I'm right.

Fern and Leticia turned to me as their arbiter. Flip and Aeura looked on, too.

Fern did the best she could.

-Thanks a lot.

Fern, I mean, "workplace" did kinda stall it.

-What was I supposed to say? El Chino's Organ Removal Center!?

I reached for Fern, a gesture of understanding, and she shook me off. I could hear Duke's best relationship advice: *"Kid, know what not to say and when not to say it."*

Aeura didn't help things.

Should have let me! I play dumb, needy Asian better than anyone. But nooo...

-Shut up!

--Shut up!

---STFU!

I asked Flip to pull over and everyone got out, steaming. The blue, blue Atlantic ocean across the highway and the low desert landscape was a calming momentary reprieve. Flip must have been wondering what he'd gotten himself into. The diplomatic intern tried to get some momentum for going back to Cabo and trying to involve the state police. Leticia wasn't having it. Todos Santos was only miles away.

Please, Flip. We can't go back now, and we can't trust any Mexican police.

We all believed that 💯.

Peer pressure times four on Flip.

OK, we go, but I head back by 6 p.m.

That gave us the whole afternoon. I tried to isolate Fern before we got to the car.

I'm sorry, babe.

-I'm sure you are.

Fern, come on. This isn't about you.

The minute I responded with that sanctimonious line, trite AF, I hated myself. So did Fern. She moved by Aeura and got into the front seat to avoid me. Know what not to say and when not to say it. Thank you, Dad. One day, I'll learn.

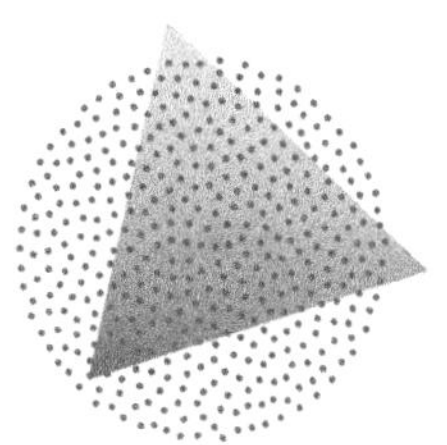

4.

right Now

 The seabirds that had been resting atop it scatter into the cloudless azure canopy above this sleepy seaside town. We have four hours to beat the bushes and find VJ. Flip parks in a dirt lot in front of a weathered hacienda-style restaurant off the main square. It advertised the best fish tacos in *el mundo*.

Anxious, we get out. There's an air of gaiety all around. Tourists mill about, enjoying themselves while their bus idles in the lot.

Locals come and go, with tradesmen, shoppers, and beachgoers in the throng. Todos Santos screams good vibes, sun, sand, and a *mañana* lifestyle that enchants. I could get used to hanging here, if the circumstances weren't so dire. Flip's staying put at the restaurant.

I'll be your 911 coordinator. You have my number. Any heat, call, and I'll come gunning.

The girls all have their cell phones. I don't want to think about my lost iPhone 16 that I'll still be paying for every month for the next two years. *Denial is not just a river in Egypt*, Duke would always say, embracing the concept. No worries. If we head too far into the interior, there won't be reception anyway. Ranking our Spanish-speaking skills, it runs from me, the best, to Leticia, the worst (oh, her shame). We have a two-pronged attack on the places where we believe that VJ has been at and the ones where he could be now. Micromanager that she is, Leticia googled all the addresses on the way and has written them out for us on sticky notes. She asks to partner up with me, and it makes the best sense. We'll start at the Saint Jude Hospital in town for leads on medical facilities that aren't on the internet. Aeura and Fern will go to the outlying yoga camp and the ayahuasca retreat. Leticia gives them the yellow note intel.

They're close by each other.

-Gather information only. Rendezvous here—six at the latest. Agreed?

---Thanks, Flip.

Aeura plants a sweet peck on his cheek, and Leticia and Fern follow with the same affectionate gesture. It's chaste, it's heartfelt. Not shocking, California gals give kisses on merit. It's in the DNA.

Flip blushes through his tan, shoots me a man-to-man nod, and hits the outside taco bar. We cross the street to a hotel with idling cabs. We walk as pairs, each pair seeking a taxi. I break for Fern to speak before she gets into hers with Aeura. Fern is frosty. #notsurprised

Aren't you with Leticia?

-Yes, because that's the best combo. You and Aeura can manage the language. She can't.

If you say so. You seem pretty happy to agree.

-What? Are you having your period?

I do not believe that I said that. Self-sabotage? Without missing a beat, Fern throws it back in my face.

Yeah, I am. So stay away! OK?

-Uh, OK.

I asked for that. She and Aeura take off. Why do I care? Is losing Fern's love worse than losing my phone, or losing Duke, or VJ? How do I rank these things? Leticia joins me.

Wow. She's high maintenance.

-Leticia, who isn't? Tell me.

Word. Gilly for the win.

5.

saturday afternoon

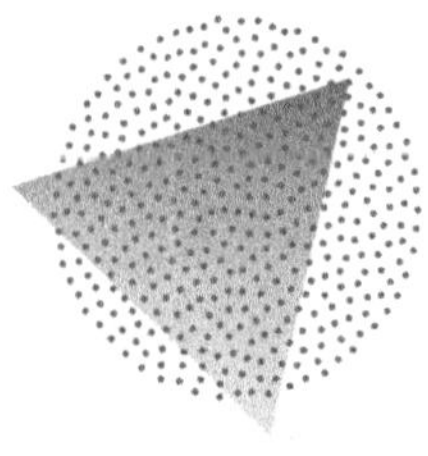

When i reached him, duke waf cleaning a faltwater infinity pool in the fhadow of the grand pink lady, the Beverly Hills Hotel, California, USA. The celebrities, including Madonna, who owned the Tudor estate on Sunset went as far back as silent picture stars. I knew the list by heart. Duke drilled it into me every time we worked there. It always made him feel a part of Hollywood. Myself, I didn't crave that validation. Thinking about him needing a liver and VJ caught on the wrong end of organ trafficking was damn ironic. It made me uneasy to dwell on it, but I had to. I wondered, if Duke had the money, whether he'd worry about being low on the recipient list. Or would he shell out for a new liver, regardless of where it came from? Dad liked being alive, no shock there.

Knowing something is wrong and doing it anyway, we do all the time. In my Business Ethics class, it's termed "cognitive dissonance." You're aware that something isn't legit, but you don't care and buy in. Like smoking cigarettes or speeding, you block it. Buying black market human organs required cognitive dissonance to the max. This business depended on that. The cartel behind it all only made it more deadly, more untouchable.

I'd called Duke using Leticia's cell phone, while our cab moved through town toward the north end to St. Jude, the regional trauma center. I was glad to hear that Duke was able-bodied, working solo, not complaining, though he'd earned the right. He asked about VJ. I kept it simple.

It's worse than we thought. I can't get into it right now.

-Of course you can. Spill.

VJ was kidnapped for his organs.

-Whoa! Time out! No freaking way—whoops!

Duke tripped over his own skimmer and splashed into the pool. When he resurfaced, phone dripping, he confessed.

I'm not well, kid.

Tell me something I don't want to know.

***

At the end of a rocky road, twenty miles into the wild, high desert landscape east of Todos Santos, was a hidden, freestanding adobe building with a faded tile roof. It sat beyond a dirt trail, deep into the Las Palmas brush, a few klicks from the yoga camp's reception tent. Except for the black Range Rover parked in front, it looked to be an edifice that was no longer in use. A scratched up, stenciled sign on dirty glass read: ATHENA. And plastered under that: CERRADO.

Inside the building, it was another story—all gleaming metal fixtures, white walls, and antiseptic quiet. No expense had been spared to create a private surgery center capable of facelifts, nips, and tucks for cost-conscious clients. But the vanity makeover business ran out of loans and cartel patience. El Chino took over, changing its mission statement with the side hustle that the doctor knew best. There was a nurse's station at the front and a break room in the rear. In between, one operating room and two hospital suites for preparation or recovery. Saturday's surgery was imminent.

VJ was no dummy. He had a good sense of what was going on, especially after seeing the dotted lines designed to dig him up like a garden plot. He'd been in a twilight since he'd drunk the ayahuasca brew, though now he doubted that it was really the psychedelic potion at all. For sure, he'd been drugged—and not in a good way. He wondered whether Leticia, Gilly, and the others he'd promised to meet were looking for him. He fought through the debilitating fog to move his hand. With his long index finger and thumb, he pinched the IV's catheter that carried the juice which was sedating him. The longer he did it, the more he made sense of his hospital room surroundings. He heard someone scream from across the hall, followed by the sound of a gurney squeaking past his room. He listened for the gurney to return. Was he next?

***

Flip Marks was halfway into a most flavorful taco dorado with mango sauce from his three-taco plate, when his consulate cell chimed. It was Consul Craig himself, calling from the Honolulu airport, on his way home. The man could talk. He'd be arriving in the morning and would expect a full report on Flip's absence from the office. He'd heard from Flip's assistant that he also took the car. Flip tried to present a case about VJ's disappearance and the suspicious death of the woman, Marlena. The consul was a State Department lifer who had found paradise in the cushy Cabo posting. He was not one to make waves, much less ripples. Craig was on top of it. He explained that the local authorities had assured him they were investigating. They believe it to be another misadventure of an ayahuasca tourist. The deceased foreign woman wasn't their business. Flip was ordered back to Cabo immediately.

Call over, Flip had his tacos and a promise to wait for VJ's friends till 6 p.m. It was only 2:30 p.m. If he weighed his interest in a foreign service career that he was already questioning against his interest in Aeura, there was no contest.

Waiting gave him more time to think about the enticing female. She was punk and she was ebullient, two styles not normally associated with each other. Aeura had been giving him hints, and that spark had him ablaze. He couldn't deny it. It was a not-so-gentle reminder of his girlfriend at Georgetown. They might have made it together, if her parents hadn't snatched her back to the Chinese mainland before they were engaged. He'd even bought the ring. It sent him into weekly therapy for the last two years. The one that got away.

Aeura was Korean American and definitely didn't have that old-school Asian vibe. Like the mango salsa he poured on the second fish taco, she had an odd zest, a special sauce he could feel. He was a romantic at heart, a closet poet, old enough to be looking for the right forever mate. Flip wasn't going to let the opportunity pass. He tried Aeura's phone to give his update. There was no answer but no reason to suspect anything more than the notorious zones of no reception in Baja South. He wondered if Aeura was in therapy, too. His therapist had told him that it wasn't a stigma anymore. It was a dating amenity. It meant that you cared enough about your mental health to invest in it. So there was that. And there was also one amazing coconut shrimp taco left.

***

Fern and Aeura agreed that the taxi ride to the yoga camp seemed to take forever. The driver knew English and was talkative at first, till they asked about a surgery hospital. That's when the grizzled local pretended not to understand any language—especially after Fern cursed him in French under her breath. Aeura could tell that Fern was on edge. Bumping through the dusty byway seemed as good a time as any to dish some dirt. Aeura had been busting to share.

What do you think of Flip Marks?

-I like him. See that photo hanging in his condo bathroom? He played polo at the Palm Springs meet. We must know the same people. My dad's a sponsor.

Hey, back off! He's my guy. You have Gilly.

Fern swallowed that thought whole. The only daughter of

Philip Fifer of the Fifer Family Financial Fund surprised Aeura by revealing that she loved Gilly but didn't think they had a future.

You know. Go the distance? I mean, with someone like Flip, I could see myself—

-Did you hear what I said?

Aeura. He's a man. With a penis.

-And I'm bi-curious, OK?

Wait. You and Gilly? You never—

-Boogied down? No, sadly. Not even a half-night stand.

This the damn driver seemed to understand just fine.

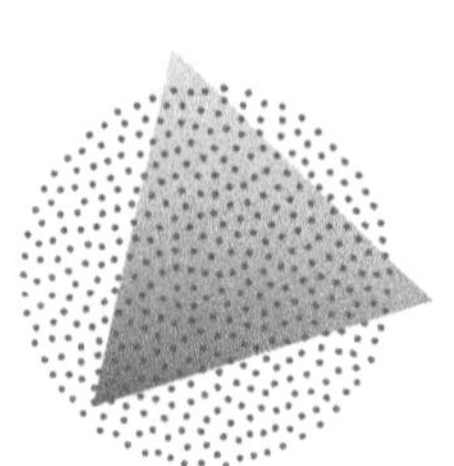

6.

right Now

 The young, immaculately coiffed orderly, a body builder in his off time, is also fluent in English. He's all about helping Leticia and accommodating her request. He slows his meal cart and straightens up to face her. Antonio, with name tag attached, is impressive, I can't lie. He speaks without any accent and is proud of it.

There was a plastic surgery facility outside Las Palmas called Athena, maybe a thirty-minute ride from here. I get off at three. I have a two-seater.

He directs that to me, the odd one out. Leticia's with it and doesn't take her eyes off Antonio. It's awkward for me, but I'm anxious to see how she plays it.

That's so sweet of you, but we have a car.

-No point anyway. Few months ago, it closed down. And believe me, you're perfect. You don't need any cosmetic enhancement.

Leticia takes in the flirting and radiates. In the era of #metoo, my LA gal pals are shameless. Thank God. Do what you gotta do. It's almost 3 p.m., and Antonio is the only one willing to help us. He smiles again at Leticia, eyes twinkling, flexes, and tells us he'll be right back. Leticia grins like she used to when she aced a debate. Let me tell you, she's only getting more and more attractive the older she gets. If VJ survives, he'd better take care of business and wrap her up. I can't help myself.

Well, Tish, you heard it here first. Your upper-body pride is sufficient.

-Antonio rocks. Eat your heart out, Gil.

Antionio went the extra mile and came back with some old waiting room magazines.

They always ran ads in Los Cabos. It must have the address. Let me see.

-Thanks, Antonio. How did you learn to speak English so well?

Oh, I was addicted to watching <u>Friends</u> and <u>Beverly Hills, 90210</u>. You are a Phoebe and an Andrea. Here it is.

Bam! Done. We have the clinic's address. Leticia thanks Antonio and so do I. He lingers, wrangling for more.

If we can meet up later, give a call.

He writes down his number on the magazine and gives it to Leticia. One more flex, grabbing his cart, and he rolls off. We look at the magazine ad and see a phone number listed for the plastic surgery facility, along with other contact info.

Let's get Flip and let the others know.

-Ya, but first, let me try the number.

Outside St. Jude, beneath a stand of shady palm trees off the walkway, Leticia calls, phone on speaker. To our surprise, it connects. A man answers.

Beau?

-Oh, sorry. I misdialed.

Leticia hangs up and then regrets it.

Did I sound suspicious?

-Who expected anyone to pick up? Did he just say, "Beau"?

Leticia's iPhone goes off, and we jump at the sound. She checks the display screen.

Gilly, it's him calling back! Should we answer?

-No. Let it ring. We know where VJ is and, if Marlena had it right, he's still alive.

We cross the plaza to the street and a cab stand. A horn honks.

Hold up! Please!

It's Antonio in an old, open Jeep Wrangler, the two-seater. He pulls by the curb to cut us off.

Sorry, Miss. Unlike me, you didn't have a name tag. Help me out.

-Leticia.

She's flattered. The local kid savors the sound of it and tells us he has a friend covering the rest of his shift. He offers to take Leticia wherever she wants to go right now. No better guide to the area. I can tell that Leticia trusts him. I'm not so sure. She looks to me for permission.

Hey, drop me off with Flip and we'll follow you.

-Good call, Gil. Critical mass.

Critical mass.

saturday afternoon

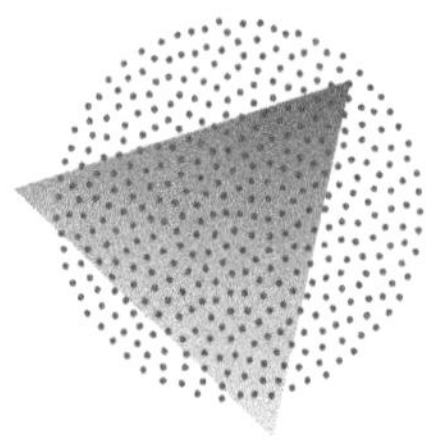

DR. foo HAd beeN WAshiNg up post-op, when he mistakenly answered the secondary landline at the nurses' station. It was an old number that they kept as a backup. There was really no reason for the surgeon to be feeling uneasy, but he questioned the call. It was from area code 310—West Los Angeles—same as Sunday's donor. He wouldn't think twice about it except that the Marlena business had been a hot mess of damage control, sloppy to say the least, and sloppy he was not. The organs he'd carefully removed earlier from the unfortunate Italian wellness seeker with the universal donor blood type were already being transported by Diego to the dirt strip airport, en route to Tijuana for distribution in Asia. He'd delivered on all his promises to his boss and had set up a lucrative pipeline.

He'd feel better when Beau returned to dispose of the day's remains and could himself be eliminated after the weekend's work. The American had proven to trust the wrong people and was therefore unreliable. El Chino had learned the hard way that this was a character trait which never changed.

Before he checked in on tomorrow's patient, the surgeon called his wife back home in Mexico City. She was barely eighteen, a blossoming innocent out shopping for her first estate in La Condesa. The doctor planned to be back on Monday and was anxious to give her whatever she wanted.

Nurse Juana passed by on her way out. Her work in the OR was finished, and she was due back at the retreat for her regular shift. She waved to the surgeon with a polite smile, her knees shaking. The patient had died, which seemed to be the point. She'd learned not to question medical superiors. The doctor was a perfectionist. He'd complimented her as an assistant. That went a long way with Juana. The young professional appreciated being appreciated, and being paid triple helped to cool her mind. She'd go to confession later and feel cleaner. She hadn't expected Dr. Foo to call her by name.

Juana. You know the other nurse here? Marlena?

-Yes, Doctor. I worked with her.

Don't be her.

With a nod, she was dismissed. Marlena had tried to warn her. Chilled to the bone, Juana left, feeling worse about her future.

***

VJ had undone the straps binding him. He'd strained his neck and let his solid, white teeth, straightened by the third-highest peer-rated orthodontist on the Westside, do the damage. He was free. After hearing no movement outside his room, VJ opened the door and, in a patient's gown, he slipped into the hallway, smooth as a semi-drugged cat. He moved to a closet across the way, got inside, and turned on the light. There were a few lab coats, a nurse's smock, a pair of Nike sneakers a size too big, cleaning solvents, and a mop in a pail. Fighting through the cobwebs, the college sophomore, son of a pharmacist, went for it. He uncapped a bottle of ammonia and took a mighty whiff. The ensuing rush hit him sure as smelling salts. Clear-headed, he focused, mixing and matching what was at hand, like a Rubik's Cube for survival.

***

The cab let Fern and Aeura off at the rustic driveway of the Green Door, an ayahuasca retreat outside Todos Santos that, according to its website, "is a soul-stimulating, natural experience." Fern asked the cab driver to wait. He did, until they exited the car, and then he squealed into a wicked U-turn, taking off. Fern and Aeura were about to unleash the kraken and light him the eff up, when Fern caught sight of an older man standing on a bench in front of the Green Door's green door, holding a phone in the air to find cell reception.

Mr. Green! It's Fern. Fern Fifer!

-Fern! Hey, kid! How crazy is this?

The old rocker hopped down off the bench with a bone-shaking grunt and embraced her like a family friend. Fern waved Aeura over.

Aeura, this is Bunky Green from Beverly Hills.

-I played at her bat mitzvah.

--Drummer on Poison's second and third album. Yes?

-Yes! I love this girl. Fern, Donny's here, too. You won't recognize him. He's gained a lot of—

---Weight. Thanks, Dad.

Donny joined them. He was husky, nineteen years old, and sporting a beard on his jowly but adorable countenance.

Hey, you put down the spoon, you pick up the fork. Badge of honor.

Donny had quit drugs and alcohol and felt the need to clarify that, no matter how self-deprecating. He and Fern hugged and laughed and then hugged some more, delighted at the coincidence. Donny gushed that he and Bunky were now both rehab alumni, here for father-and-son bonding time. Fern was perplexed.

You're sober and you're doing ayahuasca?

Bunky gave the disclaimer. No hard drugs, pills, or alcohol, but weed and 'shrooms are allowed.

"California sober." It's a thing.

Don had finished his physical but forgot to register his inhaler. He needed to drive to their cabin by the yoga camp and grab it. Fern perked at that and asked for a ride. To save time, she'd speak to the yoga people while Aeura checked whether VJ was ever at the Green Door. Aeura was all about it.

Go!

-So...you're not here to trip?

--No, looking for a friend—VJ.

---From BH?

--West LA.

You could see a dismissive cloud settle over Donny and Bunky, both snobby graduates of Beverly Hills High, decades apart. West LA was the ghetto to them, and they instinctively cared less about anyone from there. Fern ignored it and went off with Donny. Aeura excused herself from Bunky, who couldn't help throwing a love line.

Great to meet a sweet, young fan. I'm here if you feel the need.

-So good to know. Hey, were you in The Wrecking Crew, the session band?

No, but I was wrecked. The 1980s, just saying, babe…

Aeura choose not to level him with an *OK boomer* burn. Instead, she giggled the way that personal trainers do at everything their clients say and headed into the intake lobby of the Green Door. The structure was a repurposed Quonset hut with a bamboo-walled, air-conditioned lobby and some rooms beyond. There was no one at the front desk, but the *curandero* himself, the native healer, was crossing by on his way out, and Aeura went into her act. She did a head bow.

So sorry. Excuse, please. My English, Spanish not so good.

-How can I help you?

Barefoot in a white caftan, the curandero exuded goodness. Small and brown and white-haired, he took his time with Aeura. She hated to lie.

I am looking for my brother, Vansu Jin Ohara. VJ. He come here. Now he lost.

The wizened, dark, elderly man never took his eyes off Aeura. He moved to the lobby desk and called on the system phone.

Nurse, could you come to the front?

He hung up and took Aeura's hands.

She'll know. But if you're lost, I can help you find yourself. What's your name?

-Aeura.

Beautiful. That's Korean, isn't it?

Aeura shouldn't have lied. He was authentic. Nurse Juana entered, and the wise man explained that she was looking for her missing brother. Aeura head-bowed again.

He come here? VJ.

-Juana, I am off to the meditation grove. Please help Miss Aeura.

--Of course.

right Now

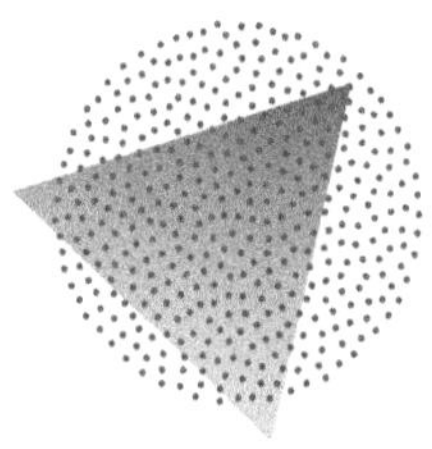

IN tHe coNſuLAte ſuv, We tAiL ANtoNio'ſ opeN jeep WitH LeticiA ridiNg ſHotguN. Bouncing along a dirt road, we blow by stands of giant, cardon cacti, the highlight of the high desert landscape outside Todos Santos. They're majestic plants—out-Joshua-treeing Joshua trees. The afternoon's peak sun beats down. Ahead of us, Antonio looks over at Leticia in the seat next to him every few seconds, and I feel jealous, which is odd. Flip's driving, and we agree about the Taylor Swift music blasting from Antonio's hot shit sound system. Don't hate me, but I prefer her early guitar-driven music. I'm not a synth fan, and neither is Flip. Leticia, by the looks of her body language, is fully engaged. We pass a road sign for the yoga camp. We're getting close. I consider asking Flip to honk to stop them. The music announcing us may not be advantageous to our mission. I'm surprised that Leticia hasn't stifled it. Reading my mind, I see Leticia's strong gesture, and the music abruptly stops as we go into stealth mode. Flip leans over to me with a sly grin.

Tell me about Aeura. Is she in a relationship?

-Uh, she was, I guess. She's—

Fantastic.

I'm about to add Aeura's sexual proclivity but decide against it. Let Flip find that out for himself. And who knows? Aeura's full of surprises. She's all that. I'll always have a special thing for her and, like she says, that makes our relationship perfect. Never consummated, always possible. Flip's cell phone sounds and he answers it.

Hold on... Carmela, you're cutting out. Hello... Oh no. Earliest, after eight tonight. Ran into a problem with the car. Please let Consul Craig know. Nothing major, but I'm delayed. Thanks, bye.

-Your office. You going to get into trouble?

Hey, I'm an intern. I'm expected to be incompetent, no?

-Excellent rationalization. You're made for public service.

The brake lights of Antonio's Jeep fire up, and he slows to negotiate a hard right turn into a narrower road—more like a path, really—and stops. We pull over behind them. Leticia climbs out of the Jeep, vigilant.

Gilly, let's walk in from here. Antonio, stay.

-Athena's just up the path. Why are we stopping? What's going on?

Antonio has too many questions for us to answer.

We don't know.

We don't. Flip's out the driver's door.

I'm going with you.

-Flip, no. Let us take a peek first and see if there's any activity. Could be a dead end.

--Be right back.

Leticia and I hustle up the pinyon pine–lined path. The air is thick with the sweet piney resin's suffocating smell. We come upon a gravel driveway overgrown with weeds where once there were flowers. Under the scorching sun, a white, freestanding adobe building glints with an ominous glow. Parked in front is the black Range Rover.

Someone's home. VJ could be inside.

-We need a plan, Tish.

Working on it.

saturday afternoon

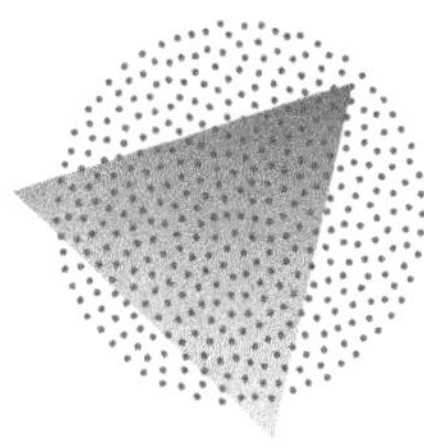

 He'd be off after Diego came in for his shift and Beau returned. His trip to the hotel to check on Marlena's friends was a waste of time. They were nowhere to be found and deemed not a threat. Walking down the hallway past the janitor's closet, El Chino was thinking about grilling up calves' liver and onions and then getting a good night's sleep, when he heard the main landline phone ringing in the lobby. He hurried to answer it.

In the closet, VJ heard the footsteps rushing by and opened the door a crack. He'd been waiting for a chance to go for the back exit. He could see the lobby and the figure on the phone.

The surgeon was expecting it to be Beau or Diego checking in, but it was Nurse Juana calling from the ayahuasca retreat.

***

In the nurse's office at the Green Door, the nervous Juana tried to make it quick. There was a young woman in the lobby looking for her missing brother. What should she do?

Waiting alone in the lobby, Aeura used the time to check out the calendar book at the front desk. She flipped it open and searched the previous week's appointments till she found what she was looking for. She didn't mean to mutter it out loud.

VJ was here.

She was by herself and then she wasn't. The nurse returned.

Ready for you now. Please, come with me.

Aeura bowed thanks and complied.

***

VJ went for it. Springing from the closet in a lab coat and sneakers, mop in hand, he sprinted down the hallway for the rear door, never looking back. It opened and activated the alarm, but he was out. He was in sunlight!

Dr. Foo was on the phone with the cousins when the fire door's alarm sounded. After the nurse's alert, he needed his local boys to hurry their butts over to the ayahuasca retreat. With Diego and Beau on their way to Athena, he had help if he needed it. But the doctor never thought that the prepped patient with the rare blood type could escape. Searching for the missing boy, El Chino moved with purpose, stopping only to grab an automatic rifle from the break room before hitting the rear door. It was jammed closed from the outside with the mop handle. The seething surgeon blasted a hole through it with a burst of gunfire and removed the mop.

10.

right now

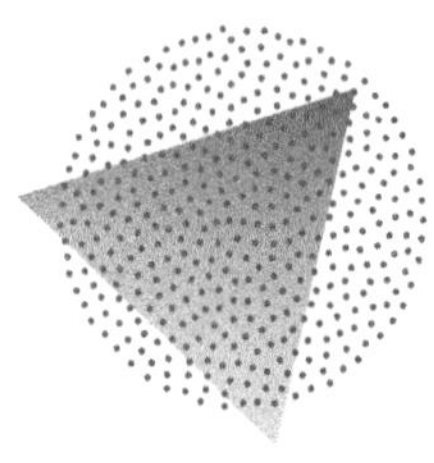

the gunshots shatter our strategy session. Huddled close, Leticia, Flip, and I lock eyes. Antonio stands up in his Jeep parked nearby.

Dios mio! Let's get out of here!

The local starts up his Jeep, motioning for Leticia. She doesn't budge.

Antonio, go!

-They're bad people out here. Come!

--It's cool. We get it, Antonio.

-*No, you don't. Muy peligroso. El cartel!*

What the shots meant isn't clear, but after the first burst, we don't hear any more. There's no turning back. We've come too far. I'm glad Fern and Aeura aren't here, and I hope they're somewhere safer. Flip goes for his car, and Leticia's right behind him.

It came from behind the building.

I catch up and hop into the back seat.

Flip, you have the gun?

-*In the glove compartment.*

--*Thanks for the ride, Antonio!*

Leticia yells it out the open passenger-side window. The local hospital worker and player shakes his head and crosses himself. We're off.

saturday afternoon

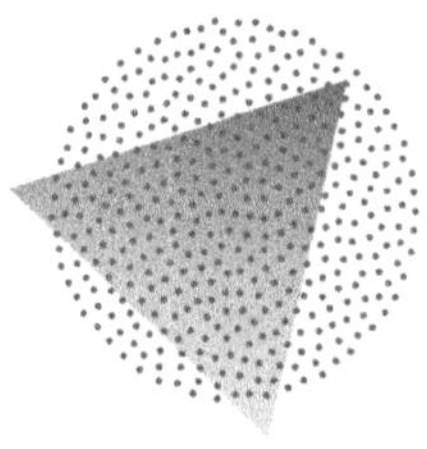

dr. foo kicked through the back door, stalking his prey. He'd been careless. He made a mental note to add security at all times during operation weeks. After methodically checking the rear exterior of the building, he scanned the territory beyond. It was open high desert brush till a rise in the sand, dominated by rare, strange, tall, spiked trees that he had learned were called boojums. They were named by the English botanist explorer who thought they resembled a monstrous plant in Lewis Carroll's *Hunting of the Snark*. The towering succulent trees had fascinated the surgeon when he'd first arrived. He had a photo of himself by an enormous, nasty-looking one. It looked like something out of the Spanish Inquisition, a vertical bed of nails. He'd had the picture framed and had given it to his bride to put on her nightstand. He liked the thought of her sleeping while he watched over.

El Chino was not rushed. There was nowhere for the boy to go. The road was the other way. He looked for tracks in the bleak hardscape and saw large sneaker prints, heading for the rise. He followed, with rifle ready. His panic subsided as the excitement of a chase took over. He reminded himself that the boy was worth more whole than full of holes and laughed at his cleverness. All was under control. They would be back on schedule.

VJ had sprinted. He was on the rise, trying to get his bearing. The young Japanese American from California, in a lab coat and nothing else, controlled his breathing like a good yoga student and focused on the best way to go. He was surrounded by strange, lethal-looking trees and low brush cacti. There were mountains not far off to the east, and his pursuer could be close. A blast of gunfire erupted, and a voice in the distance shouted.

Come back now and I won't kill you.

Somehow that didn't inspire confidence in VJ. He slipped off the shoes and, with his hands inside them, he made footprints leading away, along a path. He removed the lab coat, smudged his footprints, and tossed the white coat, which caught on a nearby spiked tree. Sneakers back on, he doubled back on all fours. Like a phantom, VJ hid naked, lying flat in a dense cactus grove, as chameleonlike as possible, in the shimmering, sun-drenched, sandy terrain. He thought invisible thoughts, using all his mental powers to blend into the earth. He was feeling full-on ninja, when his allergies—deprived of medication the last few days—kicked in.

Something had hold of VJ. He could feel a sneeze working its way into his nose.

***

With her Beverly Hills homey Donny Green Steiner standing by for support, Fern was at a stalemate at the BriteLite yoga camp's reception area. The ponytailed, tie-dye T-shirted camp manager had revealed that VJ's forwarding address was one of their cabins rented to Marlena Raskin. However, he rejected Fern's request to enter the room. Fern hoped to find some evidence that could help and wasn't about to leave empty-handed. Donny was eager to please his middle-school girlfriend. He may have been bad boy Bunky's son, but he grew up with his divorced mom. She was the daughter and heir of oil and timber titan Conrad Steiner, and they lived large.

Waving three crisp one-hundred-dollar bills, Donny secured directions to the cabin and the key for Fern. It was behind the old motor court structure, which served as the yoga camp's headquarters and residences. Donny was troubled by something he'd heard and took the moment to clarify with Fern.

Are you really still going with that Uni High guy, Fern? The pool guy's kid? Gilly?

-Yes, I am, Donny. Why?

Your dad must not… I mean, he goes to UC Riverside. Sad.

-At least he goes to college.

Hey, I was early admission to USC. I just…never mind. It's cool. Cool.

The key worked. Once inside the rustic room, Fern found VJ's laptop in a drawer. She gave Donny a celebratory cheek kiss for making it happen. He was feeling pretty good till they both heard a vehicle pull up right outside and froze. It was Beau. He'd stopped by to get a change of clothes that he kept at Marlena's before heading to the hospital. He was surprised that the door was unlocked. Inside, he looked around, but not hard enough to see Fern and Donny on the floor underneath the bed.

***

At the Green Door, the ayahuasca retreat, Aeura was done waiting. Juana had put her in a small meditation cell and had never come back. Aeura didn't expect to find the door locked from the outside. She banged on it with an urgent beat and protested. Loudly. Nurse Juana was the only one inside the facility. The *curandero* and weekend acolytes were off in the open-air gazebo, chanting.

Pacing the hallway, Juana had been promised help. Dr. Foo had told her to say nothing. It was important to keep the woman there till they came. But how and for how long? Aeura's screaming was a problem. In the supply room, the young nurse, looking to score points with the boss, found the sedative kept for those having a bad trip. She filled a syringe.

***

VJ couldn't stifle it anymore if his life depended on it—which it did. A sneezing attack erupted. His covert position was compromised. He could hear someone rushing through the brush, and he sprung up, bolting blindly to distance himself. A thunderous burst from an automatic rifle split the top of a boojum tree off to his right. His feet pounded on the hard sand, lungs burning, along with every muscle in his body. He broke for the spiky tree line on the ridge of the rise, running back toward the building. When he'd been hiding among the cacti, he had time to think of his expiring life. Marlena, that red-haired temptress, had set him up, and he felt like a fool. He was right to have slept on her couch and to have declined the invitation to share her bed. If he survived, he'd never let Leticia go.

Dr. Foo could see him running amid the low brush. He'd give up the profit on the boy's eyes to blow his head off. He'd harvest the other organs tonight, ahead of schedule. This was fun. Next week, in Mexico City, he'd dine out on the story with Juan Carlos, his boss and friend.

VJ broke for the open field, and El Chino took aim.

12.

right Now

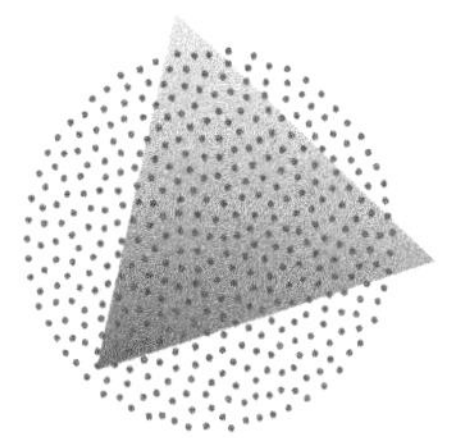

cautious, flip brakes. The SUV slows. With the increasing gunfire, we inch around the building for a better look. Beyond the open field, we see him—VJ, naked except for sneakers, running for his life. He zigs and zags and tumbles as shots miss him. Leticia screams.

Go! Go! VJ!

VJ doesn't hear us. He veers back toward the tree line. Flip accelerates toward the rise. The shooter appears, firing another blast to VJ's left. He's in no hurry. Relentless, El Chino is caught up in the hunt. VJ hides behind a tree and breaks for another. He sees us and changes direction toward the open field. He stumbles.

Gilly! The gun, get it!

I pop open the glove compartment and take hold of an Army-issue SIG Sauer. I've never held a real gun. I listen up to Flip.

The nub on the handle is the safety. Push it up. Let off some rounds to distract him!

I do as I'm told and stick the gun out the window. I point overhead and squeeze the trigger. The gun doesn't fire. I keep squeezing. Nothing!

What am I doing wrong!?

Flip sneaks a peek.

No! Sheesh. I forgot. There's no magazine.

-There's no time! He's on us.

The hunter at the tree line spins his rifle around to target us.

Duck!

Duh! Bullets demolish the windshield and tear up the seats where we just sat. Head low, Flip has one eye ahead and one hand on the steering wheel. With his other hand, he pushes hard on the accelerator. The car speeds right for a surprised Dr. Foo, who keeps firing. The cartel surgeon tries to jump away at the last moment but backs into a boojum tree! He's snagged in it, twisted around. Before he can untangle himself, our car hits him, pinning him face first into the spiky tree. The boojum, hollow at its core, teeters over and crashes on top of our car. The consulate car comes to a halt.

It's so quiet. And dark. Steam from the ruptured radiator fills the air and our nostrils. The tree is above, blocking the sunlight. Blood drips through the shattered windshield into the car and onto me. It's not my blood, not Flip's, and not Leticia's. No one can say a word—we're all still processing. We count our blessings. We're intact. The hunter not so much.

Gracias! Gracias!

VJ's voice breaks the stillness. As quickly as we can, we break out of the front and back doors of our wrecked ride. VJ looks like a god, naked, glowing under the desert sun. Except for the Magic Marker's dotted lines, indelible on his chest for a butcher's template, the dude has never looked better. VJ's shocked to see us, over the moon and beyond.

Gilly!? Leticia! Tish!!

He and Leticia gravitate to each other like silly love magnets in slow but sure motion. Arms wide, they clasp into the tightest embrace, and I swear I'm crying at this sight. VJ in big Nikes and nothing else and Leticia swallowed in his arms. The kiss goes on for so long that Flip and I turn our attention to the tree on the car. We lift it up enough to see an Asian man, face and torso impaled in spikes lethal as an iron maiden. Blood still gurgles from his pierced neck. Flip feels for a pulse and gets none.

Pierced the jugular. He bled out.

-It's El Chino. Local head of the cartel.

I stare at him and feel no remorse.

How do you know?

-I know.

Between Marlena and the cousins on the boat, his reputation preceded him. He was the man and now he's dead. Exuberant, Leticia and VJ, molded into one, join us.

VJ, meet the amazing Flip.

-That was crazy rizz! You nailed him!

--Flip's our own action hero.

The consulate intern won't even humble brag.

I had to do something. I forgot the bullets!

We all laugh and hug, and it's glorious. Leticia kisses my cheek, Flip's too. VJ has a dopey grin.

Gilly, you came, bro!

-Dude, we all did.

--Fern and Aeura are looking for you nearby.

-We love you, dog. Fab Five forever.

Overcome, VJ, a *Game of Thrones* nerd, thanks the "Old Gods and the New." Flip drapes his sport jacket on VJ, helped by Leticia, who looks like the weight of the world is off her. She lets it all out and brings VJ into another needed kiss. I lean against the Kia, fishing inside the back door for a YETI water bottle on the seat, and take a sip. Flip takes a swig, too.

I think we're—

-Marked men a long way from home?

Bull's-eye. We're not safe.

The enormity of the situation is creeping in. Flip and I stare at the medical facility's blasted-open door, expecting hard cases from El Chino's gang to emerge at any moment. We've killed a cartel capo. Nothing will change that. If I had a phone and reception, I'd call Duke and tell him I love him. Fern next. I think of her and Aeura and imagine them waiting for us at the restaurant knocking back margaritas. I got nothing to offer. Oblivious to our situation, VJ and Leticia keep the intimacy going. I don't blame them. It's up to Flip and me.

Any ideas what we do?

-First thing...

Flip gets behind the wheel of the car, hits the ignition, and it starts up, surprisingly, engine humming strong and sudden like our hearts. He backs it up and out from beneath the tree, which hits the hard sand, corpse and all, with a liberating thud. Before Flip has a chance to change gears and we can all pile in, we hear a sharp *snap* from under the hood and the *flappity flap flap* of the Kia's fan belts breaking. The engine seizes, the consulate car is toast. Flip lets out a low moan, and I feel him. This time he asks me.

Is there a second thing?

Off the ground, I pick up El Chino's automatic rifle, knocked free from the dead man's hand. Flip brightens.

That'll help. We know it's loaded.

-Guys!

Looking over Leticia's shoulder in their endless embrace, VJ spots him first, Diego—the leather-coat–wearing thug at the hospital's back door. His stocky frame fills the portal. He studies the area.

Dr. Foo! Dr. Foo?

On the rise, we're exposed—a tableau of four gringos and a wrecked car. Leather coat sees us. Yes, he does. He'd have to be impaired not to. After being drugged and confined, VJ lets loose with abandon. My friend, the smartest guy I know, taunts Diego, arms out wide, sport coat open, in all his natural glory, dotted chest blazing in the late afternoon sun.

He's dead! Muerto! SOR-RY! Not!

-VJ!

--Dude! Was that wise?

Can't make it worse, bro. Felt super sweet!

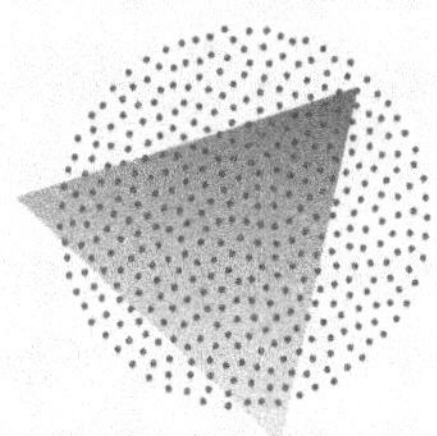

AEURA

saturday afternoon

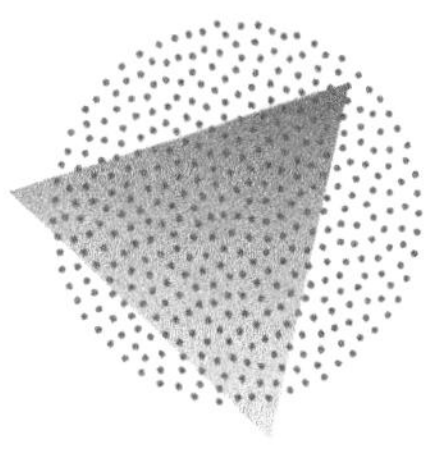

Locked in the windowless room, Aeura's heart was racing. No one had heard her commotion. It was clear that she was in danger. Her inquiry about VJ had touched a nerve. Aurea's mind flashed back. It was two years ago—almost to the day—when she, Gilly, and their friends had exposed a murderous Beverly Hills conspiracy. *Experience counts*, she said aloud, instincts kicking in. She'd tried to use her cell and call Flip, but there had been no reception. The thought of the handsome, cosmopolitan intern—make that the *very male* intern—was a pleasant wrinkle as she searched the room again for anything useful. The small space was spartan and gave her no weapon better than her camera. Aeura was ready when Nurse Juana knocked on the locked door.

I'm coming in. Please, there was a misunderstanding. Pardon.

The ambitious young nurse, taking initiative, had the syringe hidden in the sleeve of her smock. Feeling confident, she entered with the most effective professional smile and closed the door behind her.

Sorry to have made you—

Juana was surprised by Aeura's "clueless Asian with camera" act. The Nikon was focused on her and clicked away.

-Hold please. Smile.

The more photos and angles Aeura snapped, the more impatient Juana got. Juana was in good physical shape and had even trained in an MMA gym as a teenager, which could work in her favor, if challenged. She let the needle with a knockout sedative slip down into her hand, and she moved hard on Aeura to grab her.

During the previous spring, Aeura, ever the traveler, had a brief obsession with Argentine folk dancing, specifically the Malambo. It's the gaucho dance of agility and strength. Aeura swung the Nikon by its strap above her head like she was a cowboy on the Pampas and let it fly. The heavy, metal camera smashed into Juana's temple, and she collapsed. Aeura crept closer, expecting the woman to bounce back up. Juana moaned but didn't move, not even after Aeura poked her. The slender, nineteen-year-old, goth punkster thought that she'd overpowered Juana until she saw the needle stuck in the nurse's arm. The sudden fall had caused Juana to inject herself with the dose meant for Aeura. The nurse was out cold and snoring. Aeura gave thanks with a few spirited steps of the Malambo and a rhythmic handclap finish.

Olé!

***

Fern and Donny stayed stiff as cadavers, hugging the pine floor beneath the queen-sized bed in the rustic cabin near the yoga camp. They could see Beau's snakeskin boots moving around the space. He changed clothes, hit the head, and farted loudly. He also unlocked a drawer to retrieve a .38 revolver and bullets. Under the bed, it was a challenge to stay still, to say the least. Fern was more than OK with Donny being so close. He smelled like Invictus by Paco Rabanne, a quality aftershave that her dad also used. Donny always had good taste. It was Fern's idea to not park Donny's rental Lexus in front of Marlena's abode. That decision was fortuitous and made their intrusion less obvious while they waited out Beau.

The second that Marlena's ex left the cabin and drove off, they were out from beneath the bed. Fern knew that he was involved in VJ's situation and wasn't going to let the opportunity pass. She grabbed hold of her Beverly Hills homeboy and was out the door.

We have to follow him.

-What?!

Donny, I need you!

-I'm supposed to meet Bunky!

Donny! Who authored your English essay in eighth grade? Did you get your only A ever!?

-Oh, OK.

They took off in his rental car on the only road out.

***

At the hospital formerly known as Athena, Diego was not a man to make decisions quickly. He could see that the gringos had an automatic rifle. It was probably the one missing from the break room. He had a pistol with a full mag but didn't like the fact they had the higher ground and cover behind their crashed car. With Dr. Foo missing and presumed dead, the Todos Santos–raised thug had to be sure before he told Juan Carlos back in Mexico City. El Jefe and El Chino were friends, and Diego didn't want to take any blame for his demise. Juan Carlos was crazy. Diego thought about getting his old Land Rover, which was parked out front, and charging their position, but there was risk. It burned him that he'd been passed over for promotion by Juan Carlos. El Chino got the position, and his arrival changed things in Baja South. The new business became the priority. Diego found it messy in more ways than one, but he did as he was ordered. The OG liked having his hands in the drug, taxi, and fishing businesses. They were stable. Now the doctor's trouble was his to own, and he had to be careful. At the rear door, using binoculars to look out at the rise again, Diego could see an official seal on the side of the disabled vehicle.

Out front of Athena, Beau parked his Jeep next to Diego and Dr. Foo's cars. In a fresh T-shirt and jeans, he used a key fob to get inside the medical facility. If he'd looked behind him before the door closed, he'd have seen a silver Lexus as Fern and Donny silently pulled up in the driveway.

***

At the Green Door, Aeura took the time to go through the sleeping nurse's bag and snagged Juana's car keys. Aeura needed to catch up with the others. She tried to call Flip again. Shock of shocks, the cell coverage was nil. She'd have to find reception somewhere. Aeura kept her head down and walked through the hall of the ayahuasca retreat, making a quick stop at the open pharmacy closet to see what she could grab. On her way out of the lobby to the red exit door, she was glad not to encounter a single soul. In the parking area were an assortment of vehicles. The sun was getting low, the day cooling off. Aeura hit Juana's car remote button, and a dirty Toyota pickup's rear lights flashed. Before she could get in the vehicle, a voice froze her.

Hey Fern's friend! A little help.

It was Bunky, the boomer. He was agitated and not pleasant or flirty. His son, Donny, was supposed to be right back. The ceremony was starting. That's why they were there. He demanded to know where Fern was and what she was up to. Aeura tried to calm him.

I think she's at the yoga camp. I'm going to go check. Come with me.

-I can't now! When did you get a car?

Loaner. I'd better go.

-This have anything to do with Fern and the damn pool guy's kid?

Bunky grabbed her wrist and held her back. His comment about Gilly tore into Aeura's soul. She shot back at the elitist attitude and boomer entitlement.

Ya! Welcome to the new world order. #eattherich

Aeura was a Gen Alpha crusader, not about to let him get away with marginalization of the poor. But Bunky was not going to let go of Aeura till he had answers about his missing son. It got intense, and they both ignored a white van arriving and parking in the space next to the Toyota. That changed when two Mexican thugs, one with purple hair, got out and took notice of their spat.

Sent by Dr. Foo to help Juana, the cousins approached the altercation. Bunky dropped his hold on Aeura's wrist with an innocent smile. The older hard case stared at Aeura. She felt obvious and vulnerable. They could be there because of her. She lowered her eyes. The thug spoke English.

This your papa?

-No.

Ah. He bothering you?

Considering his question, Aeura didn't mean to pause as long as she did. It was reasonable doubt enough for the purple-haired hood to unload a sudden punch into Bunky's midsection. The rock drummer and legend in his own mind doubled over and dropped to his knees. The older gangster spit at Bunky on his way to the red door.

Have respect for women, hippie.

Aeura got into the pickup as quickly as she could. A distressed Bunky yelled as she took off.

Find Donny!

2.

right Now

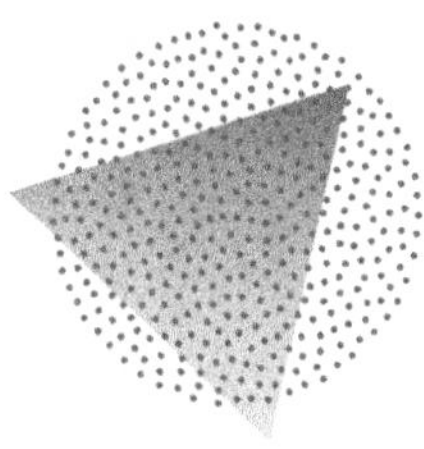

 I don't want to think about the picture in his wallet of his young bride or about my lack of empathy for a fellow human being. I know in my heart that he was evil and is no more. On the rise, above the rear of the medical building in the middle of nowhere, we're in a stalemate it seems. A situation that won't last. Our older brother in arms stands guard with the automatic rifle, while we all consider the options. Flip thinks we should surrender and talk to leather coat. After all, Flip is a representative of the US government.

That should have some weight.

-Good weight or bad?

Leticia and I are wary. We agree that it's best if we can get word to the consulate first.

There's a steep hill beyond the spiked trees. We may be able to get a signal there.

-Call in the Marines.

--Whatever it takes, guys. I want to go home!

VJ is naked no more. He has recovered a gym bag in the car trunk and looks tight in Flip's Georgetown Hoyas shorts and blazer. With VJ rocking gray-and-blue tube socks planted in his Nikes, I can hear the Duke humming that ZZ Top classic "Sharp Dressed Man." VJ models, with serious rizz of his own, a man on death row with a reprieve. For how long? I won't go there.

Leticia keeps eye out, with Flip as a spotter. There's no movement at the rear of the hospital. Leather coat must be inside. He seems to be alone. Flip sees our point and gives me his cell.

Consul number is on speed dial. Push 1.

-I'm going with him. See if I can reach Fern and Aeura. VJ—

--I stay back and spot.

VJ surprises Leticia with a kiss.

What's that for?

-In case I don't see you again.

VJ tells her he's kidding. He's not. We all understand the danger we're in. Flip waves us off.

Make it quick.

-Dude, with f-ing alacrity.

Leticia and I move single file toward the foothill of the mountain, snaking through the grove of spiked trees, with phones raised above our heads. It's after five, and we'll be losing light soon. I'm not one for hiking and laugh at the thought of Fern and me last January doing a New Year's Day forced march in the Santa Monica Mountains with her trainers' group. She hates hiking, too.

Well, there's something you have in common.

-Thanks. I think I'm going to lose her.

Fern? No way.

-Since Fern came back from France, something's different.

Do you love her?

-I do. And she loves me. Just may not be enough.

That leaves Leticia swirling about her and VJ's relationship. She's certain, more than.

It's forever, Gilly. Checks all the boxes.

I envy Leticia and VJ. They nourish each other. Maybe it took a life-and-death experience to reveal it. Maybe that's what it takes. I'm about to relay to my high school crush this pearl of relationship wisdom when my hand vibrates and Flip's phone rings with the most generic and most welcome tone. We stop in our tracks in a high clearing to answer. It's Aeura! My heart soars. We have cell reception, and we have Aeura!

Flip?

-It's Gilly. We need help. I have to call the consul office. You OK?

Now I am. They tried to drug me when I asked about VJ.

-Aeura, VJ's with us. He's all in one piece. Stay safe. I'll call you back.

I end the call, push the speed dial, and hold down the 1 key. The call connects.

U.S. Consulate, Cabo San Lucas.

It's Flip's assistant, Carmela—her voice the sweetest music. I delivered the SOS message for Consul Craig. We're good.

3.

Saturday, Late Afternoon

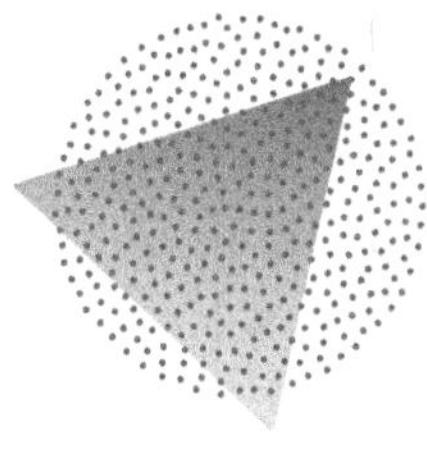

JUAN CARLOS POSADA HAD SURVIVED AN EPIC, RUTHLESS RIDE FROM HIS APPRENTICE DAYS as an enforcer in the bloody back alleys of Guadalajara to the pinnacle of power in Mexico City. More than anyone, he'd taken the cartel to heights of respectability and near legitimacy. The territory they now controlled, in treaty with their brother cartels, was in balance and stable. Their profits were growing, especially in Baja California South. The gang wars and reign of terror that had preceded this were over. El Jefe ruled with an iron fist, enabled by connections to the highest level of government and industry. He was respected and feared like an influential corporate CEO, and he always dressed the part. On the seventeenth hole of the exclusive Madeiras Country Club's PGA tour quality course, the day could not have been turning worse. He excused himself to his foursome, which consisted of a top banker, an oil lobbyist, and the deputy secretary of the Interior, and answered his ringing cell.

Earlier, on the fifteenth hole, after a double bogey, Diego, his second in command in the south, had interrupted his game to tell him that a patient had escaped from the surgery center and Dr. Foo had been killed. Foo had become a friend, a model of productive efficiency, loyal to a fault. He'd agreed to Foo's new business because he trusted the cultured doctor, and now this disaster could expose it. Most disturbing, a U.S. Consulate car was involved and damage control was paramount. Sitting in his electric cart, El Jefe checked the number on the display and answered his cell phone. He spoke in English with a strong regional accent.

Consul Craig. Thank you for calling me back.

Craig had been alerted that his intern, Foster Marks, and a group of Americans had suffered an accident and needed rescue in the high desert outside Todos Santos. He was going to send some Marines, who were normally at the airport, to extricate them ASAP from the problem, with apologies.

That's not necessary. A swat team of federales have been ordered to arrest them for murder.

Consul Craig sputtered words of confusion. Juan Carlos filled in the part about the consulate vehicle being used to mercilessly run down and kill a respected local doctor.

Your people refuse to surrender. They're armed and dangerous. Federales will handle it.

-I...I—

I know. You're sorry. As always, your understanding will be appreciated. Best to the family.

Call over, Juan Carlos, in the finest TravisMathew golf fashion, returned to the game in a better mood.

In Cabo San Lucas, Consul Craig canceled the Marines.

***

Fern! I have to get back. My dad's going to—

-Just do it. I can't. He's seen me before. You'll be fine.

Donny was freaking out. Fern had hijacked him and the car, and he wasn't sure what to do. The rental Lexus idled by some neglected scrub brush in the driveway of the private hospital that was once Athena. Fern braced her 90210 homeboy by the shoulders of his navy-and-white CK tank top.

When he answers the door, play lost lookie-loo and look around inside.

-No! That guy has a gun, Fern. This is dodgy AF.

***

Inside the facility, Beau had planned to get the human waste from the afternoon surgery and dump it in the wild cougar preserve. Diego changed that with the shocking update. *Adios El Chino.* The two men stood in the open rear doorway, eyes trained a way off on the disabled Kia SUV and on the two men staring back from the rise.

Flip and VJ were vigilant. Using the Kia for cover, they stood behind with rifle in clear view for Diego and Beau to see. They figured the standoff meant that Flip and VJ held the edge in firepower. For how long—that was the question. Leticia and I had been off searching for cell reception longer than expected. Not that our presence would help without more weapons. It was nerve-racking, Flip couldn't deny. VJ was amazed and impressed that the young consulate intern had joined in the rescue.

Very grateful human here, though it seems a tad beyond the call of duty.

-Blame it on a girl.

Serious? I know the feeling. RIP Marlena. Who are you talking about?

-Aeura. I want to know her better.

Wow, cool. There's a lot to know.

A crackle in the sandy underbrush behind them sent their heads spinning. Leticia and I returned, mission accomplished.

Consul Craig got the message. Marines are on the way!

I added that Aeura had a car and was looking for Fern, who was still unaccounted for. Leticia had also rung up the local kid, Antonio. She left a message for him to notify any local police he could trust. So they were covered. VJ was ecstatic. Flip was more measured.

I hope they make it here before we lose light.

-Gilly said that American lives were in jeopardy. Couldn't have been clearer.

Leticia gave it her vote of confidence. I asked to relieve Flip on watch, and the tired Georgetown alum handed over the AK-15.

Ever fire one?

-No, but I devoured many, many YouTube clips of school shooters.

Close enough.

Across the open field, the golden hour sunset cast Diego, .357 in hand, in a sickly glow. He hated having to depend on Beau. He never got why Marlena was with him. The cartel lifer wished that he hadn't been ordered to throw her off the roof of the Palmilla. He'd liked her. He'd enjoy eliminating Beau when the time came.

Do you have a gun?

-Yeah, in the car.

Get it. They can't leave the area.

-It's just us?

For now.

***

Outside, at the front of the remote medical facility, in the rented silver sedan, Fern and Donny were mid-argument, when she caught sight of the entrance door opening and Beau stepping out. Without missing a beat, she grabbed an oblivious Donny and yanked him into an intense, full-lip smooch that rocked his Richter scale. He tried to speak.

Fern???

She squeezed his nuts and removed her tongue from his mouth.

Play along.

-Oh...

Donny saw her eyes shift off, and he got the message. The fallen Prince of Beverly Hills, here for a bounce-back, relaxed and got with it. The windshield quickly steamed from heavy breathing.

Beau had retrieved his gun from his Jeep, when his interest was drawn to the unfamiliar silver car. He walked over, .38 in hand. He could see Donny, with shorts at the ankles, pulling Fern's T-shirt over her head. He smothered his face in the lacy bra, cupping a breast. His right hand went lower. They were making all the right noises. Interrupting them, Beau tapped on the windshield with the pistol. He was more amused than on guard. Donny opened the driver's door a crack.

Beau pulled it open all the way, lowered the gun, and stuck his head in the idling Lexus.

This is private property.

-Uh, sorry. We, uh… You know…

Hey, you. Let me see your face.

Masked by the white Prada T-shirt over her head, Fern pretended to not know that Beau was talking to her. She had every reason to believe that he'd recognize her from the Pioneertown melee.

Donny nudged her.

Sweetie…

-He has to turn away first. I'm so embarrassed…

Fern folded into a fetal position. Donny hitched back up his Greyson Montauk designer shorts and shrugged at Beau, looking for understanding. Beau chuckled and turned away. God knows why. Fern yelled to Donny.

Go, GO!

Getting smarter by the second, Donny hit drive and the Lexus rocketed off like an F-1 silver streak, catching the cartel wannabee/bartender bad boy by surprise. Beau thought about firing at it but didn't. Dust blew around him in gusts. What the hell. Not his worry.

***

At the Green Door, the ayahuasca retreat, the final ceremony before the sacrament morning had ended. The initiates were moving off, and the *curandero* was lingering with a few people, including Bunky. The healer couldn't ignore the presence of the two thug cousins who'd been scouring the grounds for the intruder. The *curandero* excused himself from his acolytes to deal with the hoods. They immediately apologized to the holy man and explained that they were only doing their job. The *curandero* made it clear that they had to leave, and the men didn't challenge him. The *curandero* deserved respect, and the locals gave it.

The cousins had come up empty in their search and went inside to question Nurse Juana again. She was finally coming out of the cobwebs of being drugged and gave the men a full description of Aeura. The cousins—not geniuses—wondered whether the person they were looking for was the Asian girl they'd seen in the parking lot when they'd arrived. The older cousin recalled.

She drove off in a red pickup.

-My red pickup!?

At the same time Juana realized that her keys were taken by Aeura, the cousins realized that they'd let Aeura slip away. The local muscle had already screwed up killing Marlena on the boat and now this. Such was the tenuous life of a henchman. The older gangster made Juana promise to never say they saw Aeura leave, and Juana made them promise not to say Aeura dosed her. Henchmen code of ethics: Cover your ass. On their way out, Bunky waved at the cousins with a taunt.

I've just filed a formal complaint against you with the management.

Purple hair came over and punched Bunky in the stomach again.

***

Donny Green's right Allbirds loafer was in spasms, tapping on the Lexus's accelerator as the car jerked along the narrow back road toward Todos Santos. He was experiencing a nervous afterburn from the experience, and there seemed to be only one cure. Leticia calmed him.

Donny, we're good. Relax. Pull over.

Donny turned off the rough paved road, put it in park, and took a shot of his inhaler to catch a breath.

That was super cool. I did OK, huh?

-You slayed it. Not as good as your Harold Hill in the high school musical.

Ha. <u>The Music Man</u>. A definite high point. You remembered!

Fern gave him a supportive hug, and he literally burst into tears.

I've always loved you, Fern. I'd do anything for you.

-You just did.

She gave him a kiss on the cheek, and he tried to make it more. Fern held him back.

Donny, whoa—

-I learned everything I know about a woman's body from you. The G-spot, Fern.

It was true. Fern couldn't deny it. They were twelve and had a heated "I'll show you mine, you show me yours" night in a Beverly Hills Beach Club cabana. It gave them both an education.

-That wasn't the only time. We masturbated each other. I can still hear you having an orgasm.

Donny, you need to get back to your dad. I have to find my friends. We found the surgery place.

-One more kiss. Please.

Fern granted it and was surprised how natural it felt with Donny. She was glad he'd gotten hold of his addiction. Even if he was only California sober, it allowed him a fresh start. He could lose weight—in the past, he'd always been thin. Plus, with a position guaranteed in his mother's family empire, a girl could do worse. All these thoughts were dancing in Fern's head while they kissed and snuggled.

Coming up the road in a red Toyota pickup, Aeura recognized the silver Lexus parked up ahead as the same car that Leticia and her friend had driven off in. As she got closer, she could see the Donny and Fern in an enthusiastic embrace. Aeura drove up alongside the car with a polite toot of the horn. The couple broke free from the deep smooch and looked up. Aeura chuckled. Fern was mortified.

Aeura?

-No worries, I never judge. VJ's ok! They have him!

What!? Yeah!!!

-He's with Gilly, Leticia, and Flip. They're trapped on a ridge not far from here. The consulate is sending in US Marines for them. We did it!

Fern and Donny hurried out of their car. Aeura was out, too, hugging Fern. They were all congratulating themselves. An unnerving rumbling sound in the distance got louder and louder before its source came into view. It was an assortment of military vehicles carrying Mexican *federales* soldiers in combat Jeeps, a geared-up SWAT team in an open troop truck, and two machine-gun–topped urban assault vehicles. Keeping up with the convoy was a white van with the two cartel cousins. The older one looked off at the red pickup idling by the side of the road and pretended he didn't see it. Aeura hid behind Donny and Fern till the procession, van and all, passed and the dust settled.

F-ing F! This is totally F-ed!

-Aeura, those are not US soldiers!

We have to warn the others. Follow me.

Aeura sprang for her purloined pickup. Fern grabbed Donny's hand, dragging him toward the Lexus. The Beverly Hills boy offered some resistance.

--Uh, Fern—

-Donny, drive!

# 4.

right Now

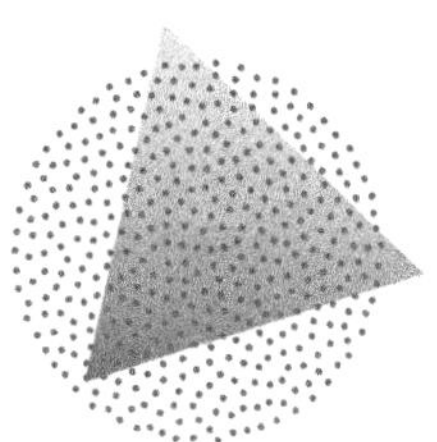

 Darkness has set in. On guard with the rifle, I have a good view of the rear of the hospital. Flip and Leticia are napping in the disabled car as we wait for the Marines to arrive and escort us out safely. Leather coat and Beau have been out by the rear door on and off for a good half hour. VJ sits on a rock next to me, talking about the life and death of Marlena. He is stoic, emotionless.

I don't know whether to celebrate or mourn. She used me.

-She also tried to save you, dude. We wouldn't be here without her help.

That makes me feel a sliver short of a lame-ass fool. Thanks.

I have to know, and I put it to him. Were they intimate? He's gotta be straight.

Gilly, I had a golden chance, and I didn't take it. What's wrong with me?

-You love Leticia.

Ya. A lesson learned about fidelity. Would you have?

I think about whether I would have slept with Marlena, kids, and the answer is yes. I have too much Duke Montrose testosterone in me maybe. Or maybe I don't know where Fern and I are headed and am keeping my options open. It's hard to sustain a relationship, that much I know.

Fern would strangle you if she heard you say that.

-I'm expecting Fern to suggest that we have a more open relationship and see other people.

What? Dog! Serious?

It's true that I'm expecting Fern to go that route. I'm trying to hide any hurt and look at it in a positive way. In my heart, I'm sure that if we do have the stuff to be a forever thing, it will reveal itself.

VJ stretches out in his borrowed sport jacket and Georgetown gym wear. He looks like he's won the lottery. The pure bliss of being alive. He's making me so relaxed that neither of us hear the army coming to destroy us till it's almost too late. VJ's mistaken and lets out a cheer.

Here we go. The Marines have landed!

-No! Duck!

I see the gunners first. VJ's almost caught in the raking machine-gun fire blasting at us from the two urban assault vehicles—one on each side of the hospital building! Leticia and Flip are as confused as we are. Fight or flee? The answer's obvious. The blaze of bullets is literally the only light we have. Heads down, under fire, we grab what we can and retreat into the shadows of night and up into the grove of spiky trees. We must tread carefully but still hurry. Leticia and I lead the way to the foothills. Leticia has the only operating smartphone. She gets her flashlight app going. Flip is beside himself. He left his consulate cell phone behind.

Gilly, you're sure you gave Carmela our SOS?

-Yes! She promised to get it to your consul.

OK. They'll come! We're Americans! They have to.

Somehow I don't feel the same confidence. It feels like we're on our own. Every second that Leticia's flashlight is on wastes precious battery life, our only hope for communicating with the outside world.

Tish, kill it. We need the juice to call out when we get higher.

-We won't get higher without this light!

She's right, of course. Usually is. This is an obstacle course, an anti-death march to the mountain.

Hold on! I got tangled.

Don't move.

Leticia goes back, and under the flashlight's tight beam, I remove VJ's T-shirt fabric from the hungry cactus tree. An unexpected quiet descends. We hold our breaths. The gunfire has stopped, no movement is heard. The federales force has stopped advancing in the dark. Flip asserts himself.

We go back. Wave a white flag.

-Flip, they were shooting to kill on first sight.

--I'm with VJ. A cartel fix is in. Those are government troops—here for us!

How can that be? They must have been notified by the consulate that our boys are coming.

---*Maybe they know that they're <u>not</u> coming.*

I'm compelled to mention this. We all agree, even Flip, that we must keep moving to stay alive.

5.

saturday night

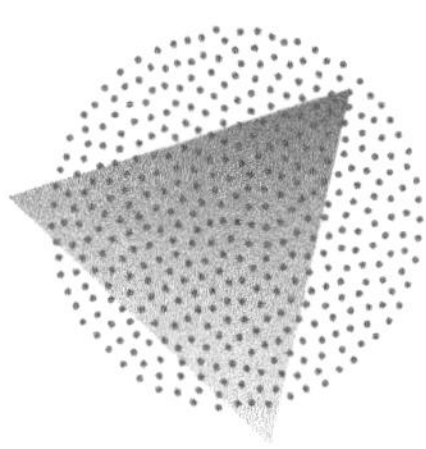

reLAXiNg oN the bed, buNky WAs bAre-chested iN MArgAritAviLLe boxers, smoking a joint, when the casita door opened. It was Donny, returning with Fern and that little cutie who got him punched in the stomach twice. The group charged into the retro-chic motel room on a mission.

Sorry, Dad. It's an emergency. Can you cover up?

What?! Fern!

-Hi, Mr. Green. We need to use the landline phone. Aeura…

The punk goth cutie shot Bunky a contrite smile and sat on the bed to use the bedside phone. Bunky got up, put on a spa robe, and took another drag.

It'll take you to their 1970s switchboard so they can charge you. It's on me.

-Dad, I'll—

Hey, I don't want your friends to think I'm always a dick.

He offered Aeura a hit of the pre-roll he was working, and she took it like a peace pipe.

Sweet. Can I take a selfie later with Bunky Green?

-You got it. I'll even put on pants.

While the others used the bathroom and got their phones plugged in to charge, Aeura first called Flip's number. It went straight to voicemail without a ring. She then tried Leticia's cell, and it connected.

Leticia!

In the foothills of the Sierra de la Laguna Mountains, Leticia, VJ, Flip, and Gilly were huddled, native style, on mossy ground inside a cropping of boulders, under the moonless night sky. Only Leticia's face could be seen in the light of her display screen, listening on speaker. The others hung on each scratchy, in-and-out word. Leticia tried to be as clear as possible.

Aeura! We need help.

-We know. A federales force was headed your way.

That's why we fled up the mountain. We're in some conservation area.

With near-zero battery life showing, Leticia wasn't sure where to turn. She'd tried calling the consulate emergency number, but it clicked off before anyone could answer. Flip feared the reason.

Our cells are blocked.

-Is that possible?

--*The cartel rules.*

Aeura said the obvious for Bunky's benefit. The joint fell from the old drummer's trembling lips.

Cartel! What the—?! Donny?

-*Shh! She's kidding.*

--*I'm not.*

It's OK. I know my way around made guys. Music biz, just sayin'...

---*Aeura, hold on. Gilly has something.*

In their remote high desert lair in the foothills, Leticia handed the phone to Gilly. He took it off speaker.

In the morning, they're going to come for us. Aeura, what can you do?

-*Turn on the Find My Phone app. Enable me to track your location. I'll screenshot it.*

Got it. Doing... Is Fern there?

In the yoga camp casita, Aeura passed the big black landline phone to Fern.

Gilly?

Call your father. Maybe he knows someone who can help.

-*I will.*

I love you.

A nanosecond and Leticia's cell cut out, going silent as silent can be. Gilly handed it back. He was glad that he'd said that out loud. He didn't need for Fern to say it back. Above them, a whirring sound tore through the stillness.

What's that?

-*Drone!*

Gilly and the others folded into the rock crevasses and prayed for invisibility. The night drone combed the area, its spotlight sweeping past them.

***

Gaiety was peaking at an over-the-top Taylor Swift–themed quinceañera in a swank Mexico City hotel ballroom. Juan Carlos was in attendance with his teenaged daughter, Rosa, and his wife to celebrate Rosa's BFF's sixteenth birthday. It was a cringeworthy nighttime affair for the gangster businessman, though his precious gals would disagree. When the star of the night was on the stage doing a Taylor-like lip-sync of "Willow" to her adoring, singing-along Swiftie friends, Juan Carlos was glad to have a phone call to distract him. He moved out to the hallway to catch up with Diego in Todos Santos. The cartel CEO had been thinking about the late Dr. Foo's business and the untidy particulars left behind. He wanted Diego to make sure that it was shut down entirely and that all traces of the operation were eliminated. Diego knew what he meant but asked anyway.

People included?

-Yes. Use your discretion. Any outsider intimate with the details.

Diego figured that meant Beau and the surgery nurse. The leather-coat–wearing henchman felt upwardly mobile, talking directly to the boss, and tried to rise to the occasion. He updated the situation about the escaped patient and his friends with a reassuring tone. There was no reason for any concern. Diego was in control. He had the federales camped for the night, ready and awaiting orders. A military drone they'd launched had spotted the Americans about two miles east of the surgery facility, up the mountain and inside the region's fenced wild cougar preserve.

You're kidding? That's where they're hiding?

-Yes sir.

This made Juan Carlos's night. He had to rein in the hilarity. At daybreak, the soldiers would move in to eradicate them. The fresh kill would be left for the cougars. Perfect, efficient. El Chino would be proud. Back inside the ballroom, the birthday girl and her friends were going strong. Into it, Juan Carlos clapped to the beat, dancing in place like a hardcore fan, to the ebullient approval of his daughter and wife.

6.

right now

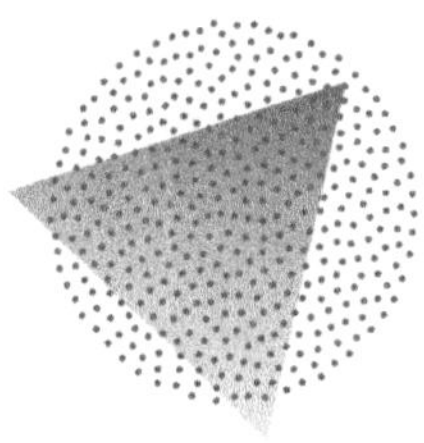

it's before dawn, of that i'm sure. The sun will be up soon and, with it, the federales under the direction of the cartel. The U.S. Consulate has apparently abandoned us. We're twisting in the winds of fate, and I'm reminded of one of Duke's favorite country songs, "Jesus, Take the Wheel." It's a resonant, early Carrie Underwood song about an unavoidable car accident and a plea for divine intervention to make it through. It's about faith. Faith that's slowly seeping out of me. Where's our *deus ex machina*? For those who never elected to study freshman Mythology 101, it's the golden chariot sent down from the sky by Helios, the sun god, to save an unsavable situation.

Dream on. I wish I could turn off my brain and rest like the others. Leticia and VJ are asleep in each other's arms, using a mossy rock for a pillow. Flip, too, has nodded off, with rifle still in hand. We have few bullets left, he says, another comforting thought. I've tried to sleep, but this darkness is terrifying. It feels like death. I have the uneasy sensation that eyes are lurking, watching me in the dark, but I lack the courage to get up and dispel the notion. I can hear movement in the underbrush, and I don't care. "Jesus, Take the Wheel." Please. I'm sleep-deprived, dehydrated, and hungry. Our supply of water and snacks has been exhausted. This has not been a great semester break.

Gilly.

I hear my name whispered. It's Aeura's voice. I can't be dreaming.

Huh? Aeura? Over here.

-Hi, peeps!

It's Aeura, like a spirit in the night. Leticia and VJ stir and gasp in the best way. Flip pretends he was never asleep, eyes widening at the sight of the adorable punkster. If there was any light at all, I'd see the devilish smile on her face.

Knew you'd be hungry and thirsty. I got loaded with the drummer from Poison and my favorite underappreciated grunge band, Top Spin. Meet Bunky Green.

She's not alone. An older man is with her. He flicks a BIC, and we see him in the light of its flame. He gives a wink. He's in a jogging suit, red-faced and out of breath.

It's quite a hike up. I don't know what I'm doing here. Remind me.

-I promised to do ayahuasca with you.

--Where's Fern? She OK?

Her and Bunky's son, Donny, are busy… I mean, not like that, Gilly.

--Well, they were an item at Beverly Vista Middle School.

Disregard Bunky. They're working on the rescue, phase two.

Aeura has a backpack full of goodies, and we pass it around and savor them. We don't have much time. Aeura and Bunky parked the pickup truck at the foot of a back road, an overgrown, gravel service path that leads into this conservation area.

Conservation area? Gilly, this is a wild cougar preserve. You didn't see the sign?

-What?! It was dark!

When I locked on your phone's location and saw where you were, I thought, wow, strategic.

--Did you see any cougars?

No one has, but we're stricken with the thought. We dare to look harder around us, the darkness lifting in the first fingers of dawn. Leticia stifles a sudden scream, pointing. A shadowy family of big cats stares right at us, a stone's throw away, manes tensing, teeth bared. VJ and Leticia clench hands, fingers tightening, tasting panic. Defensive-minded, Flip, Bunky, and I step back and look for a place to run. Aeura takes over.

Nobody move. Look down at the mama's feet only. I know cougars. Cougars are cool.

-Aeura, you're not making this up.

--Should we climb up on the rocks?

No, they can leap twenty feet. Give me your jacket, Flip. Her feet people, look at her feet!

The bigger male snarls, with an agitated shake of his large head, eyes narrowing. We all concentrate on mama cougar's paws, frozen. Aeura twirls the jacket over her head with arms raised. She stretches up to look as big as she can and howls, pogoing wildly in place like a punk rock groupie. The cats look uncertain, diffident, and they back away without a challenge. Flip is flipped. We all are. Bunky has no filter.

Am I too old for her?

-Yes.

Flip makes that clear. Aeura hands him back the jacket to applause from us humans.

Something I picked up from my Nigerian friend.

-Oh, the cocaine smuggler.

--What was that?

--They're coming!

We don't have to strain to hear the unsettling groan of military machinery. A squad of armed men and vehicles is coming our way. Their lighted SWAT helmets spread across our horizon.

We got this. Follow the neon glow sticks. Come on!

Aeura hustles off the same way she came, and damn if it isn't all that. Plastic lighted markers glow in the shadows of dawn, helping us traverse the steep hill on the dark side of the mountain.

Hey, wait for me! BTW those sticks are mine.

Bunky trails us. He struggles to keep up.

Suitcase staple. Essential for finding the drum kit on stage in the dark. Ow!

Bunky's down. Ahead, unaware, Aeura, Flip, Leticia, and VJ rush onward. I hesitate and go back to help him. With a grip under both his armpits, I get Bunky back on his feet. The SWAT force is grinding its way closer. Behind us, a burst of gunfire blasts into the body of the consulate SUV that we left behind. I drag the father of Fern's friend up the path. Bunky tries to help himself and put weight on his foot. It's a nonstarter. Hopping, he loses balance, falls back into me, and kisses my cheek.

Thanks. I'm not supposed to be here.

-None of us are.

Bunky's masking the pain by chatting on, ankle twisted. I brace him and prepare to be his crutch.

Don't chase your fantasies, kid.

-Aeura will do that to you.

Spoke the voice of experience?

We hurry as best we can, arms around waists, locked together, hobbling with urgency down the hill like a synchronized Olympic duo. We follow the bright red markers after the others along the neglected stone path. The old rocker's a load and he knows it. He tries to be as weightless as he can.

Hey, you're the son of the pool cleaner Duke. Big fan of your pop.

-Nice.

Fern's guy, too, from what I hear from my son, right? You lucky dog.

-I guess.

I know what he means. How did a kid from the wrong side of the 405 ever hook up with a Beverly House beauty like Fern? Pushing on, I vow to stay with Fern just to spite Bunky and the haters. Daylight widens, brimming orange. What the day will bring I don't know, but I have an awful suspicion. Leading the way, Aeura doesn't lack for confidence, and even Leticia follows without question, despite the fact that we have nowhere to hide. On the mountain, off the mountain, this is cartel turf and we're a long way from safe ground.

Sunday, Dawn

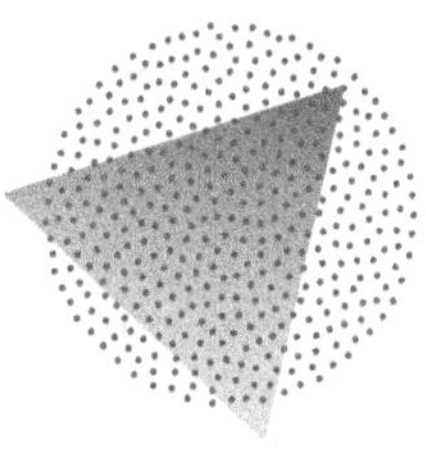

Diego was in no hurry. The leather-coat–wearing gangster was savoring the moment. Local boy makes good. Headset on, he was the point man for the operation, in communication with the SWAT captain from his position at the rear of the bush hospital formerly known as Athena. He lounged on a folding beach chair and ate a leftover bean burrito from the break room fridge. It was his tenth anniversary working for Juan Carlos, and he felt that he'd earned this position of authority.

The whole Dr. Foo operation had crashed and burned, and Diego was going to benefit. In fact, it was teed up for him. He'd update Juan Carlos in Mexico City the moment that the Americans were killed. The SWAT captain, a cartel-pleaser, had been ordered by the boss to move in slowly and steadily and to fire on sight. Juan Carlos was not interested in their surrender. And most of all, he expected all loose ends eliminated.

Unfinished business nagged at Diego. He had Beau and the nurse being held in the facility lobby under the guard of the two cousins. He planned to send them up the hillside afterward to help clean up the carnage—before they became part of it. Killing Beau made sense to Diego, but he'd liked the look of the nurse and wondered whether he should take advantage of the situation before she was cougar meat. He headed for the lobby.

Beau and Juana were tied up, begging the cousins to help them. Their pleas fell on deaf ears. Before Diego had Juana untied, the SWAT captain reported that the Americans were headed down the back of the hill. He'd ordered his attack vehicles to move ahead and surround them in the clearing, where they appear to be headed. The squad can meet up there. The road out is now blocked, and it's just a matter of time.

Take your time, Diego thought as he grabbed hold of Juana and headed to the break room with her. Beau called out.

What about me? I can help.

That got a good laugh from the cousins. The purpled-haired young thug waved Beau's own gun at him, whistled, and grinned.

In time, chico.

riqHt Now

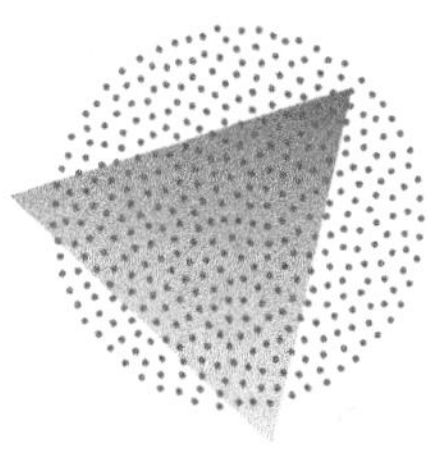

IN pursuit of us, two urban assault vehicles with swat warriors hanging on the sides, crest the hill. Like the stretch run of a mad, three-legged race, Bunky Green and I hop, skip, and jump our way down and reach level ground. It's dizzying, bright. Aeura's at the wheel of an old red pickup, Flip by her side. She screeches up to us, dust whirling. From the open cargo bed, VJ drops the tailgate and yells.

Your Uber! Hop in.

-Ya! Thank you! Five stars!

I push, VJ pulls, and we get Bunky aboard. I follow him in, slamming the tailgate as the pickup squeals off down the dirt path. I catch my breath and sink down to the truck bed. Across from me, I look into Leticia's face, her eyes oddly vacant. Her jaw's as tight as her grasp of VJ's hand. This is endgame, she believes. I can't help myself.

I love you both.

-Sorry, guys. I'm so sorry!

VJ cries. Leticia sets her eyes on me.

We're in a tumbrel, Gilly. You know?

What!? It's so Leticia to be intellectually challenging me at a time like this. She was my first lover, and I'm happy to have that bond with her, BUT she can be trying.

Tumbrel? I got nothing. You win.

-It was an open cart used to convey condemned prisoners to the guil-lotine during the French Revolution.

-Oh, that tumbrel. Ya.

Up ahead, where the dirt lane meets the road, federales soldiers have blocked access with a troop truck and barricades. Further behind us, the two urban assault tanks are on our tail. I yell up to the truck cab.

Aeura, game over. Flip, white flag!

-No worries. We're not going that way.

--Hang on! Fern promised me!

What?!

Aeura steers off road, following the blinking dot of a GPS app map on her cell that Flip holds up for her to see. In the rear, we bump over the uneven desert hardscape, jarred hard like a smack of reality, and look for something or someone to anchor on. The truck picks up speed, veering through the low-lying flora. I have to shout to be heard.

Fern promised what? We're surrounded. What can she do?

-Rearrange deck chairs on the Titanic.

Deadpanned, Leticia's going out in style. VJ's eyes are closed and he's chanting. Bunky, a spaced-out old hippie in a Michael Kors jogging suit, mutters loud enough for us to hear and sympathize.

I'm not supposed to be here.

And then I see it, like a fiery golden chariot. A helicopter streaks across the glowing sky, burning bright and closing in on us like our very own deus ex machina! I blink for focus. The chopper lowers. Aeura drives for it. Leticia has a moment of doubt.

How do we know it's for us?

From the chopper PA, we hear the distinctive piano coda of Eric Clapton's "Layla."

Fern's playing my ringtone!

I'm not going to lie. Trite as it sounds, Fern makes me feel special AF. The chopper touches down. A camouflaged armed mercenary lowers the steps. Fern, in her fourth outfit of the trip—a nautical navy skirt and blouse—with this Donny guy, helps us aboard the chopper that Flip identifies as a Black Hawk. I make sure to go last to help Bunky in. He still trolls me.

Fern and Donny made it happen. They're a power couple.

-Ya. Money isn't everything.

Correct. It's the only thing.

Gag me with a silver spoon. Where's Duke when I need him?

Arriving too late, the SWAT assault vehicles below us fire harmlessly at our fast-rising chopper. We steady our altitude and head east into the healing arms of *el sol*. Belted in, I strain to kiss Fern. She meets me halfway. We test the laws of gravity and lay into a long lip-lock of longing. Sweet breaths mingle, sweet words. Please God, may this helicopter ride go on and on and on.

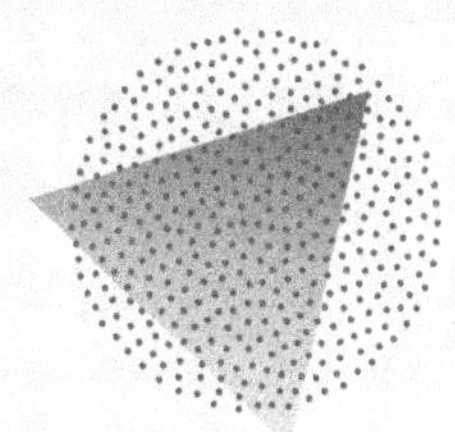

ferN

ſunday morning

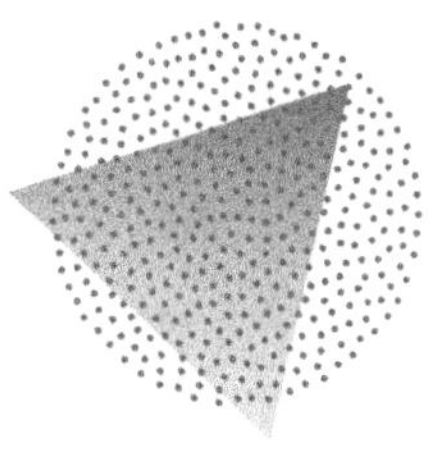

At the baſilica de ſanta María de guadalupe, the most magnificent church in Mexico City, the urgent messages were piling up for Juan Carlos on his muted cell. He was with his wife and fifteen-year-old daughter and didn't want to look panicked, but he was. Oh, he was. The Americans had eluded their fate and escaped with the aid of a pay-for-hire mercenary team. Two credit cards were used in that transaction, one in the name of Fern Fifer and the other in the name of Green Steiner, both residents of Beverly Hills. Juan Carlos was doing all he could. He'd already sent his best man, Carita Ramos, to clean up the situation.

The intelligence that they'd received was that the Americans who posed a clear and present threat to the cartel were hiding in a safe house somewhere in Mexico, awaiting extraction. The unraveling incident was now being played out behind the international doors of power. The escaped Americans were wanted for murder and were being urged to give themselves up to Mexican authorities. So far they hadn't. The US ambassador to Mexico was due back in-country on Monday morning to arrange for their surrender. Juan Carlos needed to find out before then where they were holding up. Determining their location was the priority, and the mob executive was using everyone in his network to uncover the answer.

He was painfully aware that even he had a boss, and there would be hell to pay if the cartel was held accountable. The use of the *federales* had complicated matters and embarrassed the president himself. The exposed actions of Consul Craig would ruin the US diplomat and make him a weak link, capable of linking Juan Carlos to the crimes. With the church service over, the Armani-suited gangster explained to his family that he had to take care of business at his office and that he'd meet them later for Sunday dinner. He exited the church ahead of them, but he didn't get far. There was a limo waiting for him at the curb. He hesitated to get in, until two large men in black made the decision easier, grabbing him roughly and depositing him in the back seat. Juan Carlos could see his terrified wife and teen daughter watch him being driven away.

***

Diego cursed the situation he was in. On his phone call earlier to update to Juan Carlos, he'd blamed the soldiers for the gringos' unthinkable escape. A helicopter rescue? Who could have foreseen that? And who could have afforded it? Surely Juan Carlos understood why it failed. The leather-coat–wearing henchman had thirsted to be more than a henchman and, at the moment, was looking for anything but responsibility. He packed up his things at the bush medical facility, intending to lock it up and split. Muscle from the mainland was coming, and Diego wasn't going to be around to greet it. He was off for an auntie in Costa Rica and a new identity—if he survived the day. He was ready to run.

Nurse Juana had been more than compliant, and he'd been reluctant to kill her. It hardly seemed to matter now. Diego suspected that he was as marked for death as she was. He felt secure in letting her live and even offered her a ride to the Cabo airport, where he was headed. The nurse thanked him with tears in her eyes and kissed his hand. She followed him to the lobby, where the cousins were holding Beau at gunpoint. Diego told them to get back to Todos Santos and await orders. They were OK with that. Beau pushed the issue.

What about me? Diego, por favor.

-I'd leave the country immediately and forget everything.

The thug was feeling gracious. It was music to the ears of the bartender from Pioneertown. Unbound, Beau stood up with a smile and brushed himself off. The purpled-haired gangster had some information that he wanted to share with Diego. He said that he got a call from his older sister about her son Antonio. The boy bragged that he was tight with one of the wanted Americans. Diego's antennae went up.

De verdad?

-Claro que si.

It was true. That hit a nerve in the doomed henchman who saw an off-ramp to extend his life's horizon. He dropped his bags, shot Beau in the forehead, shot Juana between the eyes, and sat the cousins down to hear more before calling Juan Carlos with the news.

2.

righT Now

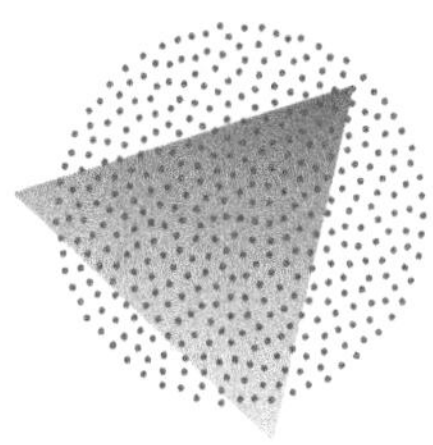

pArty! We all agree. It's time we let loose and celebrate life. It's late afternoon on Sunday, and we're safe in a safe house arranged by Fern's father. I'm not sure where we are, but it's fabulous. It's a multistoried villa built into the cliffside of a remote island somewhere off the west coast of Baja, Mexico. There are enough supplies in the kitchen to feed us in style. Enough wine to satisfy the drinkers among us. In the kitchen, Aeura, Flip, and a healed-up Bunky slice and dice and season, preparing a joyous dinner of capered lemon chicken and veggies. The comedy duo of

Fern and Donny entertain us with the whole absurd tale of how two Bev Hills kids with adult Bev Hills credit cards sitting in a Todos Santos restaurant could hire global mercenaries and a helicopter for the extraction.

And that's not counting the bonus frequent flyer miles I racked up.

-Donny has it locked.

Fern compliments her homeboy. The others laugh and I join in, though it's bothering me. The small airport we landed at is called Sala de Espera, which translates to "waiting room," perfectly fitting our situation. The mercenary duo will protect us till Monday, when, we were told, we'll be flown home by the US ambassador himself. We have no internet here and no way to communicate with the outside world. That's for safety reasons, like the order we were given that we stay inside. The pool beyond the picture window sparkles without us and it's hard to resist, but we understand. The dock below us stretches into the azure sea and berths a sleek cabin cruiser that looks perfect for cruising—just not for us. So there's nothing to do but enjoy the simple pleasures of each other's company. Listening to Donny and Fern explain how they floated $250,000 in credit to book Nightwing, Inc., has Leticia, VJ, Aeura, Flip, and Bunky in hysterics. Yeah, I'm jealous. Bunky rubs it in.

Bravo, sonny boy and Fern!

-We promise to do a GoFundMe when we get back.

--That's all right, Tish. Donny's mother spends more on handbags every year.

Everyone laughs and toasts Fern and Donny. I stare outside. The two mercs who rescued us are guarding the exterior. They aren't much older than me and are groomed like ex-US military, which they are. They've had a long day and will be relieved of their shift by 9 p.m., they've told us. We'll miss them. Aeura senses my distance and puts the spotlight back on me.

I think we can finally laugh about your decision, Gilly, to sleep in a wild cougar park.

-Saved our lives, didn't it?

--Hear, hear! Scoreboard! It made the federales wait till first light.

VJ has my back. I get the group love and need it. I wonder why Fern doesn't come over and kiss me right now. I want her to, but she lingers with Donny. How can I ever sustain a relationship if I'm always worried about being on the receiving end of a quiet dump? I'm feeling way too much emotional turbulence. It felt less stressful when my life was endangered. Just kidding. But if I'm worried about losing Fern, that means I care, right? First world problems, I know.

Each one of us, in our own way, is getting our soul back after the ordeal. Leticia is tipsy and, with her phone charging, she cues up a Spotify pop playlist. The spacious living room booms with Beyoncé.

Hit the mood lights, Gill.

I flip a wall switch and, outside the house, under the eaves, the water misters for the gardens accidentally come on, with their billowing fine spray. It soaks our guard in cooling mist.

Oops.

Wrong switch. Off goes the luxury water feature. The sentry stationed on the sunny patio of the villa gives me a thumbs-up, enjoying the surprise wet-down. The next switch sends the interior mood lights swirling. A big whoop from the group.

I have a surprise. Lower the music.

It's Aeura. She holds up an eye-dropper bottle and makes an announcement.

It's DMT—chemical ayahuasca—what they use at the Green Door for their brew.

-Now you're talking. Love this girl.

--Easy, old timer.

Flip and Bunky face off over Aeura. If they only knew her. I take that back. She may be sexually uncertain, but she's a love worth having. Aeura confesses that she snatched the bottle from the Green Door after being held captive in a meditation room.

I wanted something after denting my camera. The word is "micro-dosing," my friends.

-I'm in.

--I can't think of a safer space.

VJ's all too eager. Leticia gets sucked along. Bunky and Donny are a go.

This is perfect. Without the chanting.

-I'm with Dad. No chanting.

--No better time and place. Children's portion for me, please.

With that, Flip gets a chuckle out of Aeura. He's not missing this. Fern looks at me.

I dare you.

-No, I'll be the outside man. I can't.

Gilly! What are you worried about?

-Getting high. That I'll like it too much. I'm the son of the ultimate stoner.

Fern's bummed. I encourage her to do it if she wants. It's cool with me. I'm high enough from all we've been through. I reassure her with a quick kiss.

All's well. I am the guard.

-Hey, good one—last line of a Kerouac poem, "Mexico City Blues."

Aeura joins us. Besides me, only she would know 1950s Beat writer Jack Kerouac's work.

Ready for your trip?

-Not me. Just Fern.

Fern sticks out her tongue to receive a microdose from the dropper, and that's that. I give her an encouraging nod.

Bon voyage.

The music is back on, something Bad Bunny–like. Fern is ebullient, joining the other psychedelic inductees pogoing their way through the "doors of perception," as Aeura describes it. To my surprise, Aeura does not take her dose.

I can't leave you alone as the watcher. I've done DMT. I know who I am.

-Thanks, Aeura. Welcome to reality.

--Everybody! The sun's setting!

VJ demands that we catch it. We all crowd the big, wide window to watch the miracle. A red ball of steaming hot radiance lowers and refreshes itself, disappearing into the cold, blue water of the Pacific. We cheer the performance. Life is good.

3.

SUNDAY EVENING

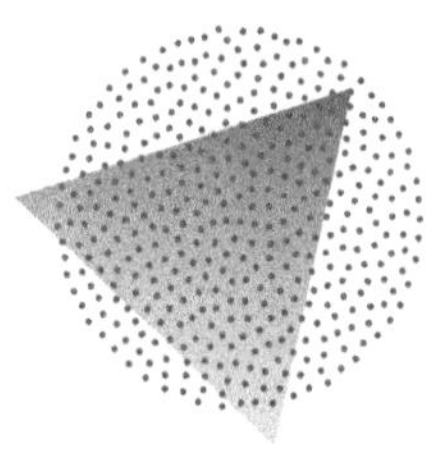

IN THE FIRST HOUR AFTER ARRIVING IN CABO SAN LUCAS, Mexico City–based Carita Ramos had his first long-neck, glass-bottle Coca-Cola of the day (he would ingest a dozen) and garroted Consul Craig in the garage stairwell of Craig's condo complex, not far from the consulate office. The senior foreign service officer never saw it coming. The pro did as directed. In his white linen sport jacket, the dandy drop-kicked the body all the way down the stairs. He took whatever was valuable, to make it look more like a random, follow-home robbery gone wrong.

A sudden change of plans gave Juan Carlos's hand-picked pretty-boy assassin plenty of time to get back to a local crew waiting at the Cabo airport. An occasional surfer, Carita had been looking forward to visiting Todos Santos, but there was no wet work to be done there anymore. The focus had shifted. He was winging north to la Isla de Cedros, a private island off the coast of Central Baja. Such was the busy day of a working hired killer. On the island, they'd be joined by a demolition man who'd finish the job. Taking it as a slight, the egocentric assassin wondered why that was needed as he chugged another raw sugar Coke.

***

Juan Carlos made it back for Sunday dinner with his family. He had their chef make his wife's favorite, *octopus al pastor*. It was going to be OK. He had a reprieve. Thanks to his man Diego in Todos Santos, they'd been able to geolocate and lock on the whereabouts of the Americans. It helped that Leticia's charging cell phone was open and the calls from the pressured hospital aide, Antonio, had gone to voicemail. The eradication plan was in motion.

After the serious threat to his life, Juan Carlos was leaving nothing to chance. The attention of the US authorities on the plight of the young Americans could not be minimized. He'd have their safe house blown up and blamed on a gas leak. Better than having them machine-gunned by Carita. The meal was delicious. His daughter, Rosa, hadn't touched her food, and Juan Carlos tried not to comment or even notice. Instead, in passing conversation, he mentioned to his wife that he was exploring having Rosa's quinceañera in the luxury suites at AT&T Stadium in Dallas at a

Taylor Swift concert. That got the morose teen's attention. Rosa shrieked and her appetite returned. His impressed wife kissed his cheek. Juan Carlos prided himself on being a good parent.

***

Antonio spent the day in same way that the heartthrob of *Beverly Hills, 90210* would in this situation. And it came to Antonio—Dylan, played by the late Luke Perry, whom he worshipped, would either binge drink whiskey, snort heroin off a babe's bare shoulder, or follow his uncles to stop the worst from happening. Antonio choose door number three.

***

Back in the states, daddy Duke was more horizontal than vertical this Sunday. Major depression had set in for the pool guy with liver disease. He'd gotten the call late that afternoon that there was a liver waiting for him at UCLA hospital in Westwood. He needed to come to the hospital immediately, but Duke was gone for the day, two hundred miles north in San Luis Obispo to attend the funeral of Abby Jo's ninety-year-old father. Abby Jo had told him not to come, but Duke didn't want her to be alone. When he insisted on coming, Abby Jo was ready to celebrate rather than mourn. Her elderly pop had dementia the last few years, and the death was a blessing. The planned overnight stay, a one-night romantic vacation at the famous Madonna Inn, had cost Duke the chance at a new life. Not able to get back to LA in time for the transplant, he was passed over.

At least you know that you're at the top of the list.

-And now I may be at the bottom!

No matter how Abby Jo tried to spin it, Duke was inconsolable, in bed by six o'clock, without dinner, pot, or lovemaking, which was so unlike him. In didn't help that both he and Abby Jo were in a state over Gilly's silence for almost two days. No messages, no way to reach him. With nothing but time, while Duke slept, Abby Jo revved up her laptop's search engine and her phone's contact list and started digging. By the time room service delivered an avocado salad and dessert, she'd already learned of the tragedy in Cabo. The U.S. Consul was killed, a victim of street crime. Abby Jo wondered whether it was connected to the intel chatter she heard of a search for missing young Americans in Baja. They were wanted for the murder of a surgeon, Dr. Foo. By the time she finished the inn's world-famous Black Forest cake, smoked two cigs to the stubs, and gulped down a Tito's-infused double espresso for ballast, the freelance fifty-eight-year-old investigative journalist was aware that Foo was the disgraced cartel capo known as El Chino who'd been involved in organ trafficking in China. With urgency, Abby Jo shook Duke out of his slumber.

They killed a cartel biggie. They're targets now!

-What? Who?

The kids. Must be frightened out of their minds.

 4.

right Now

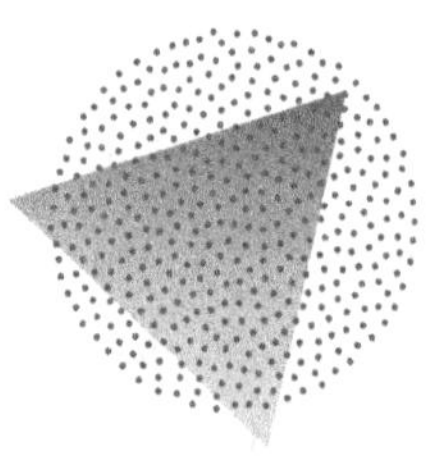

out of their minds, yes. At least everyone but Aeura and me. The microdose of ayahuasca has kicked in, and the others are tripping. *It's better than watching TV*, says Aeura. In the living room, with Ed Sheeran quietly crooning on the sound system, Donny and his dad Bunky are close, hands on shoulders, staring face to face, wiping away each other's tears in an intense noncontact hug.

Gilly, did you hear what Bunky just told Donny?

-Sorry, missed it.

He said that every father drops feathers on his son and hopes the right feather sticks.

-Is there a feather guide to be sure which feather is right?

Stay tuned.

Aeura quips. We're having the best time. She's good company, with a goofy, running play-by-play of the psychic explorers. We watch Fern. Lost in a song, the Beverly Hills Barbie plays an imaginary, incendiary piano. The fingers on her left hand tickle the imaginary ivories in upbeat time. Her right hands stretches, playing the chords. Synched to her rhythm, Flip shreds an air guitar, sliding up and down the neck to squeak out the most soulful sound. Inside the essence of their unheard music, they jam, feeding off each other's energy. It builds.

They're ripping it up.

-Definitely not Ed Sheeran. More like Lynyrd Skynyrd. Is it OK to yell "Free Bird"?

We're cracking each other up. Aeura declares that VJ's smile has gone nuclear, and she's spot on. Taking Leticia by the hand, my boy and his love prance off for a bedroom, losing layers of clothing with every step till they are naked.

Two flesh poets.

-Bent on creating magic—and maybe more, if no birth control.

We're having fun at their expense, happy they have release from the reality that we've faced and are facing. Across the room, Flip puts down the air guitar and wanders back to Aeura and me seated at the big, iron-hinged oak dining table. We sit in throne chairs and welcome him. He has no eyes for me—only for Aeura—and stands before her. Like a zombie partner, Fern joins me and traces a finger over my lips. I wrap my lips around her finger. In response, she pulls it back and puts both her hands on my face, framing it. Flip does the same to Aeura's face. Like dealing with a new species, I'm uncertain what to say or do and I follow Aeura's lead. We smile at them, sending positive, gentle vibes. Fern and Flip share a glance and, mouths agape, eyes wide, laugh at something we don't get and wander off, entranced. They're on a different plane of existence than us, and it's best that we keep our distance.

It's different when you have a curandero, a real healer guiding it.

-You know me. I don't judge.

Ha. Said that myself yesterday when I saw Fern kissing Donny. Now she's with Flip. What's—

-Up? How do you sustain a relationship when love and making love isn't enough?

That's a brain twister.

Aeura gets it. Crazy that I'm thinking about kissing her, though I wonder whether it's inappropriate. Her lips are familiar and soft. Maybe sensing what I'm sensing, Aeura changes the channel on our home entertainment. She stands tall.

Let's see if there's a wine cellar in the basement. The red is running out.

-You must want to get me in a cool, dark place.

Did I just say that? Delayed reaction from Fern's extracurricular activities? We find the door to the basement. A nautical clock on the wall shows it to be just after 8:31 p.m..

Ah! Second shift of guards should be here soon. Feel secure?

-Totally. And the night is young. C'mon.

Aeura takes my hand. We hit the light switch and descend into the basement. Forgive me.

5.

ʃuNdαy NiqHt

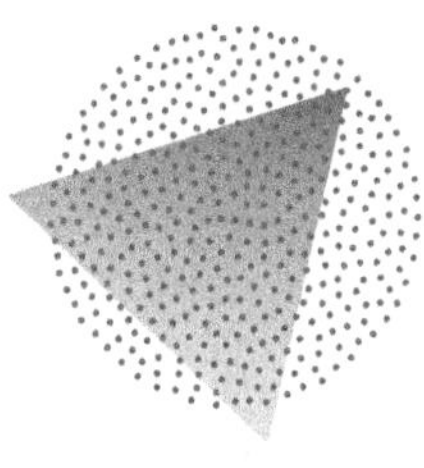

tHe cαrteL cHαrter ʃLiqHt ʃroM cαbo WAʃ IN Itʃ ʃiNAL deʃceNt to the small island airport off the coast of Central Baja. Stretched out on a plush lounge couch, not belted in, Carita wasn't fidgety at all after downing four more Cokes on the trip. He was, however, primed for action. He'd sat by himself and had binge-watched the HBO series *Barry* on his cell phone's six-and-a-half-inch screen. It was about a hit man turned actor. Carita found it very believable and funny.

He didn't know the local muscle aboard the flight with him

and considered them rubes. The way they ate and talked, those accents! The one with the purple hair seemed to blow his nose too much, and the handsome, professional killer was sure the guy was on coke. Of the trio from Todos Santos, only the one in charge, Diego, seemed solid. He was obviously trusted and was in direct contact with Juan Carlos, who was calling the shots. Diego knew their plan moving forward. Carita cleaned his Glock in the hopes that he'd get to use it. Before landing, the leather-coat–wearing Diego gathered the team. Their first objective was to take out the two new Nightwing guards who'd be arriving at the airport for their shift.

Amigos, we get to guard the house.

-So no one gets in?

So no one gets out—till the demo man is done.

The King Air bounced to a stop on the one runway of la Isla de Cedros, and the hoods deplaned. From the baggage hatch at the back of the plane, they grabbed their bags and equipment. No one noticed the stowaway in the far corner beneath the cargo mats. Antonio was freezing, despite the two horse blankets in which he'd cocooned. Crawling out of the belly of the plane, the warm night air of the island gave the young player strength. He'd made it. He tried to imagine Leticia's surprise.

Would he have a chance with her if he saved her life? Like the mad, bad, dangerous-to-know Dylan McKay, lovestruck Antonio followed his heart with all his heart. Unlike Diego though, the young Romeo, hospital aide, had no plan forward. What he had was family. He hurried to catch up with the men headed for a hangar.

Hey, Ricardo!

The street punk spun around—his shock mixed with panic.

Antonio?! What are you doing here, nephew?

-Uh, helping.

It was true. Antonio just didn't say who.

6.

right Now

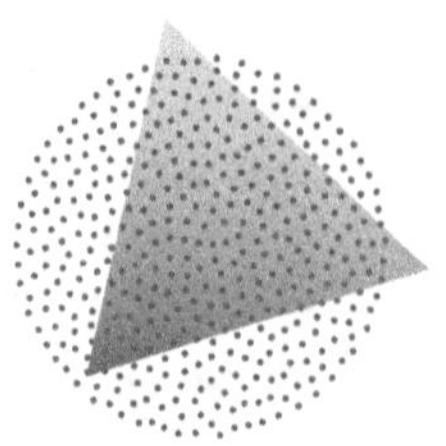

 I mean, if tensions were rated, it would be the most desirable, the most maddening, without a doubt. Even if nothing happens between Aeura and me, the feeling I'm feeling is sublime. I'm alive in the moment. Aeura says it like the Keats poem about the Grecian urn. The lovers on the pottery piece are depicted in pursuit of each other. The takeaway is that they never consummate so the heat never lessens. It's eternal. The lady knows these things.

Fumbling abound the basement of the villa has been interesting. In our search for the wine cellar, we've found the electrical room, the private water tank room, supply closets with many shelves of canned goods, dishware, and towels, and the maid's quarters. With only a few more doorways to go, I like my chances with a big oaken door. Presto! It swings open to reveal an over-stocked wine cellar. Aeura turns to me, mock unimpressed.

Thank you, Gilly. Looks adequate for the night.

She rewards me with a kiss on the cheek, and I don't know how to take that. She shrugs.

-Just playing. You?

I kiss her back for real. I want this. I hold her, and her body sinks into mine seamlessly. I feel like I'm tripping. Aeura says what I'm thinking.

Should we?

I don't answer fast enough. There are footsteps in the hallway, echoing off the stone floor, and we freeze. I break the embrace and peek out of the wine cellar.

Antonio?

-You're in danger. They're going to kill you!

The hospital orderly from Todos Santos is standing before me, in the flesh, and I'm not tripping.

7.

ſunday night

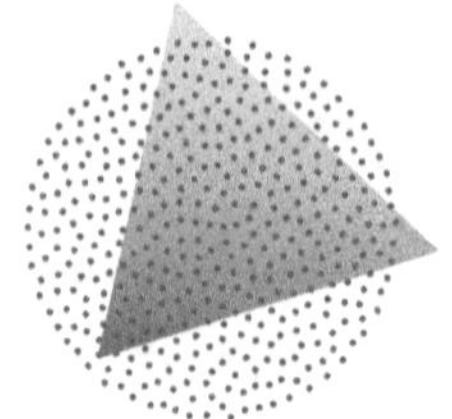

if waſ nearing midnight. Diego had deployed the cousins and himself, each on one side of the villa. The west side faced the water, was on a cliffside, and was trickier to control. It didn't help that the hit man from Mexico City had refused to guard. Below his pay grade. So the west side was without a sentry, which bothered Diego. He was sweating in the balmy, breezeless night, and the arrival of the demo guy from Tijuana couldn't come quickly enough. In the meantime, their orders from Juan Carlos were clear. They waited, they guarded.

Inside the windows, he could see the oblivious young Americans up late, partying or something. He didn't want to look too hard or someone might get suspicious that they weren't Nightwing. On a chaise lounge on the patio, lounging in the shadows by himself was Carita Ramos. He was a cartel star, and Diego could see why, given the way that he'd handled the elimination of the second shift of mercs. Diego had won some trust with him by allowing a stop at a store to load up on his drink. Guy was hooked on sugarcane Coke. Juan Carlos had directed that the two locals from Todos Santos be unarmed, which Diego didn't understand. The leather-coat–wearing gangster was glad to be armed, in case he and the cousins were seen as expendable.

The purple-haired thug, Ricardo, and his older cousin, called Torchy, were both in the uniforms of the security company. The wiry Ricardo had to make a few new notches in the belt to keep up a dead guard's camouflage pants. He hadn't mentioned to Torchy that their nephew Antonio had stowed aboard. He did tell his aunt's dumb kid to get lost, stay out of the way, and above all, stay away from the house, which was gonna blow. Walking over to Torchy's side of the villa, Ricardo couldn't hold it in any longer.

Psst... Antonio's here. You hear?

-Antonio? What's he doing?

Uh... Helping?

-How?

Ricardo didn't have a good answer and wished he'd told Antonio to hang close.

8.

riɡɦt ɴoW

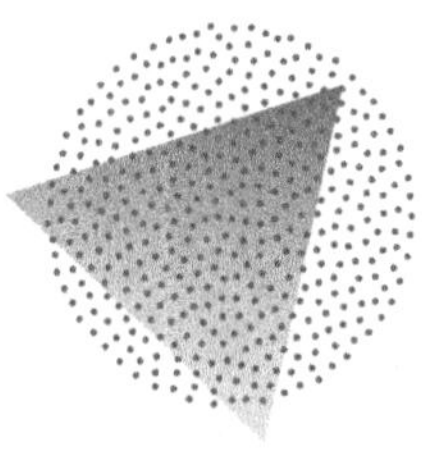

ᴀɴtoɴio ʃɦoWʃ ᴀ℮uᴦᴀ ᴀɴd ɱ℮ ɦoW ɦ℮ ɡot iɴ. The last door in the basement leads to stone steps and a sub-basement cave that opens on the rocky shore near the foot of the dock. There's a boat tied up there. It's a way to escape—if we can trust him. Aeura doesn't.

How did you know about this back door?

-I didn't. Went down to the rocks to take a dump and saw the cave. Please, I came here to warn you. Leticia, actually.

I believe Antonio, and Aeura believes me. He says that their plan is to blow up the villa with us inside. We have to move quickly and gather the others. I'm thinking ahead, and it's not clear or comforting.

Do you know boats, Antonio?

-I'd be lying if I said yes. You?

That's a big no from landlubber me. The trip with Marlena was enough boat for a lifetime. Aeura's no boater either. I'm thinking, hoping, counting on Flip being the captain type. We need to gather the others. Upstairs, we can see the new guards from the dining room window. The purple-haired one Aeura recognizes from Todos Santos. Antonio verifies this.

My uncles. They can't see me in here.

He keeps out of sight. Aeura and I close all the thick velvet curtains and get to the others. In the living room, sitting cross-legged, Fern and Donny stare deep into each other's eyes as they chant a Buddhist prayer in unison. Bunky and Flip are flat on their backs, comparing the ceiling's intricate architectural moldings to an inhabitable solar system, in a conversation that only they can fathom.

This is going to be like herding cats.

-Not really. Seekers! There's a lunar eclipse outside. Come!

That gets Bunky's attention. He's all about it.

Donny, our first eclipse!

-Wow. Oh, Dad. I love you.

I love you more.

They're on their feet and charged to the nth. I help Fern up and Aeura helps Flip.

Eclipse?

-Flip, ever captain a power boat?

Never. Eclipse, where?

--I can. Faster the better. I water-ski every summer on Lake Tahoe. We need a boat to see the eclipse?

-Fern! Amazing! You're our captain.

Oh, thanks, Gilly. I missed you.

Angelic, she beams at me and throws down a mighty hug. I feel so guilty. Antonio searches the room.

Where's Leticia?

-Bedroom with VJ… I mean… I'll get her.

Aeura hurries off. Fern couldn't look more adorable. Flip thinks so too. Hmm…

Gilly, did you know that Flip is half Jewish?

-It's true. On my mother's side.

We were at the same bar mitzvah in Rancho Mirage in 2014.

Luckily, Aeura interrupts with Leticia and VJ, bed-headed and wrinkled. They're wide-eyed, especially Leticia, who notices a familiar face.

Antonio!?

The Todos Santos lover boy grins at his lady fair.

Hi, Leticia. I had to come for you, doll.

-Ah…

---Who's Antonio? Is he here for the eclipse?

----VJ, he's the guy that you're going to follow down the stairs.

I hand them each a bottle of water from the fridge, and the sextet—Fern and Flip, Leticia and VJ, and Bunky and Donny— get in line behind Antonio. He leads the trippers down into the basement. I peek out a window and see a non-uniformed guard drinking a Coke, twirling a machine pistol. From the living room, looking toward the sea, under the faintest moonlight, I can see the dock. A good stretch of shore is exposed, from the rocks to where the boat is berthed. If any guard bothers to look, there's a good chance that they'd see us crossing.

We'll need to distract them.

-Wish we could drug them.

Ha. Did you notice, in the water tank room, that little container system for the garden misters?

-Yeah. So?

So, how much of the liquid ayahuasca do you have left?

Aeura synchs on that notion and shakes a nearly full vial in response.

9.

SUNDAY NIGHT

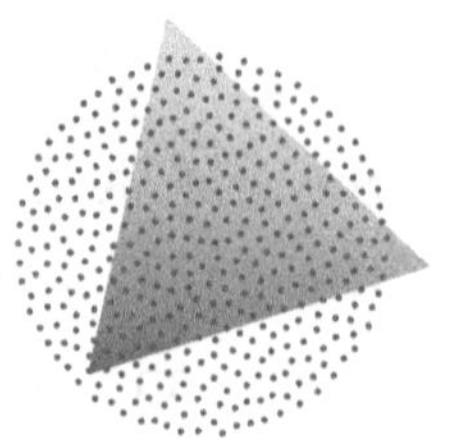

diego, in his position on the east side, was caught off guard by the water-mister feature that was springing to life under the villa's eaves. He could hear that Ricardo and Torchy were also surprised by it. Rather than stepping away, Diego stepped into the increasing spray to catch it fully on his face. The cooling mist felt healing, and he indulged. It tasted good, too. On the patio, Carita had to laugh, watching the local hard cases get wet. In the warm night air, it wasn't unwelcome. Feeling left out, the Mexico City assassin wandered over to the house's massive front door to get cooled himself. It hit the spot. Carita sipped at a glass-bottle Coke and soaked in the delicious mist.

***

It worked. With the trippers huddled in the basement waiting for the signal, I peeked through the curtain before joining them. The doctored mist's contact on skin and tongue absorbed fast, and hilarity ensued. The purple-haired street thug was focused on surfing an imaginary wave and riding it all the way into the imaginary sand. His older cousin, Torchy, was frozen, staring at the back of his hairy hand till he collapsed on the ground in a fetal position. Yes, I did switch on the house music system's outdoor speakers. The first thing to come up in the queue was opera—to be specific, an Andrea Bocelli/Zucchero duet from Puccini, and it was grand. The cartel quartet seemed inspired. The leather-coat–wearing OG was leading an invisible orchestra with all the passion he could muster. The armed hood in white linen tiptoed like a diva pirouetting, mouth open under the spray, arms up, and pistol raised to the heavens. A pair of headlights approaching in the driveway sent me hurrying to the others. It was time to go for it.

***

The demo man's rented van stopped in front of the bluff-side villa, and he got out to unload. He kept glancing over and scoffing at the goofy behavior of the cartel men, who were caught up in some operatic aria outside the estate. The obese explosives expert from

Tijuana opened his two suitcases of explosives and yelled over the music, somewhat annoyed.

Who's Diego?

-Hola, amigo! Welcome!

Diego waved and approached and approached—a bit too close for the demo man, who firmly rebuffed the friendly embrace that mellow Diego offered.

Get back! What's wrong with you?

-Hermano, chill.

You chill! I have to concentrate. Turn the music off!

With C-4 plastique bombs in his arms, the exasperated bomb guy waddled around the perimeter of the villa to place them.

Turn the music off!

Diego yelled it into the night, and Carita heeded the call. He blasted through the windows, shooting up the inside of the house in search of the music's source.

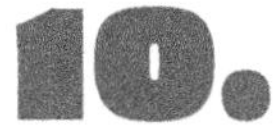

10.

right now

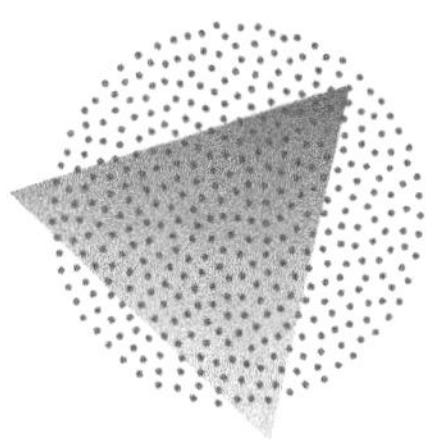

the sound of gunfire above quickens our pace down the stone steps, single file, following Antonio. I can't figure what's in this for him, but I'm thankful that he's with us. I know that the Todos Santos hospital aide is smitten with Leticia and hate to break it to him. He has to know about VJ by now. Or maybe he doesn't care. *Love knows no bounds or freeway exits.* Duke always says that. For Antonio, this is way more than pursuing a long-distance date. This is risking your life.

More power to him and much respect. At the cave opening, Aeura and Antonio gather the trippers who are getting confused. Bringing up the rear, I can hear the resistance still echoing in the rock tunnel. Rebellion!

How can there be an eclipse if there's not even a full moon?

-I need to sit down.

--I heard fireworks. Let's check it out.

---Anyone else hungry?

----Yes! Let's go back upstairs. Couch time!

-----No!

I shout that as quietly as possible. Catching up, I tell the truth. With a finger to my lips, I get their attention, addressing each.

Fern, Leticia, VJ, Flip, Bunky, Donny, the cartel is here. They're going to kill us if we don't get out to that boat. This is not a drill. This is a lifeline.

The chirping ceases. There is immediate silence from the seekers. A flash sobriety sinks in. And, as if my leaden words weren't enough, the cliffside house above us explodes to rockin', freakin' smithereens!

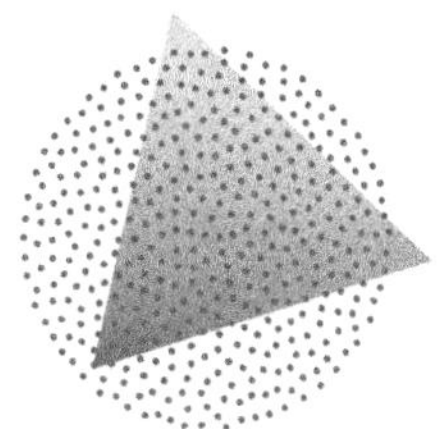

Sunday Night

the conCuſſion from the bLaſtſ ſhook the ſurrouNding LaNdſcape. The royal palm trees swayed. Smoke and flame dominated the night on the bluff where the villa once stood. The aftermath of debris and smoldering conflagration reflected across the satisfied face of the bomb guy from Tijuana. It was a beautiful sight for the pro, interrupted only by the plaintive wail of the stoned, purple-haired thug Ricardo. He carried the lifeless, blood-soaked body of his cousin Torchy over his shoulder and dropped him at the feet of the oversized, explosives expert.

He's dead!

-He got too close. I warned you all!

Ricardo lunged for him, quick as a stoned cat, hands on his fat neck. More stoned, Diego hustled to intercede.

Ricardo, stop! Please. Torchy's not dead.

-He's not?

Ricardo loosened his grip on the demo man. Sparks of hope filled his every pore. Diego, floating in a rarified bardo, propped up the dead body like it was in the unmade third sequel for *Weekend at Bernie's*. As the incredulous blast technician and Ricardo watched, Diego animated the torso like a puppet, with jiggles and jostles, whistles and nudges.

Ricardo, see? Sing, Torchy! Dance! Ai ai ai ai! There is no death.

Literally, a lacerated chunk of Torchy's skull fell off. Outraged Ricardo went after Diego, hand around his neck, meaning to kill him. Diego's hand slipped into his waistband and took hold of his gun.

Pendejo! Say hola to your cousin.

Diego shot Ricardo point-blank in the heart, and he crumbled. The TJ man was packing his bags fast, anxious to split, cursing under his breath.

Amateurs.

Another wail, more pitiful. This time from a distraught, ayahuasca-infused Carita. He held a distressed canvas traveling bag in his arms like a dying child. It was filled with broken glass, and it dripped gooey brown liquid. Heartbroken, overcome with emotion, the assassin screamed at the big man.

Your damn blast shook my bag! It broke all my Colas!

-Serious!? Are you crazy? Buy more.

Where? You notice a 24-hour mercado around here, jumbo?

-You better believe Juan Carlos is going to hear about—

The imported talent from another gang never got to finish the threat. Carita shot him in the mouth. He fell straight back on the lawn. Diego was coming down quick and quickly panicking.

No, no, no, Carita! He was borrowed. You shouldn't have done that!

The hit man turned his pistol on the leather-coat–wearing Baja henchman, but Diego's gun was already on Carita. It was the picture in the dictionary you'd find for "Mexican standoff." So obviously so, both men laughed. Diego's cell sounded. With a nod, Carita gave him permission to answer. Diego checked the display screen, though he knew who'd be calling that late.

It's Juan Carlos.

-Give the good first. The Americans were eliminated. Olé!

Olé!

The two loaded men lowered their loaded pistols and took a moment to celebrate that thought with psychedelic self-realization and a hug. From the seaside below, twin engines roared to life. As the phone kept ringing, Carita and Diego looked down with consternation at the dock a distance away.

Dios mio! They're getting away!

-Don't answer that phone!

12.

right Now

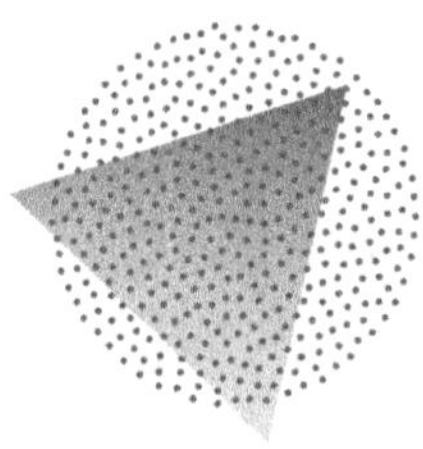

At the helm of the Sea Ray Sundancer, a thirty-five-foot cabin cruiser, Fern is in control like I've never seen her. Steely focused on the complicated pilot console, she is in super-Fern mode. The Beverly Hills babe revs the two 430-horse-power inboard engines to clean out the lines and checks the gauges.

It's a miracle. We have full tanks—250 gallons!

What's a miracle is Fern. The other ayahuasca-enabled friends are functioning as well as possible. Aeura and I couldn't be more relieved. Even Bunky and Donny, who have gone below to check for provisions, are pulling their weight. Flip is first mate and is also the guy who hot-wired the ignition.

Just a little something I picked up at boarding school.

-Ah yes, the mean streets of Switzerland. Been there, done that.

Aeura, pull in the bumpers. Cast off the lines, Flip. Let's rock.

--Hold on. I'm not coming. Good luck to you all.

Antonio, our angel, says his goodbyes and stops before VJ and Leticia. She embraces him.

Antonio, you can't go back.

-It's alright. I have my family. I'll be fine.

We can't even begin to thank you.

-Just promise me one thing, Leticia.

Anything.

-If this guy ever treats you badly and you want a new man, know that I'll be waiting.

Oh, Antonio. You are a love.

Leticia gives him a kiss on the lips. Antonio builds it with sweet heat, getting his money's worth. VJ squirms with discomfort.

OK, there you go. Better hurry, dude.

-VJ's right. Ciao!

Like a cocky TV teen idol, Antonio takes the high road and waves, stepping back onto the wooden dock. He pushes the boat off and turns toward the bluff.

We watch him under the stars, walking toward the wrecked and burning villa. It's quite a dramatic exit. We motor off. I'd be lying if I didn't report Leticia gasping in the good way. I point it out to VJ because it's what we do. The bar for Leticia got higher. He fields it clean.

Thanks, bud. Bring it on.

I notice the muzzle flash from atop the bluff before we hear the gunshots. Antonio's under fire! He ducks behind a metal barrel. Bullets eat up the dock's lumber around him. He yells to us.

Help!

-Turn around, Fern!

It's instinctive for me but also dangerous. The gunfire is on automatic, nonstop, with uncertain range. The shooter is high up with a clear view. Fern hesitates. Leticia screams.

Do it!

We all echo it. Except Bunky, who isn't so sure.

C'mon, the guy made a choice to stay behind. Is that on us?

-Some hippie you are!

Aeura leads us all in outshouting him. Fern's right hand tightens on the wheel.

OK, everyone. Get down and hold on!

Like a ski boat's hard right turn, Fern accelerates and takes the cruiser spinning 180 degrees. I'm doing all I can to make it out to the bow, holding on to whatever I can for dear life and the best view ahead. Closing in, I spy Antonio hunkered down and I free an arm, waving for him to see.

Antonio! Jump!

With no hesitation, the Todos Santos hospital orderly, far from home, breaks for the dock's edge and dives into the water, disappearing from view. A barrage of bullets follows right behind. They ping into the water ahead of us.

Fern, slow down. I lost sight of him.

Antonio doesn't emerge. Worried, Leticia's head peeks up from the deck. The bullets are getting closer. VJ ducks her down and raises his eyes above the gunwales.

There he is!

Antonio's head pops up, and he swims hard for the back of the boat, doing a watery version of the zigzag. It works. He reaches out, and VJ pulls him up and onto the deck with one smooth move.

Dude, when you got the rizz and make an exit, don't come back.

Antonio spits water and laughs. Fern warns to hold tight once more, and it's whirling around we go, speeding as far away from the shooter as possible. I join Fern at the helm and hold her while she steers. We say nothing for the longest time. Sitting next to the captain's chair, Fern's head drops down and settles on my shoulder. My head meets hers, and like Siamese twins, we channel our feelings directly into each other. I can feel the depth of her affection. I hope she feels mine.

Nothing can change that, I'd like to believe. Of course, there's always a *l-i-e* at the core of *believe*, as Duke likes to point out. Fern purrs.

I think we're safe.

-Except they know that we didn't die in the explosion.

Oh, there's that. Get some rest, Gilly. I got this.

She does.

13.

monday, before dawn

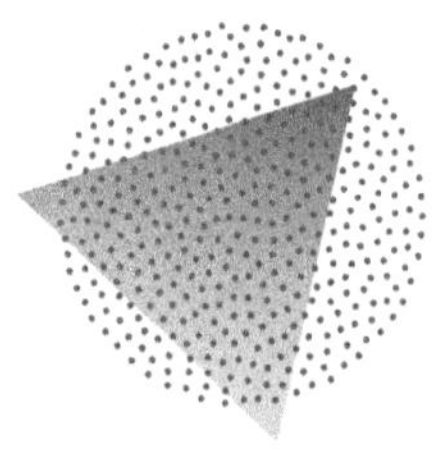

juan carlos could finally sleep. With a call from his man Diego that the house explosion had claimed the lives of the Americans, the mortal danger to his position, his life, and the life of his family was eliminated. He learned a lesson in this. He'd tried to delegate and expand the business in Baja South and had lost control. The last thing he thought about before he drifted off was to remember to have Diego killed. Though he'd done his job, he knew too much.

***

On la Isla de Cedros, cleaning up from the infernal blast and coming down off their ayahuasca buzz, Diego and Carita had formed an alliance. It did neither of them any good to have the real result of the operation come out, so Diego had lied to Juan Carlos about the demise of the Americans. He neglected to mention the other friendly fire deaths, too. It was a matter of his survival. He knew that blowback from the screwup was only delayed, and the escaped, resourceful, very alive American kids would surface. The missing demo man was also a major time bomb, threatening their story. Juan Carlos would learn the truth soon enough. Diego planned to be in Costa Rico by then, finding another line of work. He thought he'd make a good maître d'.

Carita and Diego had been working hard on the fake news. They were singed, sweaty, and smoky and were (well) done. They'd planted the bodies of the cousins and the demo man in the pit of the fire, to help with the alternate facts. The burned-beyond-recognition remains would slow identification down. Carita himself didn't plan on running or on altering his life at all. He was doubling down. The microdose of psychedelics had given him real insight. He liked himself and was confident that his needed skill set would survive Diego's deceptive narrative. He was also absolutely over Coca-Cola and vowed to never have another sip. Carita had successfully executed his part of the job, minus killing a rival gang's bomb tech. That was embarrassing, and it was why he agreed to help Diego. Carita figured he'd get a call in the morning from Juan Carlos to kill Diego anyway. It was just a matter of time.

****

Back in the states, in their West LA bedroom, while Duke sawed Zs, Abby Jo burned through her DC contacts prying intel out of the State Department regarding Gilly and friends. She'd promised Leticia's mom, VJ's folks, and even Philip Fifer that she'd have something. Fifer, with all his clout, had been stonewalled.

Abby Jo's persistence finally paid off. In a span of five minutes, she got three separate bits of info—one, that they were alive and being held in a remote location; two, that they were missing; and three, and most recent, an updated report that clarified the situation. While waiting to surrender, the wanted Americans and their abettors were presumed killed in a gas explosion. The chain-smoking, burnt-out freelance journalist was devastated. She stubbed out a cig halfway through and trembled. She didn't know how she'd break it to Duke. Maybe after breakfast, she could find the words. She stood in the darkened room, trying to decide whether to go to bed or make coffee. Duke turned right to her, eyes wide open.

Gilly's dead?

She only had to nod.

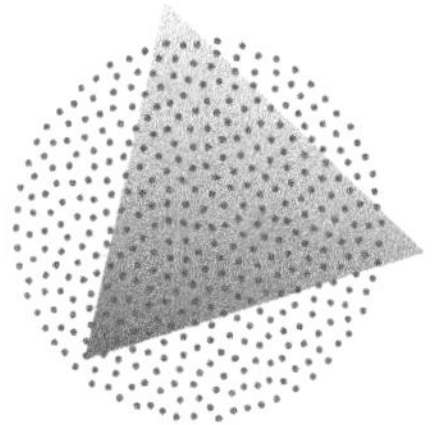

right Now

 and brings a little warmth to my face. I did sleep for a few hours under a tarp on the stern and had zero dreams, good or bad. That was a relief. I shiver, stretch, and survey the scene. We're moving at a good, steady clip, heading north on flat seas. I make my way to the pilothouse with a couple of bottles of water. I'm surprised to see Flip at the wheel.

Good morning.

-Ya, it is. I thought you weren't captain material.

Hard to screw up when Fern put it on cruise control and autopilot.

Thankfully, Fern's getting some rest with the others in the cabin area below. Flip's shaking off the effects of the drug, a little ashamed. We gulp at our water bottles till the plastic cracks. Flip lets out a mighty sigh.

I don't know what I was thinking when I partook.

-You were thinking that Aeura would, too. You're a guy.

Ha, yes. Desire! I did get to know your girl. Fern's quality.

I know that but am uncertain how to take it coming from Flip. Is he a rival? Probably. We should both live so long.

Where are we headed?

-She set the course for El Rosario de Arriba. There's a marina there.

That could be risky. No?

It seems obvious to me. The cartel men at the villa saw us flee by boat. They'll be watching marinas. Flip agrees. Back in the pilothouse, Fern agrees, too, but says, *What else can they do?* El Rosario is halfway to the border. Fueling up once is imperative if they're going to reach it. She's right, and I suddenly feel vulnerable in the Pacific, with no back door for escape. Flip sees my discomfort and adds his own.

Sitting ducks. I keep scanning for police helicopters. We're wanted for murder, don't forget.

-Made it this far, Flip. Can't cave now.

Except we have no one we can trust. We can't even use our phones.

-I know.

Gilly, my consul chief never sent help for us. He let this happen.

Flip winces, feeling some inner pain. I feel him. He lets it out. During the trip, he bad tripped.

I spiraled down a deep hole, Gilly. The U.S. Consul…Craig is freakin' cartel.

-If I say, "That blows chunks," am I minimizing it?

Flip laughs. He needs to. I let the salt spray hit my face and get serious and rhetorical.

How far will they go to stop us?

I remember the Armenian mob's tactics a few years back. We were a threat to their billion-dollar payday, and they went after our loved ones to crush us. Will the Mexican mob use the same playbook? I feel the need to warn Duke and Abby Jo, all the folks. Hold on. We do have one secret weapon. They may not be aware of Antonio. I get a surge of positivity.

Someone will hear us, but Antonio's got a clean phone.

-Gilly, they won't stop. Goes up too high.

My hopes bounce harder than our speeding craft over the suddenly swelling sea. The others are rising, appearing on the deck like confused zombies in the thickening marine layer. What a perfect day to die.

15.

Monday Afternoon

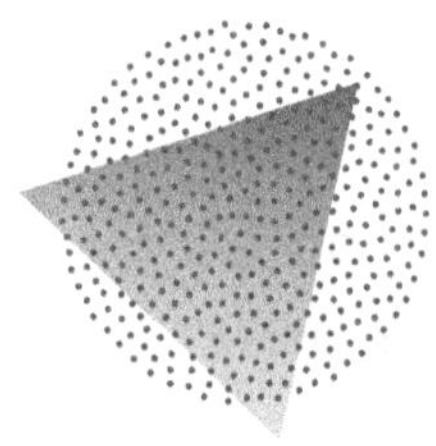

there was no darker time in the life of duke montrose, the happy-go-lucky cleaner of the pools of beverly. The news from Abby Jo that I and my friends had perished in an explosion on some remote island off the coast of Central Baja destroyed the Duke. He was paralyzed, unable to get out of bed. Don't get it wrong, Duke was never a doting dad or a constant beacon in my life. After his ex-wife, my mother, was killed in an auto crash, Duke was forced to be a full-time father and really wasn't prepared. But he wasn't the worst. For all his failings as a functioning adult, Duke knew I was the best part of him.

Abby Jo understood what she had to do. To buoy her boyfriend, she went to Marty's Hamburger Stand on Pico Boulevard in Rancho Park and got his favorite, the combo. Dad didn't take the bait. He let the fully loaded hamburger with the hot dog inside attract flies on the nightstand by his bed.

Abby Jo had worked the phone to get details that confirmed the explosion at the villa on la Isla de Cedros. She'd spoken to Fern's father, who got the same information. He was a rock and helped by calling Leticia's mother to deliver the blow. Abby Jo called VJ's folks. His father, understandably in denial, kept pressing the point that until the bodies were identified he was holding out hope. That gave Abby Jo, the most cynical of all, the tiniest spark. The gray-afroed crusader used the password of an old lover—who, conveniently, happened to be a lawyer—to access the LexisNexis database and retrieved Aeura's mother's private cell number. She left an urgent message for the Houston-based woman.

Since Aeura helped expose her mother's part in the Beverly Hills IPO fraud a few years back, she no longer had a relationship with her mom. But Abby Jo felt that the woman should know her daughter's fate and called her cell, texted, and even reached out on LinkedIn. Persistence had always been at the top of her skill set. So far, the disgraced Houston socialite had not bothered to call back. When Abby Jo's cell chimed, she figured it was Aeura's mother. It was UCLA hospital. They had a liver match for Duke and had scheduled surgery for 11 p.m. that night. He needed to be at the hospital by 7 p.m. and to not eat anything after 2 p.m. Abby Jo didn't even bother to ask Duke. She told the office that he'd be there with bells on.

In the bedroom, she turned on the light and opened the curtains. Hidden under the covers, the grieving Duke groaned.

Close them!

-It's 1:05 p.m. You need to eat in the next forty-five minutes. We have—

Go away!

-…to be at the hospital four hours before your 11 p.m. transplant surgery.

What? They have a match?

-You heard me.

I don't care. What's the point of extending this agony?

-OK, I'll cancel. Let someone else enjoy more sex, drugs, and rock and roll.

Abby Jo walked out of the bedroom and slammed the door. On second thought, Duke emerged from the web of covers. He was screaming.

Don't cancel!

The heartsick pool man sat up and reached for the combo sandwich. Duke's dripping tears moistened every delicious bite.

***

Stay together as a group or split up?

-Continue cruising north or hit the road?

Aeura and I laid out the choices. Which was our safest path? The high afternoon sun was filtered by ballooning cumulus clouds above us, providing the sweetest canopy we could ask for. We were about an hour out from the marina in the sleepy port of El Rosario de Arriba. Fern believed that our remaining fuel should be more than enough to reach it. Then what? We were last seen in a boat.

Do we ditch it or fuel up? The boat's maps show that the federal highway which goes north to the border begins at that port. There are buses, maybe vehicles to rent. We pooled our cash and have close to $1,000, thanks largely to Bunky, Donny, and Flip. Credit cards, it was agreed, should be avoided. Our whole crew—me, Aeura, Fern, Leticia, VJ, Flip, Bunky, Donny, and Antonio—was now nine in number. We'd been wearing the same clothes for the last few days and looked like a ragged tribe on *Survivor*. Despite the fact that we were a united force, it would be awkward and risky to travel together in stealth mode.

With the boat cruising open water on automatic, we were spread out around the deck to talk it through and shared the little bit we had to eat. That consisted of seven protein bars and a bag of questionable strawberries. Water was running low. No one was complaining. We were alive. There had been no land, sea, or air attacks on us. Do we dare think that they've forgotten or don't care? The ayahuasca microdose had given the seekers a hangover and a welcome calmness. Bunky, the oldest among us, stood up.

Will do whatever the group decides. You all rock.

-I'm with my pop. Your call.

--I'd like to touch grass, guys.

---We need to get supplies, whichever way we go.

VJ and Leticia were back up to speed and making their voices heard. Antonio couldn't take his eyes off of Leticia. He stood up.

Let me off before the port. There's a dinghy. I can check things out at the marina, you know?

-I'll go with him. I'm non-white, too, won't stand out.

VJ was not going to let Antonio play hero ball alone. Capitan Fern had gone over the boat GPS's digital views. The long channel into the port showed a few places for us to anchor and land a dinghy. If Antonio could get cell service in the town, he could call and get help.

That'll be a challenge. Who doesn't the cartel control? Who you going to call?

-*Ghostbusters!*

Knee-jerk, we all chimed in. We couldn't resist and choked with laughter. Except Flip. He wasn't amused.

They'd be more trustworthy than a U.S. government official.

He had a point. Aeura and I reminded the others.

If the cartel's searching for us, we have to warn our families. We can trust them.

-*Gilly's not being paranoid. They could be in danger.*

That iced the tribe.

***

In Mexico City's financial district, Juan Carlos looked out from his high-rise window. He'd been busy all morning using his trucking company resources to arrange a massive fentanyl move for El Jefe de Jefes. Juan Carlos truly hated being part of smuggling this heinous narcotic. It was worse than heroin and cocaine in its destruction of human lives. The drug was a plague on young people. It was because of his problems in Baja that he was forced into this penance. He absolutely needed to get back in the good graces of the boss of bosses, starting today. His sole consolation was that the giant load was bound for the states and out of Mexico. He worried about his daughter and her friends being tempted by its insidious allure. He couldn't understand how educated kids or adults could be so stupid as to take it. Yet, against their own common sense, they were eager and the Tijuana cartel raked in the windfall. Juan Carlos's phone messages were backed up, and his assistant reminded him that, among others, he owed Mr. Ramos a call.

Put him through.

Carita was sucking a cherry Tootsie Pop, getting through the first day of withdrawal from his carbonated addiction. He'd used his Platinum American Express card to access the VIP lounge at the Cabo airport and had been awaiting further orders, since he and Diego had made it back to Baja South. The hit man had participated in Diego's lie and felt it was time for a lie of his own.

Juan Carlos, I must apologize.

-What happened, Carita?

Diego didn't tell you everything. We lost the bomb guy.

Juan Carlos was confused. He'd heard nothing from Tijuana on a missing man.

You will. He got too close to the blast and boom, was killed. Terrible, ironic.

-Thank you for telling me.

Juan Carlos was in a hurry to get off the phone call. The cartel CEO needed to get ahead of this and apply some swift, sturdy guardrails. Carita held him. He was about to throw Diego under the bus.

Please, there's something else you should know.

-I have to go. Make it brief!

The Americans were not killed. They escaped.

16.

riɡʜt ɴow

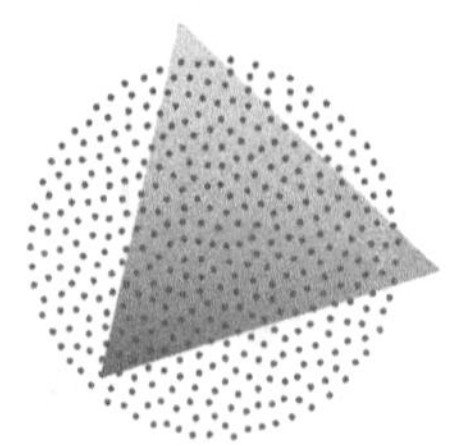

 We're anchored in an inlet a football field off the channel banks and about a mile from the El Rosario de Arriba marina. Only Flip and I are on deck. We occasionally wave to passing fishing boats coming in for the day. No one has threatened. It's a lazy golden hour. Still, Flip keeps a flare gun at hand. It's our only weapon. The others are below so as not to draw suspicion. I can't deny it, it's getting tense. VJ and Antonio have been gone for over two hours. I see only one way to get an update.

I'm going off to check. Hold the fort.

-No dinghy. You swimming over?

Hey, Southern California represent. We get wet.

I pull off my shirt and take off my Vans. The evening is warm on my skin, and I can use a wash, for sure.

Clear it with the captain, first.

-Aye aye.

I duck my head down below and laugh. Leticia, Fern, Aeura, Bunky, and Donny are playing cards. A light-hearted vibe abounds. Kibitzing goes around the table.

Gilly, this isn't strip poker.

-Could be.

--Ya. Make it a night we'll never forget.

-Donny, you mean never remember.

---Either way, deal me out. Gilly, what's happening topside?

----All OK. Permission to go ashore. Need to check on the scout party. Should've been back.

---Permission granted.

Capitan Fern seals it with a kiss. In the corner of my eye, I see Aeura grinning. Is she happy to see Fern's affection for me or judging it? I toss a mock salute to the assembled.

Flip's on watch. Don't go anywhere.

Back on the deck, I use the stern pad, give a hang loose hand sign to Flip, and dive in. The water is colder than in Baja South but refreshing as hell and clear. I lean into my stroke, stretching, and rewind the image of Fern's send-off and Aeura watching. I come to a conclusion. Neither has had on makeup for a while. Both are more beautiful without, though neither of them would ever believe it. What strange, wonderful creatures I've been privileged to know.

I can feel the channel bottom with my toes, and it's rocky—big, slippery stones that I hate. I swim till it's so shallow that rocks are hitting my chest and then I literally crawl to shore. Shaking off, I see where the dinghy was left and a path that leads to the town. Barefoot, shirtless, tanned brown, I look local myself in my board shorts. High reeds obscure the curvy path ahead. Someone's coming. Someone's drunk, singing the Friends theme song.

Antonio?! Dude.

-Hola, Gilly!

He carries two bags of mercado goodies and is as happy drunk as a sitcom sidekick.

Where's VJ?

-At the restaurant waiting for us.

Is it safe?

-Totally.

He tells me that when they first got to the marina, they purposely poked around so people would see them. They found nothing but good, hardworking folk. Friendly, too. They went to the only restaurant in the sleepy outpost and sat, like bait. No one bit. So they ordered and had a few.

That's when we saw the news story on TV.

-What story?

The Americans wanted for murder were killed in an explosion.

-No way!

They're not looking for you, Gilly.

I'm overwhelmed. We have an advantage now. We can get home.

Did you call our folks?

-And warned them. VJ's parents are staying out of town. Fern's, too. Leticia's mom is going off the grid till her daughter's safely back. She seems nice.

And my dad?

-Never answered.

He turns it off when he's sleeping. I should have said text.

-Here, I have a one bar. Go for it. Dial 00 first.

Thanks!

He hands me his cell. I type in Duke's number and compose a text as cryptic as a compliment sandwich.

IT'S GILLY. I'M OK. TAKE CARE

The message sends.

***

In the West LA rent-controlled apartment, Duke's cell phone is charging on the bedside table. It chimes with a text message alert. The bed is vacant, the room empty. At the apartment door, Abby Jo enters with arms full of bags and a jug of juice in each hand, breathing hard from negotiating the stairs. She coughs through the words.

Duke, I need help. I got everything we need for post-op. Honey, come now.

No Duke appears. Abby Jo balances the bags and jugs and makes it to the kitchen table, a feat unto itself. She starts putting the groceries away, yelling loudly enough for him to hear.

Thanks a lot! Duke? You drinking clear liquids? Ninety minutes, we're out the door, sweetie.

There's no response. With concern, she checks out the bedroom. No Duke in the bed, covers tossed. The en suite bathroom is empty—no Duke on the throne. Before she exits, she notices his cell on the bedside table. It displays Gilly's text. Abby Jo absorbs the good news right down to her Birkenstock toes. She howls with unbridled happiness. Immediately, there's an urgent tap on the bedroom window. It's Duke, outside in his pajamas on the fire escape. With a doobie in his mouth, he raises up the window.

Come out!

-Gilly's alive!

I know. My cup runneth over!

Duke takes a celebratory toke and helps Abby Jo out the window. She ducks her afro and steps onto the ancient iron grill balcony in the last light of day. Duke closes the window.

Fern's dad called. Invited us to hunker down in La Quinta till... Oh no! No!

-Till what? Where are the kids?

--Shhh! These bangers have been sitting in that rent-a-wreck. They're getting out.

Looking below to the street, Abby Jo sees what Duke does. Two dangerous-looking, tatted-up Mexican OGs cross the street toward their building with unholy purpose and machetes.

What fresh hell is this?

-Not a social call.

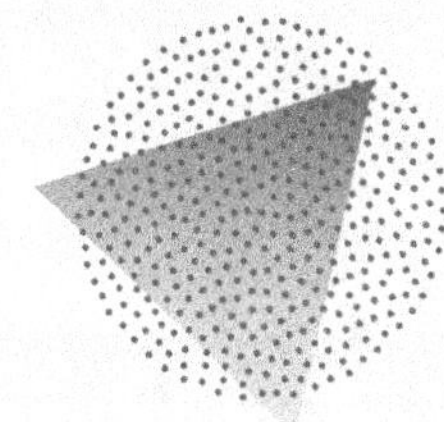

GiLLY

MONDAY NIGHT

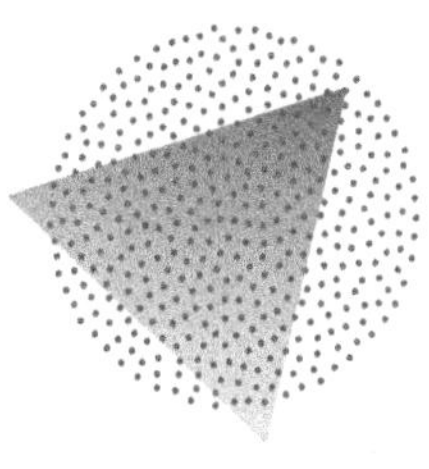

the evening breeze wafted through the open adobe windows of the best and only restaurant in el rosario de arriba. Our team of nine dominated Las Casuelas and were treated royally, probably because we were the only customers other than the two fishermen at the bar. Anxious for fresh clothing, we all bought their T-shirts, which didn't hurt either. The food was right out of mama's kitchen. Chile rellenos were the specialty, and we ordered all they had, plus cerveza and chips—lots of chips—and a pile of *pico de gallo*. Even I had a beer.

The heat was off us, we wanted to believe, though I couldn't stop wondering for how long or why we were reported killed.

My better angels—Fern, Aeura, and Leticia—agreed with me that cartel soldiers knew that we'd escaped by boat before the explosion and should have told their superiors. We'd traveled a whole day and had encountered no sign that anyone was after us. With the resources and swiftness that the mob had already demonstrated, this seemed incongruous. I mean, we had to come to grips with the fact that our mercenaries, hired by Fern and Donny, were infiltrated or killed by the cartel. That would have taken a lot of clout and intel, which is scary.

And oodles of cash. I feel like we should get a refund, Donny.

-The cartel can't let you tell your story VJ.

--They bribed an American consul, for God's sake. They control the country!

---Too many loose ends to consider on too many beers, boys.

----Exactly. Can we enjoy the meal? We're a day away from home.

Antonio, VJ, and Flip were convinced that the mob men, including Antonio's uncles, lied to cover their asses and that we're safe for the time being. We all agreed that other than Antonio's phone, no one who still had one should even turn it on. Our boat, named *El Vagabundo*, based on the embossed letters on its hull, was tied up at the marina in town. In the morning, the three girls, VJ, Flip, and I would head north for the border and surrender ourselves in the United States. Bunky and Donny had all their papers and weren't wanted for murder. They opted for a bus to TJ. I don't blame them. Antonio was torn. He wanted to make sure we—that is, Leticia—got safely back, but he was two days AWOL from his work at the hospital. Leticia let him off the hook.

Antonio, we'll see you again. I'll see you again. That's a promise.

-Me too, bud. Promise.

--Thanks, VJ. So glad to hear that, bro.

-Come to LA. I'll hook you up. Dude, we're stocked with fabulous females.

VJ reaches out in a DAP handshake.

Brotherhood?

The Mexican Romeo from Todos Santos meets it clean, and they finish it like brothers. Flan for dessert hit the spot, and the sweet syrupy topping felt as good as it gets. I kissed Fern, and our honeyed lips smacked perfectly. Our waitress told us that the band was coming in soon and lots of their fans, too. She had a wicked grin and said it could get wild. Our crowd of funsters liked that prospect. Over coffees, we toasted Bunky for picking up the bill, and I thought about cutting Fern from the bunch and walking her back to the boat early. Before I could, she whispered in my ear.

Let's cut out.

-Si, si.

✳✳✳

In West LA, after grabbing what they needed and escaping down the collapsible fire ladder into the alley, Duke and Abby Jo changed Ubers twice. They were only going less than a mile to UCLA hospital in Westwood, but Abby Jo insisted. They were a good hour early for intake and relieved to take sanctuary in a security-controlled facility. Duke was running hot, unnerved about the future for his boy, his girl, and his liver—not necessarily in that order. Abby Jo was used to analyzing situations, and she spun the gangbangers' appearance as a positive.

You've been hitting the Tito's?

-If they're looking for you, dummy, then Gilly's still alive. They must not know where he is.

Oh yeah. So that's where I come in.

-You are the pinch point.

Machete meat.

They were directed to the general lobby to wait till called. The room was cheery, comfy, and carpeted, with plush couches and TVs all around—some on CNN, some on Fox News. The veteran activist Abby Jo saw the irony.

Ah. Good people on both sides.

-Can you get me a water?

Got it right here. Settle in and try to relax. It's going to be a long day.

From her massive shoulder bag, she handed him a bottled water and took out her laptop and powered it up.

You have Gilly's number on your phone. Want to call it?

-No. Could be risky for him.

Then erase it.

-Good idea.

Duke cleared his phone, and Abby Jo caught up on her emails. One from a reporter friend at The Washington Post confirmed that the kids were presumed dead, pending ID of the bodies found at the site. She passed that on to Duke.

Huh, dead? Tell it to the OGs. According to you, they didn't get the memo.

-Keep your phone nearby, in case Gilly calls back. I got to have a smoke.

Abby Jo went back out through security to the front of the hospital and stood near the semicircle drop-off with another pariah, a sad, young nun in a habit. She bummed a cig.

Do you have one to spare?

-Of course.

Abby Jo took out a Marlboro Gold, handed it over, and lit it for the nun. The girl of God took a good drag and smiled, turning away, perhaps ashamed. Abby Jo smoked in peace, keeping to herself, with only good thoughts allowed. Duke was getting a liver. That was miraculous. She'd never been religious; however, in the presence of a smoking Sister of Christ, it seemed like a good time. She invoked the Jesus of her Cincinnati upbringing and said a silent prayer for Duke, her significant other, boyfriend, common-law husband, booty call. A white Prius with an Uber sign pulled up to let people out. It was the same Uber car in which she and Duke had arrived. Abby Jo would bet the house on it. Her extreme satisfaction of being correct was supplanted by the extreme reality of the two tatted, gang-bangers exiting the Uber and running up the steps to the hospital.

MF'ers!

-I beg your pardon.

The nun was shocked. Panties in a panic, Abby Jo surrendered her lit cigarette to the surprised young nun.

Sorry, Sister. Gotta go. Matter of life and death.

-I'll pray.

And smoke for me, too.

With a cig in each hand, the surprised bride of Christ watched Abby Jo rush back in.

***

In the ritzy Polanco district of Mexico City, Juan Carlos had been in his study all night, glued to a computer screen like a freshman college student cramming for a test. He went over the Americans' possible escape routes by boat. He'd used his Cabo network to get word out to the marinas north and south of la Isla de Cedros to be on the lookout. He knew that eventually they were going to have to gas up or tie up. To speed up the process, he quietly reached out to his Los Angeles contacts to get some bad boys to find the Americans' families and squeeze them for their children's locale. He didn't publicly change the narrative that they'd died in the explosion, nor did he privately reveal the truth to El Jefe de Jefes. Tijuana didn't yet need to know of the utter screwup.

Juan Carlos was buying time for at least another day to eliminate the threat to him, his family, and his entire operation. The odds of silencing the Americans were diminishing with each hour, so he worked all the angles. He'd make sure to have his wife and daughter on a plane to Dallas first thing in the morning. His sister would take them in and hide them—and him, if necessary. Before the cartel CEO shut down, he got a text from a marina night watchman in El Rosario de Arriba, Central Baja. A cabin cruiser with Americans had tied up. An elated Juan Carlos texted right back for confirmation that it was *El Vagabundo* and put in an urgent call to Carita Ramos.

2.

riqHt Now

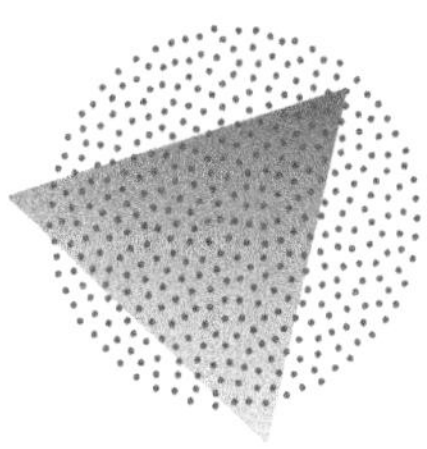

tHe NiqHt couLd Not be More SAtiSFYiNq. I'm not an experienced lover and have never asked Fern her sexual history. We pant with toasty sweet breath and laugh in an afterglow of pleasure shared. I have no idea how long we have lain within a clearing behind a boatyard that lines the marina. Probably not that long at all. We snatched some loose tarps and put them down for bedding and went at each other like hungry lions. The sky above us is an awesome wonder. We kiss for each shooting star blazing across the celestial canopy. Fern invents constellations to crack me up.

And finally, there's Gilly the Stud. Five stars that make up, an erect—

-Do you love me, Fern? I mean, like Leticia and VJ's forever?

What?

-No what. You hesitated.

Gilly, we don't want to have this conversation. We don't know if we'll make it through tomorrow.

I press Fern anyway. My bad. She stands and dresses, and I wish I hadn't taken us in this direction. Why am I so insecure that I need to push the point? A school shrink once scarred me with abandonment issues. He called me a "textbook child of divorce," and I can never quite bury that label. Fern holds me in her arms and lets me have it.

I love you. And that doesn't change, whatever happens.

-What's happening?

I plan to move to Paris in the spring and study architecture. I've been waiting to tell you.

My reaction is visceral, unguarded. Like an all-in poker pro, I see her return to Paris and raise the ante, on one knee, in mock dramatic jest. I swear.

Oh cool. In the spring, I plan to ask for your hand in marriage.

-Cute. And I'll say no. You dope, get up. Put your shorts on.

Shhh...

-I need to get back to the boat. Plot the course. Please.

No, Fern. Listen. Hear that?

She focuses, and we move for a better view of the road a distance away. We see them, a shadowy group of maybe twenty people trudging onward in the night, with belongings on their backs.

Migrants?

-I think so. Walking to the border.

Fleeing for our lives, too, we feel a kinship with them, though who is more vulnerable is anyone's guess.

We make our way back to the marina. The overhead lights are off. Still, it's easy to spot our trusty craft. It's the only non-fishing boat on the long dock. Fern and I aren't the only ones spotting. Ahead of us, alongside the boat, are two locals. One holds a flashlight. The other takes photos of the illuminated name on the hull, *El Vagabundo, Isla de Cedros*. They don't see us. Uneasy all over again, we retreat into the night.

3.

MONDAY NIGHT

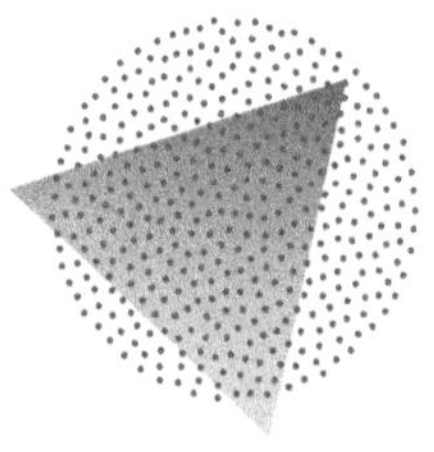

CARITA RAMOS WAS LAYING OVER IN CABO AT THE AEROPUERTO HYATT AND TAKING ADVANTAGE OF ITS SPA, when he got the call from Juan Carlos. He thought that he was going to be asked to track down Diego. He was wrong. Charters were waiting to wing him north to a little fishing village where the young Americans were spending the night. He had orders to leave no one alive. In the hotel sauna, the hit man had detoxed from the psychedelic spray and felt like a new man. The thought of killing again seemed rich and wonderful. He took the hotel shuttle to the airport with renewed vigor and a handful of Tootsie Pops.

***

At the UCLA hospital in Westwood, Abby Jo hustled to get ahead of the two hard cases who looked lost in the lobby. They had overcoats on, and she had a solid idea what was underneath. Though she felt protected in the facility, she was bent on stopping any interruption or delay—or worse, police lockdown—that would prevent Duke from getting this transplant surgery. It was almost his intake time. At an unoccupied nurses' stand, she hopped behind the desk and did her best "helpful receptionist" impression. Seeing the two men, Abby Jo waved them over in her friendliest proper voice.

Can I help you? Are you looking for a patient?

-Montrose.

While the Latino gangsters fidgeted before her, Abby Jo pretended to be looking it up on the computer.

Oh, I see. Mr. Montrose was just transferred to our UCLA Santa Monica Medical Center. Do you need the address?

On a notepad, she wrote it down for them—or at least what she imagined the address was—and they nodded. Abby Jo watched them lumber away and removed herself just as a nurse came by and gave her an odd look. Contrite, Abby Jo shrugged and returned the pen to the desk.

Oops.

In the waiting room, Duke was standing with a nurse and three doctors. He was going in. She hurried to wish him luck and love. He handed her his cell.

In case he calls. Why you shaking? I'm the one who's scared.

-I'm not. I'm quaking with joy. For you, for us, for Gilly. He's alive!

She hugged Duke, and he was off with the surgical team. He was safe. No need for Duke to know more tonight.

* * *

In the remote Baja port of El Rosario de Arriba, the Las Casuelas eatery was lit. In the parking lot outside the establishment were at least six Harleys, a dozen pickup trucks, and an old school bus, re-bannered for a band called Guapo. The music was loud and strange. Fern and I entered into a different restaurant than the one we left. It was going off, and a good time was being had by all. The band was mariachi punk, fronted by a young lead singer with raven hair and a nose ring. They were doing a mariachi version of the Ramones's "Blitzkrieg Bop." Bunky was on the bandstand with them, adding percussion on cowbell. They sounded pretty damn good, and the crowd, including half a dozen bikers from an outlaw club called Los Sucio, was into it, singing and dancing. Each of them looked like an even more intimidating version of Danny Trejo, the LA icon.

We searched for our friends to tell them the upsetting update. On the dance floor, Leticia and Antonio were going at it with abandon, *Dirty Dancing* style. In the corner, Flip and Aeura were smooching. (I should have seen that coming.) Donny was asleep, head down on the table, and VJ, with his skills, was taking on all comers at the foosball table.

The lead singer, whose name was Maya, had her eye on Antonio and motioned him up to the bandstand so she could gyrate with him during the song. Flattered, the Todos Santo homeboy took the bait, leaving Leticia on the dance floor, momentarily partnerless. She went right over to the foosball table.

Dance with me, VJ.

-Tish, you know I don't dance.

Dance. With. Me.

VJ got the message and obeyed. I had to laugh, knowing how tough she can be in a relationship. VJ knew what he was getting into. He also knew that she was worth it. Fern and I waited till the set ended, with Bunky sitting in and playing drums on a high speed version of "Hotel Californ." His drum solo echoed into the rafters, with the crowd urging him on, and the big finish led to cheers. Bunky was old, but he could beat those tubs. The band took a break, and we got everyone to follow Fern and me outside to huddle. The air was intoxicating for our intoxicated team.

Listen up, kids.

No one did. In the Las Casuelas parking lot, the good time had them warm and reeling, chattering, full of spirit and spirits. Bunky got some weed from his new band buds and was sharing a Jamaican-sized spliff with Aeura and Flip. VJ was getting an earful from Leticia and smiling through it. Antonio shrugged, feeling responsible, and strode off to give them space.

Donny couldn't stop yawning. To his credit, he was the first to ask Fern and me.

Is something wrong? Can we go back to the boat?

-Thank you, Donny. No, we can't.

--Peeps! Our boat's being watched.

-It's not safe anymore.

--We're not safe.

I clarified that and meant it, meeting the eyes of each. That brought everyone down, and worry set in. The alternative ways to get to the border were limited. Public transportation seemed risky for the whole group at once. It was a five-hour drive, if we could buy or rent a van. My eyes were fixed on the band's ride, parked in front of us.

Or a bus? How tight are you with Guapo, sir?

-They love my discography. Hardworking players. Driving back to Ensenada after the show. Whoa! Could we hitch a ride?

Ensenada would get us an hour from the US border. Before Bunky could answer, Antonio volunteered.

--I could talk to the singer, too. Maya and I had a little thing.

-So we noticed, Antonio.

Leticia felt obligated to utz him. VJ approved. What Antonio didn't mention was that the singer reminded him of one of the few Hispanic characters on Beverly Hills, 90210. Joy, Kelly Taylor's half-Mexican half sister, was played by the alluring Ruth Livier, whom Antonio and his mother agreed should have been in the main cast. Maya—the Joy look-alike—and Guapo were going back inside for the last set, and we headed in, too. I lingered for a private moment with Aeura. We can usually tell each other anything.

What are you doing with Flip?

-Same as what you're doing with Fern. Life is short, G. I can't wait for you.

She threw that down and stepped ahead to rejoin Flip. I knew she was high, and I didn't want to read too much into it. She'd never been with a man yet, either, so there was that. Up ahead, VJ was waiting for me outside the entrance.

Dude, think you could be overreacting? News said we were dead.

-But we aren't, are we? We need to hit the road. The boat's hot.

***

The boat was. Under the warming first rays of Tuesday morning, the sleepy marina of El Rosario de Arriba buzzed with the sound of a seaplane. It landed gracefully, skimming the channel water, only disturbing some feeding brown pelicans, and drifted to a stop next to the moored *El Vagabundo*. Carita Ramos told the pilot that he wouldn't be long. He stepped across the wing and right onto the deck of the boat. The cartel hit man was dressed in a white sport jacket, collarless shirt, and plaid golf shorts. A cherry Tootsie Pop was perched in his mouth, moving occasionally from side to side. He'd been traveling all night, catching charters and some wicked turbulence. With no sleep, his mood was as dark as his heart. He was told that there were as many as eight Americans on board. His job was to erase them all. He wasn't interested in making a whole day of it.

Who the hell are you?

On the upper pilot deck, sunning himself, shirt off, beer in hand, was Torrez, treasurer of the Baja chapter of Los Sucio, the outlaw biker gang. Torrez was the size of a Viking refrigerator and had skulls tattooed across his chest. He stroked his thick mustache, considering the sight of Carita. The professional killer hadn't expected this. His right hand hung low beneath the jacket flap that shielded his Glock. The stocky biker came down the ladder and faced Carita, who blinked, pretending to be polite.

Sorry to disturb you, señor. Are the owners of the boat on board?

-Owners? That would be Los Sucio.

From the cabin below, two other gnarly, enormous Mexican bikers emerged, curious and waking up, catching up. Carita gave a wave to Bluto and Flippy and directed his pitch.

Ah, just looking for the gringos who arrived on this boat. Do you know where—

-No. Boat was abandoned. It's ours now.

--Law of the sea.

---Go away!

No need to be rude. I understand that intel has a value. Let's talk. These kids. Where—

Carita persisted. Torrez was not a people person. A diabetic, he'd passed out during the night and had no memory of the Americans at all. He'd woken up in the bushes and heard that their club owned a boat. As treasurer, he liked acquiring surprise assets and didn't want anything to change that. The biker hulk removed the cherry lolly from Carita's mouth and stuck it on Carita's white jacket.

Go suck somewhere else.

The other two burly brothers of Los Sucio, not the sharpest tools in the kit, laughed, but their laughter was short-lived. Carita pulled out his automatic pistol, and the deck ran red as a Tootsie Pop, with the blood of the three outlaw bikers. The inconvenienced assassin would have to beat the bushes now to pick up the Americans' tail. Juan Carlos had offered him a significant bonus. Carita planned to score it and salvage the remainder of what had been a difficult week. With a group of gringos that large, someone in the town had to know more.

right Now

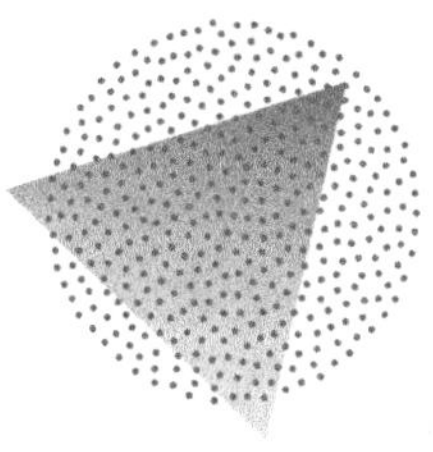

The traffic is light on the Federal Highway north. Bunky called in a favor, and the Guapo quartet invited us along on their ride home. Antonio's pull with Maya definitely helped seal the deal. The Baja Romeo's still with us. Since I was the only sober one, the band let me do the driving. With one road to navigate, it is a no-brainer. I can't get lost. This once-yellow 1995 school bus handles better than you'd think. The sun is gentle on my left shoulder, and I'm into the monotony of the road, holding my speed and keeping between the lines, passing the occasional overloaded produce truck. It's hypnotic and soothing.

My passengers are all sleeping off the excesses of the evening. In my rearview mirror, I see the band at the back of the bus. Maya, the lead singer, is paired with Antonio, who confessed to me before we boarded that with Leticia so set with VJ, Maya is a soft landing. Plus, unlike everyone else the mariachi punk singer hangs out with, Antonio has no tattoos and that turns Maya on. Whatever works. Whatever advantage in the game of love is cool with me. I can see Leticia, half-awake, gazing back to see Antonio canoodled with Maya. She can't be jealous, can she? Ah, you always want what you don't have. That's a core Duke Montrose belief. The others are conked out—Fern, Aeura, Flip, VJ, Bunky, and Donny, each oblivious to the random bumps on this cracking asphalt excuse for a highway.

Since I pushed Fern into sharing her future plans, I have to deal with them. No matter how I try to frame the picture, I don't see myself living in Paris. This quiet dump has been so quiet, I didn't realize that it's been happening to me for months. I mean, I did, but denial is an easy anesthetic to block the pain of a breakup. I could try to talk Fern out of this dream of hers. If I loved her without reason, I think I would—or I would go with her unconditionally. Does that mean I don't? When I mock proposed to her, it didn't come out of the blue. It had crossed my mind months before to really do it. The image of us married, in student housing, her maybe pregnant, is all I need to know that it's not a pressing option. We need time to grow ourselves. Time, however, is a luxury we may not have.

I stop thinking of relationship BS and start worrying about after Ensenada, the last leg of our trip to Tijuana and the US border. We have all the information we need to expose the cartel's crimes and their murderous cover-up. Have they forgotten us? Were the men watching our boat not a threat? On that hopeful thought, I take a swig of bottled water and try to relax. The accordion/keyboard player of the band steps to the front and directs me to pull off at the next side road. Bathroom break? He shakes his head no and grins. I don't understand why we're stopping when we're so close to the city. His name is Javy and he won't say why. I do as I'm told and steer us onto a dirt path. Deep mud ruts jar everyone awake and yammering. Javy laughs like a hyena and gives me further directions. He sends us down a narrower lane that the bus squeaks through, with leafy branches scratching at the windows. My fear meter for clear and present danger jumps.

After a stand of dense eucalyptus trees, I come to a clearing, brake, and stare ahead. The band members cheer, joined by our chorus. Before us is a natural, bubbling, steaming hot spring rock pool, fed by an idyllic waterfall—right out of a music video. It's a locals' local treasure, and all we need to do is enjoy it. I open the doors with a flourish. Our bunch piles out quickly and, just as quickly, sheds clothing, racing to be the first to jump in. Javy claps my shoulder and rushes off. Fern slides in behind me and kisses my neck all around.

Thanks for manning the wheel. I missed snuggling with you.

-You did?

Go figure. Or not. Best to carpe the diem.

5.

tuesday morning

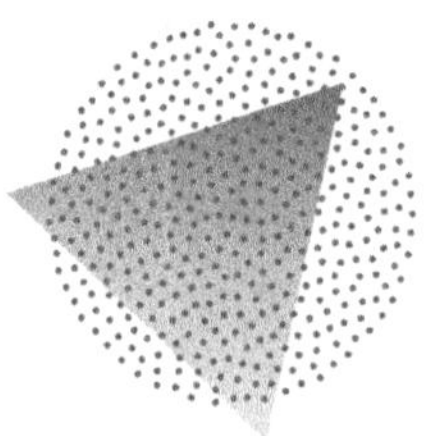

At his hilltop seaside estate outside of Tijuana, El Jefe de Jefes—the Boss of Bosses—had taken a cold plunge after his workout with a trainer and was feeling tip-top. A phone call from his lieutenant in TJ changed that. Their top explosives expert had never returned from a job in Central Baja. The esteemed Rodrigo Santos, El Jefe de Jefes, had loaned Juan Carlos the man from a brother cartel to help alleviate a mess that was created in Baja South. Rodrigo wondered whether the mess had ever been fixed. Juan Carlos had assured him that the Americans wanted for murder—and their threat to his operation—had died in the explosion. Rodrigo had exacted a price from Juan Carlos and used considerable resources in the upper level of government to smooth over things for him.

The kingpin's ire was palpable. Something didn't compute. A phone call later, he learned that Juan Carlos had put out an alert to the northern state police and border patrol to stop and hold a band tour bus, marked GUAPO, with the Americans in it until his man could arrive and take charge of them. That tore it for Rodrigo, who knew that he'd been lied to, and the level of cartel exposure was significant. He didn't have to deliberate on a course of action. He was going to hang Juan Carlos out to dry. He canceled Juan Carlos's APB. Let the Americans get home and sink his whole outfit. The country could use the PR of a good cartel cleansing, he told himself. More territory for El Jefe de Jefes when the dust cleared.

***

Duke's surgery was declared successful. In the UCLA's surgery center's waiting room, Abby Jo had nodded off with an open bag of nachos spilled over her mom jeans, when the nurse came to get her. In the recovery room, Duke was not fully awake so she stood by his bedside and squeezed his hand. That did the trick. He turned and looked up, groggy, confused. Abby Jo had a sandpaper personality, but her touch was smooth and gentle. Her hand brushed his face, and he felt alive. Doctors entered and the nurse apologized. They needed to examine him. Ushered out, Abby Jo headed for the entrance and the smoking area. Outside, she was surprised to see the young nun again. This time, the nun had her own smokes. Buddies in hospital woe.

Loved one inside?

-My mom. The men you followed in last night are back. They've been sitting in that car.

Acting casual, the novitiate waved her cigarette in their direction. Abby Jo saw the two OGs in the back seat of a dark four-door. A third banger was at the wheel. A fourth, in the passenger seat, was on the phone, staring right back at her. Stricken, Abby Jo choked on her cig smoke. The sister put a hand on her shoulder.

Should I call the police?

A fit of serious, spasmatic coughing prevented Abby Jo from answering. Before it ceased, the sedan with cartel soldiers pulled away from the hospital entrance. The tough guy riding shotgun threw her a peace sign as the car drove off. Flummoxed, Abby Jo turned to the smoking nun.

You prayed, didn't you?

***

Juan Carlos didn't go into his office. His wife and daughter had flown to Dallas, albeit kicking and screaming. He worked alone in his Mexico City mansion, guarded by three of his better men, who were on the perimeter. It was unsettling that he hadn't heard from Rodrigo. El Jefe should have been aware of the missing bomb tech by now. Juan Carlos expected a tirade and was prepared to take it. He'd do whatever it took to make it up. The escaped, very much alive Americans were another matter. Juan Carlos had delayed the ID results, so no one should have been the wiser.

Juan Carlos had muscle in Los Angeles on surveillance of the kids' families, and Carita, God bless him, was after them on the road. There was reason for optimism. A school bus on the highway wouldn't be hard to spot. When a call came in with a 310 area code, he knew it was Los Angeles with an update. Juan Carlos wasn't expecting to hear that the gang muscle working the surveillance detail were standing down. They'd been called back by order of El Jefe de Jefes.

It was war.

6.

right Now

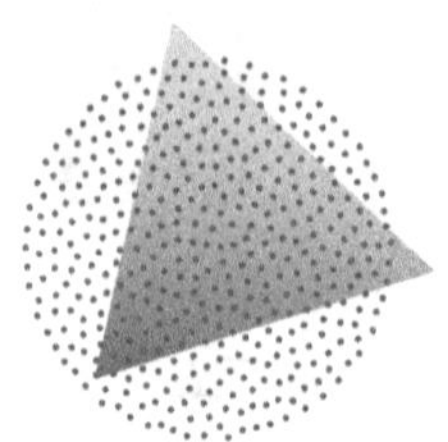

 Every inch of my skin is tingling, the liquid beads glistening in the light. Our whole group, band included, thirteen in number, dries out all in a row on the rocks, half-naked under the late morning sun. I close my eyes, and colors refract into the spectrum. Just lying between Fern on my right and Aeura on my left is a symphony of sensation. This is illegal.

Aeura twists to Flip, who turns to her, face to face, nose to nose, breath to breath. There's something happening there. I'm happy for Aeura. I think. I mean, Flip is a quality human whose foreign service future we've surely altered. We've come a long way in hostile territory and are less than two hours' drive to the border. I've been thinking ahead. With Leticia in charm mode, under the spring's waterfall, we got Antonio's promise to help us again. In Ensenada, after the band unpacks, Antonio will borrow the bus, with Maya's permission, and drive us to the Tijuana border crossing and then bring it back to Ensenada. Problem solved. We could be back in the states tonight. Maya rolls on top of him, and they're entwined. The kid continues to impress. Even VJ is down with him. Where would we be without Antonio?

I can't imagine what will make us move. Well, a police siren, for certain. WTF!! Blaring, it shatters the bliss. Everyone quickly goes for their clothes, but we have nowhere to run. A state police car pulls into the clearing, blocking the bus, and the two officers get out. They take their time looking over the bus. They're locals themselves and always check out the hot spring. The tall one with a small mustache takes a photo of the Guapo banner hung on the side. The other is a stocky, bodybuilding, lady cop, with a shape like a fire hydrant. She looks over our diverse group of Mexicans and Americans.

IDs, por favor.

Ya, right. Me, Fern, Aeura, Leticia, VJ, and Flip have none and declare it. Each of us has lost it along the way. We're passed over for the moment and fade toward the rear of the group. The band grabs documents from the bus and shows them to the squat female. Bunky and Donny have theirs. The tall policeman considers the passports and hands them back. None of them want any trouble and are extra polite. Antonio surrenders his driver's license, and there's a pause. The lady cop retreats back to the squad car. While one checks Antonio's license, the other tells us all to sit down. We comply. It feels weird. Antonio simultaneously translates.

Straight up. There was an APB out for the Guapo bus. Now there's not. Who do you know?

-We're musicians, man. Nobody.

--We have fans.

---We didn't do anything.

----I paid my parking tickets.

I'm comfortable having Maya and the band answer. The tall cop is from Ensenada and has seen the band. He's a fan himself. Power of music. To our delight, he asks for a signed CD. From the bus, Maya guarantees it, plus a band T-shirt.

Thanks. And you better hope you do have fans. Certain people were after you.

-What kind of people?

Certain.

The tall cop says that word carefully, slowly, and says no more. We all understand—he means cartel. The lady fireplug returns and takes hold of our main man.

Hey, he's the missing kid from Todos Santos. Antonio Lopez, come with us.

-Huh? No!

You're wanted for questioning in the disappearance of Ricardo and Torchy.

-My uncles? What—

Save it.

--Maya, I'd take down that banner on the bus, just in case.

---Thanks. Return him in good condition, por favor.

The tall cop winks to the band singer. The two officers escort a protesting Antonio to the patrol car and deposit him in the back seat. We can't believe it. There's a lot to process, and the band's looking at us with suspicion. Above us, the sun shuts down, covered by thick, dark clouds that cast us into shadows for dramatic punctuation.

Where will we be without Antonio? We're about to find out.

tuesday afternoon

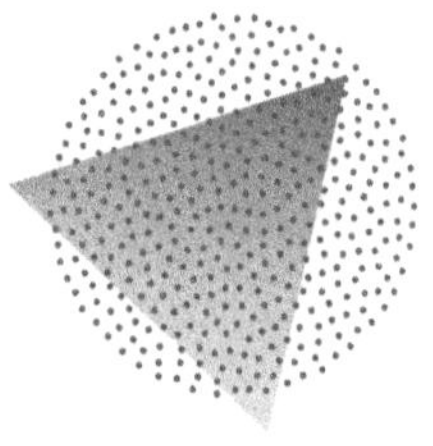

CARItA HAD LEARNED tHAT tHE AMERICANS WERE HEADED FOR tHE bORDER IN tHE GUAPO bAND buS. A little pressure on the Las Casuelas barmaid and he had all the information he needed, without even showing his gun. And a Harley, abandoned by a deceased Los Sucio biker on his highway to hell, gave Carita just the wheels he needed to pursue them. It was his motorcycle now. *Law of the road*, he chuckled to himself, blazing up the Federal Highway toward Tijuana wearing a kick-ass helmet with Bluetooth enabled.

He'd put the screws to Juan Carlos, too. His usually cheapskate boss, Juan Carlos, had agreed to transfer a large advance at Carita's request. That was all the evidence the hit man needed to understand that his boss was on shaky ground. Carita didn't want to be on a losing team and would have to be careful. He was on another cartel's turf. An hour out of Ensenada, roaring by the dirt lane turnoff to a hot spring, the wet work pro never realized how close he was to his prey.

Half a klick behind him, a Cristo Redentor school bus emerged from the dirt lane. Its band banners removed, the old yellow bus with its faded original signage on the sides chugged onto the highway and onward north. The slate gray clouds had turned black. The wind howled, screaming winter storm.

***

El Jefe de Jefes had stopped giving the problems of Juan Carlos any attention. He was lunching at Misión 19, the most exclusive restaurant in Tijuana, with the head of the Plaza Monumental, the last remaining bullring in Baja, and a talented, female toreador whose career he'd invested in. The preservation and splendor of bullfighting was Rodrigo's passion and helped him maintain a level of respectability in the community. He kept the peace and kept Mexican traditions alive. The phone call from his wife soured the béarnaise sauce on the amazing chateaubriand he'd ordered. Her youngest sister, a freshman at Universidad Nacional Autónoma in Mexico City, had been abducted.

He'd underestimated Juan Carlos's desperation and regrettably had to cut the lunch short.

***

In the tallest tower in Mexico City, in his high-rise office, Juan Carlos was expecting the call from El Jefe de Jefes. His demands for the life of the college student were simple. All authorities will assist his man Carita in finishing his job, and the sister-in-law will be released unharmed. Rodrigo wasn't going to break a sweat on this. He agreed and would deal with Juan Carlos's fate at a later date.

***

In the Policia Estatal de Ensenada, inside a small interview room, decorated gray upon gray, Antonio told what he knew. The detective with the gang unit was aware that the cousins—Antonio's uncles— were cartel members working under the late Dr. Foo. Antonio thought that they were working a job on an island off the west coast of Central Baja. As far as he knew, they were alive and well. That placed the cousins at the location and satisfied the interviewer. The cousins, among others, were suspected in the death of two security guards at la Isla de Cedros Airport. To his relief, Antonio was let go with bus fare and meal money for the two-day trip down the peninsula. Outside, the rain had started. Antonio pulled his T-shirt over his head. True to his word, the state patrolman was waiting in the parking lot in his patrol car. The tall cop opened a car door. Antonio got in.

You're really gonna return me to Maya?

-Sure.

The tall cop had printed ID photos, in color, and he showed them off one at a time—Gilly, Leticia, VJ, Aeura, Fern, Flip, Bunky, and Donny.

Your American friends are wanted for murder. Or abetting murderers.

-No, the American murderers are dead. It was on the news.

And now they're alive and considered armed and dangerous. You should warn the band, if you know where to find them.

Antonio knew he needed to get back to Todos Santos and to pray that he still had a job. Yet it was a need that somehow he no longer needed. He was living la vida loca. His new friends were a risky hang, but his own family would learn that he ratted on the cousins. He'd out-Dylaned Dylan McKay and had come too far to take the ticket home. The stocky lady cop joined them, with takeout tacos. Antonio looked at the tall cop with conviction.

Give me a phone charger and a taco. I'll find the band.

-And the Americans. If we see them, we have to bring them in.

right Now

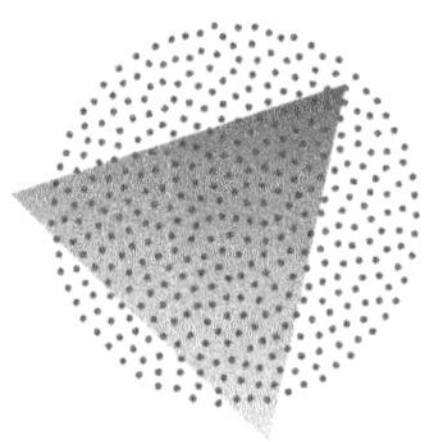

the never-ending baja sunshine is only a memory. We're on the outskirts of Ensenada, on the main road, and the rain is pounding harder than Bunky on the drums. The afternoon sky is slate black, and thunder and lightning are our soundtrack. The band Guapo and their singer Maya were kind enough to let us off at a bus depot with an overhang. They wouldn't consider selling the bus or taking us anywhere near their loft in the city. They'd heard through the grapevine that some American kids had killed a cartel chief, which explained the unwelcome attention—attention that the band did not relish.

On the bus platform with a number of working class locals and students, we crowd together to avoid the elements. It's awkward. It's uncomfortable. It's unpleasant. No one has a word to say until Francophone Fern starts the deluge.

If anyone has a phone charger, we need to send an SOS now.

-How exactly will that work? Walk me through the steps where we don't get arrested or killed.

You don't agree?

-I don't agree.

Leticia's in a foul mood, and she has been and always will be debate club captain. And Fern has never met a challenge she could turn down. Beverly Hills buddy Donny is right with her and does have some juice on his iPhone X. Aeura and VJ are having none of it.

Don't you dare. Leticia's right. How would it work?

-We send a Bat-Signal to be saved, we give ourselves away.

Anyone who's looking for us is closer to us than anyone who can come save us.

--I got to pull a dad card here. Kids, we need to split up. Group's too big. Like Crosby, Stills, Nash & Young, someone's got to go. That'd be us.

Bunky had spoken. He and Donny, with their passports, are clean to take a regional bus to Tijuana and walk across the border. According to the posted schedule, a bus is due. Flip thinks that without IDs, the rest of us can surrender ourselves to the consulate in Tijuana. It's as good as US soil.

The Tijuana bus approaches. I back a decision that gets quick consensus. We do need to split up.

Bunky and Donny, take the bus and walk over the border. Flip, go too, check out the consulate.

-What about you guys?

We five? Like old times. We'll spread it out. Take later buses.

--Hunker down till then. I got the schedule.

---Just need a little cash and Donny's phone.

Fern makes that request. Father and son shell out a handful of twenties and the cell phone, along with its password. Bunky will call our folks. Flip will call us when he gets the TJ consul up to speed. He believes that they'll send Marines to come and get us, once they hear him out. Leticia snarks.

Heard that before.

-I gotta try. Every consulate can't be dirty.

We have to hope. Goodbye hugs all around and surprising emotion. We've been a team. We vow to keep in touch, and they're gone on the #1 to Tijuana. The rain hasn't abated. We need to lay low in Ensenada somewhere safe and dry. Aeura has been looking at the free local circulars. She shows an ad to us.

Barbie II is in "dos salas de cine" at the Cinépolis 5.

-Good. That's the shopping center across the road.

I'm being facetious.

-I'm not.

--Dude, it's three tortuous, man-hating hours.

---Perfect.

Fern has the last word. We shield ourselves with discarded newspaper and head into the rainstorm, crossing the highway at the green light.

9.

tuesday, late afternoon

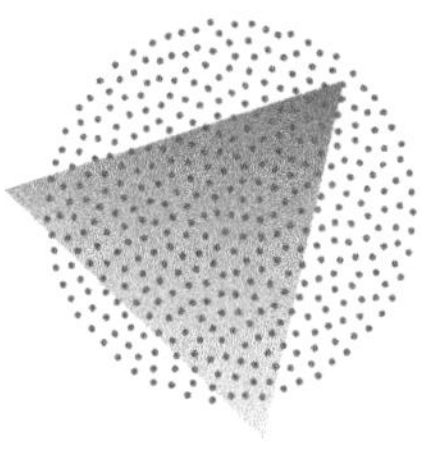

ANTONIO'S CELL PHONE CHARGED IN THE BLUE-AND-GRAY STATE POLICE CAR, while they cruised downtown Ensenada in the cold, windy drizzle that had replaced the pelting rain. The ex-hospital aide from Baja South cursed the cold of the north. He figured that the cops, no matter how friendly, were using him to find the eight fugitives—Leticia and her friends. Antonio wanted to warn them that the heat was on and had tried calling Leticia's number, pretending it was Maya's. Her cell phone was dead or shut off. He wasn't surprised. Antonio had no intention of aiding the cops and had them driving aimlessly, while he professed to having forgotten where the band's loft was. As if he knew.

The tall cop and the stocky lady officer had reported in that they'd sighted the Americans earlier and believed that they were in the city. The converted school bus they were traveling in might no longer bear the band name. The information undercut Antonio's ruse. A radio call came in, confirming that the bus was found.

The state police, with Antonio in the back seat, responded to the call, and Antonio's head throbbed with dread. The band's ride was parked in an alley, and city police had Maya and the band leaning against the bus, hands up, faces forward, legs spread. The Americans weren't with them. Her flirtation with Antonio was done, for sure. Another uniformed cop went through their papers, while Maya was questioned by a man in a white suit, sucking a lollipop. Antonio crossed himself. He'd seen the man before. He was part of the crew on the island and had flown there with his uncles. Antonio saw an opening.

That guy in the suit is not a cop, officer. He's a cartel killer.

-Copy that. Yes, he is. Pray he gets what he wants from her.

You're not going to do anything?

--Have a churro.

The lady cop offered Antonio a pastry. He pushed it away.

***

In his high-rise, Juan Carlos finished a late lunch that had the OK of a highly paid food taster before Juan Carlos had a bite. He wasn't paranoid—he was experienced in cartel wars.

Rodrigo would come at him from off angles before having to come at him hard. Juan Carlos had been working his whole network and felt he had hold of the situation. After Carita's update from the band that the Americans had been let off at the city bus depot, Juan Carlos had used his resources to track the buses north. With ID photos sent out, three of the Americans were seen on the Tijuana bus. The trio had arrived less than a half hour earlier and included the consul intern who was wanted for El Chino's murder. The cartel CEO had the border watched for the three. That left the other five with the need for a place to hang out. He'd ordered Carita to stay in Ensenada and find them. With eyes and ears everywhere, Juan Carlos expected an answer soon. He wasn't wrong. A report came back that mall security saw two of the suspects enter a movie theater multiplex.

***

For the first time in two decades, Duke Montrose had a functioning liver. At the UCLA hospital in Westwood, he was sitting up in bed with Abby Jo. His recovery was going well, according to the doctors, and with any luck, he'd be home in a few days. Abby Jo had regaled her man with stories of the smoking nun and the gangster forays. It all seemed like fun and games now. Gilly and his friends were alive. Abby Jo had pushed her pal at the State Department to find out where they were being held and for how long; however, that information was not forthcoming. Still, reading the tea leaves, with the gangsters no longer interested in Duke, she assumed that the immediate threat to Gilly and his friends was over. The bedside cell chimed, and Abby Jo answered for Duke.

She coughed twice, covering her mouth, and put it on speaker so Duke could hear.

Hello! Duke's phone.

-Hi. It's Phil Fifer.

--Phil! I hope this isn't about your pool. It may have to wait till next week.

Fern's dad, Philip Fifer of the Fifer Family Financial Fund, was a Duke client and a guy with big clout in Beverly Hills and beyond. They had a good relationship, and Duke figured the call was a "Get well, flowers on the way." Fifer didn't mince words.

There's a manhunt on for the kids. Shoot on sight.

Abby Jo gasped, convulsing, hand shaking, reaching for Duke's glass of water. Duke, of all people, started to tear up. Abby Jo had never seen him break. He'd kid about his inability to cry—even with the death of his Mom, or Sparky his dachshund, or even Prince.

Fern's distraught father had heard the dire latest from a source at the U.S. Consulate in Tijuana. One of the kids' friends, the Cabo consul intern, surrendered there, and the hope was that the others would do so soon. His voice cracked.

The situation changed. They'll be shot on sight.

-Is there anything the consulate can do?

No. They say that their hands are tied!

Fifer started crying, Duke was keening, and Abby Jo added to the waterworks. A nurse came in, took in the scene, and went right back out.

***

Bunky and Donny arrived in Tijuana and headed for the border's PedEast crossing on a shuttle bus known as a calafias. There was a line for US citizens, and the father and son got right into it. It had been an amazing adventure that neither would forget. Donny would never view his pop the same way. A divorced, absentee dad, Bunky always felt guilty that he'd shortchanged his only child. This Cabo trip had been the equalizer. It was a lovefest, and Bunky squeezed him close. Donny felt the moment and said something he'd never imagined saying.

You're the best, Dad.

Bunky swelled with that, and it helped them both curb their impatience at the slow-moving line. Bunky asked Donny to hold his place while he wandered toward the front to see what was going on. The aging rock-and-roll drummer, wearing a Las Casuelas T-shirt and a recently purchased cowboy hat, stopped in his tracks. Ahead, in addition to the Mexican Border Patrol overseeing the exit, there were camo-dressed *federales* holding color photos of the fugitives they were looking for. Bunky wasn't sure whether his and Donny's photos were among them, but he wasn't taking any chances. He'd been at the fiesta a long time and planned on continuing that. He slowly backed away. A young *federale* probie happened to look up and see him. Bunky turned, hurrying off.

Stop!

The officer screamed it. Bunky made a fateful decision to pretend the kid cop wasn't talking to him. The *federale*-in-training crouched, textbook style, took careful aim, and shot Bunky in the back. He crumbled to the pavement. Shocked, devastated, Donny was engulfed by the panicking crowd.

***

In Ensenada, Leticia agreed with Gilly on the need for the five of them to split up into two groups. She and VJ went ahead to watch the movie in one theater. They would catch the late afternoon bus, unless Flip called Donny's cell phone. Gilly, Fern, and Aeura would stagger their time, go to see Barbie II an hour later in the smaller screening room, and catch the TJ night bus after. It was almost ninety minutes into the movie when Donny's phone went off. The sound did not go over well with the packed auditorium of filmgoers in the big theater #1 at the Ensenada mall. Leticia went out to the lobby to take the call from Flip.

Flip?

-I was lucky to make it. Don't get on the bus.

Bunky and Donny?

-No word. They have our pictures, street cameras watching here. Stay out of sight.

That might be difficult.

Through the big plate glass windows of the entrance, Leticia watched two city police cars and a Harley pull right up on to the sidewalk outside the exit. She hung up and rushed back into the theater. Hushed, she ducked down and grabbed hold of VJ.

Police. Get out. There's a fire exit.

-What about you?

Go! I gotta warn the others.

Too late for that. No way out. The auditorium doors swung opened, and Carita, with his Glock pistol in hand, entered. The film stopped abruptly with a sickening sound, and the overhead lights banged on to the angry shouts of protests from the inconvenienced Barbie fans—many dressed all in pink. Carita, followed by two Ensenada city cops in black unis with hard-copy photos, searched row by row, rousting innocent, frightened people and checking them out.

VJ and Leticia were bent low and moving down the far aisle on all fours. They were headed for the front of the theater and a fire exit door. Pausing at the row closest to the screen, the duo locked eyes, gave a quick kiss, and broke for the door across the considerable open area. They were exposed, and Carita eyed them. Blocked by all the patrons on their feet, he climbed onto a seat, straddled two armrests to rise above the crowd, and let loose with a deafening barrage of bullets that all missed their mark. VJ and Leticia were already out the door.

Outside, the blue-and-gray state police sedan was waiting. VJ and Leticia tried to elude it until they saw Antonio get out of its back seat, waving for them to join him. They didn't have to be waved twice. As they hustled into the police car, the rear theater door flew open and Carita appeared. The tall Baja California state policeman, in his light-blue-with-yellow-trim uniform, was there to meet him.

We got them!

He slammed the rear door shut. Carita was not pleased.

10.

right Now

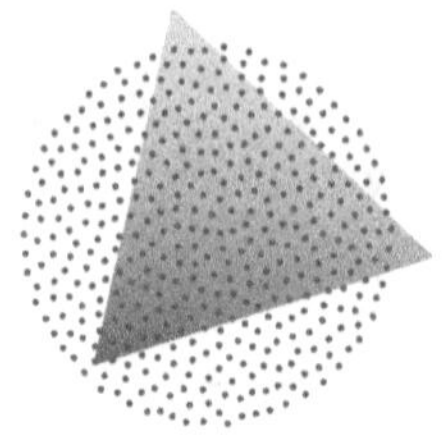

 Our movie date interrupted, we huddle low beneath the seats as the screening room lights come on. The hair on the back of my neck bristles. The film grinds to a distorted stop, and the theater manager enters, apologizing. He declares that there was a threat in the other theater but that it's over. He offers refunds and asks the movie patrons to exit at this time. The theater is closed.

Though we used the time before the movie to buy some new clothes and disguise ourselves, who are we kidding? The red wig on Aeura, the curly black one on Fern, and my pink Barbie beanie may have fooled a mall guard but not the cartel. We're quiet and we listen. People leave, and the door closes and locks. The lights go out. It's pitch black in the windowless room. Fern is the first to stand in the glorious safety of darkness.

Works for me.

-Me too. Did they forget about us?

--"The threat is over"? What did that mean?

-Is there a rear door?

Blindly, we make our moves, hands outstretched toward the imagined back wall of the room. There's no exit sign. I feel metal.

Here's a ladder. I'm going up.

It's bolted to the wall. I grasp a rung and start to climb, hand over hand. It feels good to stretch my arms and legs. I traverse my way to the top and find an iron hatchway. It has a locking arm. I pull it back and it unseals. One push reveals the colors of dusk and Venus in the west, first star of the evening. I'm outside.

We can get to the roof.

-Sweet.

--I'm coming, too.

I step out onto the tarred, flat surface and wander to the edge that overlooks the street below. Two black-and-white *policia municipal* cruisers pull away. The rumble of an aftermarket Harley muffler rudely roars. The helmeted motorcycle rider drives off. I'm joined by Fern and Aeura, who hang on each shoulder, looking down at the street scene as it returns to normal. Each of us feels fortunate AF to still be in the gene pool.

What do you think happened to Leticia and VJ?

-Hard to say. Good news, I don't see any ambulance or coroner's wagon.

--I wish we could reach them. We gave away the only working phone.

We'd planned on getting Donny's from Leticia and VJ, when they headed for their bus. That didn't occur. Without any communication, our best option for the time being is to stay put. We're safe. Aeura grins and pulls out oversized bags of Mexican movie theater candy. The red-wigged beauty teases the medley of flavors that await—Chupa Chups Melody Pops and a bag of Red Vines. And there's more. Raven-haired with wigged curls, a more European Fern's gorgeous eyes widen as she digs from her bag two quarter-split bottles of pinot noir. The Beverly Hills princess holds them up, savoring her French.

The pièce de résistance!

-Wine and candy?

--We've got dinner.

11.

tuefday Night

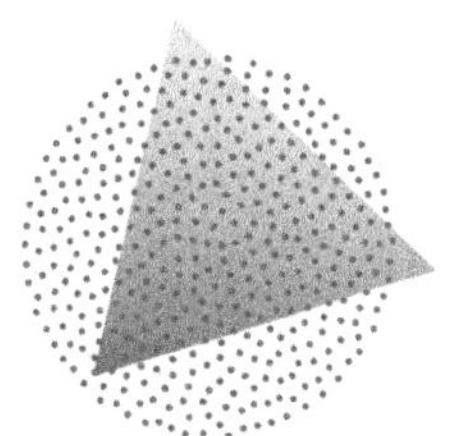

 crowded into the back seat of the state police car that was parked in the lot of a deserted warehouse. Leticia, sitting between the boys, grabbed the hand of each for support. She was always trying to control things in her life, but here she was in a bad, bad part of Ensenada, in the grimy shadows at the deadest end of the street. She didn't even bother to make a literary reference for hopelessness. She was the reference. Consumed with the morbid helplessness, she shared it. VJ chanted to bring back the transcendental eternalness of their ayahuasca microdose and to prepare their souls. Antonio tried to buoy them. He liked the tall cop, whose name, they learned, was Sgt. Alvarado. Of course, Antonio wasn't wanted for murder like his American friends, Leticia shouted in reminder.

Alvarado was outside the car, a distance away, in heated discussion with his stocky female partner, Officer Grandal. No matter how hard the back-seat trio concentrated, they couldn't hear enough of the emotional disagreement. It ended with a nod of resignation from the lady cop and a hug. She disappeared off around the abandoned building. Sgt. Alvarado lowered his head and joined the fugitives in the car. He settled behind the wheel, let the car idle, and turned to them through the grilled partition. Whatever Leticia had imagined that the policeman would say next, this was not it.

I can't bring you in. It isn't safe at the police station.

-What?

--For real?

-Thank you.

--Why are you doing this?

I have my reasons.

High above them, a police drone swept the area with a spotlight and an unnerving whir. The heat was on, and VJ was having trust issues.

Could you give us maybe one reason?

-Carita. The killer after you. You need to get to the consulate in Tijuana. I can take you.

What about our three friends? They were in the screening room at the mall.

Other than the two wanted Americans in his cruiser, Alvarado hadn't received any report of fugitives sighted at the mall. He confirmed that the search for the remaining three was ongoing.

We were at the rear of the multiplex. Only you guys came out the back.

-No way they got out the front.

--They could still be hiding there.

---We have to look. They would for us.

VJ spoke truth. In Leticia's bag, Donny's phone jangled with an incoming call. She answered.

Flip?

-It's Donny. They shot my dad!

In a high booth of a Tijuana cantina, Donny talked into a prepaid phone, his hands quivering.

I don't know what to do.

-Find the U.S. Consulate. Flip's there.

***

It was after midnight. In his Mexico City mansion, Juan Carlos was going crazy. He'd heard from his wife that their daughter was given a drugged soft drink at a Dallas skating rink. It wasn't meant to kill her—only to cause painful abdominal distress. It was a message from Rodrigo. Juan Carlos was certain of that, despite swearing to his wife it was coincidental. El Jefe de Jefes could strike at his family anytime. The little hitch that had started with El Chino's greedy side hustle in Baja South had gone nuclear. The cartel CEO believed that two of the five accused of the cartel doctor's murder were in state police custody. He felt confident that they could be stifled from giving sworn testimony—testimony that could bring hellfire to the cartel's operation and a gruesome end to him and his family.

After a high-level deal that Juan Carlos had negotiated with the damn consul, he ordered Carita to head right to the border and supervise the screening of returning US citizens. One of the Americans' accomplices, the older man, had been shot trying to cross. He was in surgery at the hospital and wasn't going anywhere, even if he survived. Juan Carlos was doing all he could to keep everyone clean. Maybe he needed to remind his boss of the leverage he still controlled.

***

One of the most powerful men in Mexico, Rodrigo had been out late at an executive board meeting of the largest bank in Tijuana and its after-meeting, convivial drink-fest. His chauffeur dropped him off. He winked at security upon entering and was relieved to be inside the quiet of his sumptuous seaside estate. He'd worked hard to keep the sheen of respectability on the cartel's multibillion-dollar enterprise, and the carelessness of Juan Carlos in managing his territory could damage all that Rodrigo had built. He'd had a full day keeping up with the costly cover-up and missteps. He didn't want to think about it anymore till the morning. Before El Jefe de Jefes could tiptoe into his bedroom and slip under the covers, his wife, who'd been waiting, flipped on the lights, sitting up in bed. She was livid and lit him up. The former Miss Avocado 2020 had received texted photos on her private line from an unknown number. The first was doctored. It showed her youngest sister with a garish red streak drawn slicing her neck. The accompanying message read: *Kill the Americans* or *blood not crayon*. The three photos attached were of the remaining fugitives still at large—Fern, Aeura, and Gilly. Rodrigo's wife's eyes drilled down.

I'll share it to your phone so you don't forget!

A few clicks and she did just that.

12.

riGHt NOW

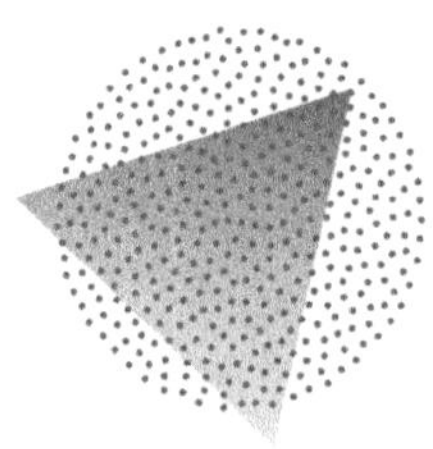

i'M ʃH*t-fΛced. My tolerance for alcohol is so low that I'm blitzed on a few swigs of a big bottle of pinot noir. I wipe the black curls of the wig I'm wearing from my eyes and focus. I know that I'm wrecked because red-wigged Fern almost beat me in leg wrestling.

Rematch!

-Wait your turn. Aeura, you're up.

Beneath an overhang, we're having fun, stripped down under the midnight blanket of a clear Ensenada sky. This rooftop has been the best lodging we could ask for. We found tarps, a few chairs, and a cistern of clean water. At first light, we'll head out if it feels safe. The drones have stopped. We have not. Aeura, in the pink Barbie beanie, takes a swallow of the last nip of our communal wine and lays down next to me, her head to my toes. We raise our right legs in a salute to combat and start the countdown.

OK. One, two, three...

-Go!

Fern yells it like a ref, and Aeura and I, with our legs raised, lock and groan pulling hard to tug the other all the way over. Damn, she's stronger than I imagined—or I'm weaker. Under Fern's unabashed encouragement, Aeura strains like her life depends on this.

Girl Power!

-It's useless, female! You're going down!

I taunt them. Our legs pull at each other and meet maximum resistance. It's exhausting for us inebriated humans. We're at a standstill, legs vibrating above us, our whole bodies trembling in the dark. We hold steady. Can we keep this up? One of us has to give. It's not going to be me.

Outlast him, Aeura. You can win.

-Never!

--Tag team!

-Not fair!

Fern doesn't care and, with hands on Aeura's right leg, adds her strength to help turn me over. It's working. How important is this to me? Very! I gather strength from who knows where and, even with Fern's added force, I have the edge. Boy Power! Aeura breaks. I slam her over and pin her leg. She rolls back into my body laughing, panting like me. We lay there close, way too close for Fern.

Not done! Move, Gilly! Let me wrestle Aeura.

-Fern! Make love not war.

The punk goth princess surprises the Beverly Hills J.A.P. with a kiss on her mouth and pulls her down with us. Fern gives in. There's a playfulness and familiarity that binds us. And wine.

Battle over?

-We all won.

--Yeah, but I have wounds. Serious.

Where?

-We'll heal them.

Oh boy, talk about stolen hours. When is a fantasy not a fantasy? Half-naked together, sweat dripping, I can't tell where I end and Aeura starts on my left side or Fern on my right. Melded, flat on our backs, they take turns kissing both sides of my neck, both cheeks of my face, and when they reach my lips, it's a three-way. If this is wrong, why does it feel so right? What will happen next, I'm not certain. Aeura is.

This night never was. Can we all agree?

-If being drunk counts, then yes.

--Majority rules. It's two against one.

That's the idea. I love you both so much.

A night of firsts could be our last. We're in tight, and our breaths and hands are racing. Aeura's pushing it. She lives rent-free in my head and elsewhere, and I'm not complaining. Fern isn't either.

Gilly? Hello?

-VJ? VJ!

My best friend's head appears from the hatchway entrance to the roof with a flashlight beam that spotlights our erotic tableau. We shrivel in the glare, like bandits in the night.

They're up here! They're OK—more than OK!

He yells the news back down to Leticia and Antonio. I look at my lovemates.

To be continued?

Neither answers, covering up, sobering up. Somehow the moment disappears faster than that dreamy dream you can't remember.

13.

wednesday, 2:30 a.m.

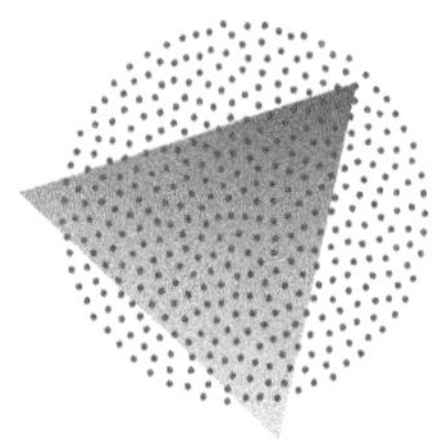

At the estación federal, the tijuana headquarters of the National police, Flip was in a holding cell by himself. It wasn't the worst—two beds, a toilet, a chair, and a table. He didn't plan on being there long. He'd been able to reach his estranged father, and it was one more disappointment. The Big Pharma CFO, offspring of a diplomat, seemed more upset at his son's involvement in such sordid business than concerned about his son's well-being. Despite Flip's pleas of innocence, Foster Senior told Flip to follow the government's advice. The glaring fact was he was wanted for murder. The US authorities had agreed to hand him over to the *federales*, with the agreement that he'd be released on bail in the morning and could take sanctuary again at the consulate till trial. Thanks, Dad!

It all added up to a more pressing fact—Flip had to survive the night in custody. That thought throbbed in the diplomatic intern's cranium as the minutes ticked on. He tried to block the paralyzing fear by concentrating on his new friends. He took a walk on the wild side, throwing in with them. His professional future was definitely hazy as a result. What choice did he have, with all he knew and had witnessed? They were the good guys in this! They'd saved VJ's life and had definitely exposed the insidiousness of the cartel. He could only pray that the truth might come out and vindicate them. He had no regrets, only that young, dumb, and full of... hope feeling that he'd have another chance with Aeura, though she seemed more interested in Gilly than Fern did, at times.

Flip had been mercifully asleep for maybe fifteen minutes, when he heard his cell door unlock. He coiled, standing on the bed, ready to fight for his life. The door opened and, in the light, he saw Donny get pushed in. He gave his comrade a hug.

Welcome. Let me guess. You surrendered to the consulate?

-Yes, that was a mistake.

At least I wasn't shot like my dad. I can still hear him saying, "I shouldn't be here."

Donny's soul cracked. He dissolved into tears.

***

In his hospital bed in Westwood, Duke Montrose slept the sleep of the just transplanted, thanks to heavy pharmaceuticals. In the recovery wing's near-deserted waiting room, Abby Jo was enjoying late-night snacks, courtesy of Philip Fifer. Sick with worry, Fern's dad had come to the hospital to share intel with Abby Jo and to bring some comfort food. The Palm Restaurant takeout included the pastrami-crusted lamb lollipops, fried onion strings, and a quart of the Palm Mule with Tito's Vodka and elderflower liqueur. Abby Jo set aside her #incomeinequality notions to appreciate the magnanimity. And the Tito's. Phil Fifer's top-ranking contact in the State Department had given him the latest concerning the Baja consul intern and Donny Green Steiner who had also surrendered to authorities for a quick court date. Fifer knew Donny's mother, Marcia, and tried to get her into the loop.

She's already in Tijuana pounding on officials. Her son's charged with abetting, unlike—

-Ours. And Aeura, VJ, and Leticia.

Marcia Steiner's a pisser, a powerhouse of Beverly Hills. Will not be denied.

-My kind of gal. Here's to her!

Abby Jo toasted Mrs. Steiner with seconds of the lamp lollipops and swore that it was a first-class pacifier. Briefly, she considered dropping nicotine in favor of a lamb habit. Marcia's ex, Bunky Green, was another story. He was in surgery, and his chances of survival were heavily in doubt.

That left the five friends on the loose. The same five who'd sunk a Glendale gang chief and a crooked Beverly Hills detective were once again embroiled with a mob and crooked cops and were running for their lives. Fifer noticed a disturbing pattern.

How does that happen?

-They're kids who never look away and don't desert their friends.

Here's to them.

They toasted that with two red Solo cups of Palm Mule. No word from—or about—any of the kids was the best news, they both agreed. It meant that they had to be somewhere and, more than likely, they had to be alive.

✱✱✱

It was still a few hours till sunrise. Passing Rosarito Beach, the Mexican landscape flew by. VJ and I were laying out flat in the back of a late model Chevy Silverado pickup, Sgt. Alvarado's personal chariot. The girls and Antonio were in the four-door truck's cab seats, warm and chatty, by the sound of it. VJ and Leticia were right to trust him. Alvarado was a good guy who was committed to protecting us from a psychopath cartel assassin named Carita. A few years back, that hit man in a white sport coat had killed Alvarado's beloved mother and black lab pup. They were collateral damage in a contracted mob killing that got sloppy. Alvarado never received justice and never forgot. He'd promised to take us to the U.S. Consulate in Tijuana, and we were already at the outskirts of the city. It was more than luck that Aeura, Fern, and I were found on the rooftop. Leticia deduced it, VJ embraced it, and they got Alvarado to find the theater janitor to let them in.

VJ—

-Gilly, relax. I'm not going to say a word about your threesome. Dude, it was...nothing.

Hey, I'm not today years old.

-So you were just in a flesh panini for a photo op?

VJ!

-Kidding. I'm zipping it. It's in the vault, bro.

The truck cab's back window slid open, and Leticia yelled to us. She'd gotten a voicemail from Donny on the phone. He was arrested and was in a Tijuana cell with Flip, awaiting charges.

Do we go to the consulate and get stabbed in jail or the border crossing and get shot?

-Trick question. Is there a third option?

Sgt. Alvarado had one.

***

There were now ten heavily armed men and an urban assault vehicle surrounding Juan Carlos's illuminated estate. He'd been nonstop busy the whole night. Rodrigo, to satisfy his demanding wife, had demanded proof of life that his sister-in-law was unharmed. Juan Carlos could only stall him. The young woman had tried to escape her captors in the city loft where she was being held. In the struggle that followed, she tumbled down the cement steps and broke her neck. She was dead, along with Juan Carlos's leverage.

The Mexico City cartel CEO had a bombshell backup plan, which had the backing of two other mighty cartels, the Juárez juggernaut and the insane Los Zetas. He'd proffered an irresistible offer to both criminal syndicates to join him against Rodrigo. The smaller cartels hated the Tijuana Jefe de Jefes and could imagine a power shift if they united three against one to carve up his territory. Juárez was sending Juan Carlos reinforcements. Help was in motion.

The two Americans in custody would be taken out by Los Zetas in the morning, after they were released on bail. But the other fugitives, with their incriminating evidence against Juan Carlos, were still out there. It was strange and bothersome, to say the least, that the two arrested at the theater were never booked and were once more considered at-large. A predawn phone call solved that mystery. Its relayed message came from a state policewoman in Ensenada.

Looking to curry favor, Officer Grandal reported that her partner had gone rogue and was taking the wanted Americans north to the border. Juan Carlos relayed to Carita the details of the truck they were traveling in, and the beleaguered cartel chief had his first relaxed meal in a blissful while.

14.

right now

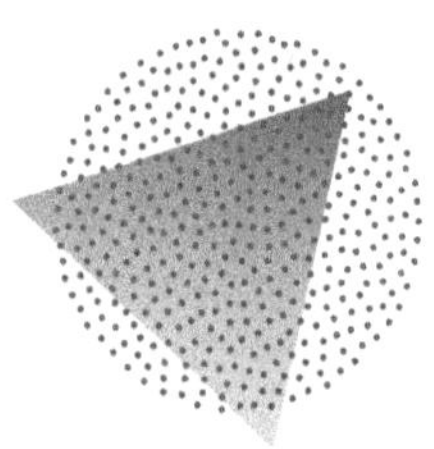

friendship park beach in tijuana runs along both sides of the us-mexican border. The sandy park lies in two countries, divided by graffiti-covered vertical steel slats, eighteen feet high, topped with razor wire. It's a barrier wall that reaches right into the same sea that the nations share. Extending from it, jutting deeper into the ocean, is a twelve-foot-long monolithic jetty, made of gray concrete, that makes it nearly impossible to go around without feeling the fury of the mighty Pacific. The ocean's perilous rip currents and crashing surf serve as deadly deterrents to those who attempt the illegal crossing.

It's late morning, and Sgt. Alvarado's Silverado is parked in the lot of a run-down, half-deserted strip mall right off the park. We sit in the pickup's bed and on the tailgate, taking in the imposing national divide, the Great Wall of TJ. When the good sergeant in his civies, with a wide-brimmed cowboy hat, presents his best bet for our escape, Leticia's hands go up in surrender.

It's impossible. We'll drown.

-Not at low tide. Migrants make it all the time. Problem is they get caught right away.

--That's good for us.

---At least we'll be in the United States.

-Exactly. Have to wait for low tide. Another hour or so. Like them.

He points at the nearby shoreline. A migrant family of six squats, biding time, considering the pounding breakers. Further up the beach, more huddled groups gather as the high midday sun beats down like punishment.

Enforcement here's a daily game. The less risk, the more border guards.

-I'm not a strong swimmer, guys.

You form a chain for safety. At its lowest, you'll be wading across.

-I can wade.

Unlike the rest of us "big-blue–adjacent" kids, Aeura did not grow up in SoCal. The smell of the sea here is so familiar. We're almost home. VJ hums "God Bless America." Leticia makes me ache.

Gilly, it's just around that corner.

-Goodbye, Baja!

--We've come a long freakin' cray cray way.

---We couldn't have done it without each other.

----New and old friends.

-And heroes.

-----Any target of Carita is a friend of mine.

The sergeant means it. Antonio returns with a load of tacos from the one open stand in the mall.

Sorry. Had to wait. Biker gang with a big order. Los Sucio, do you believe it?

-Three of their brothers were murdered in El Rosario. I'd say that Carita was behind it. He's on a bike that was stolen from them.

And no one arrests him?

-He's bulletproof, protected by the you-know-who. He could shoot you all here and walk away.

I have a sudden pang. The sooner we hit the water, the better.

Antonio can't thank us enough. It's really the other way around. He'll get a ride back to Ensenada and, from there, he still has his bus ticket home. We make plans to see him again, and it gets sappy in a good way. How many times have we said goodbye? Flip and Donny are not far from our thoughts, either. Sgt. Alvarado has heard no update on them or on Bunky. We munch chips. No one has much appetite. We're killing time. Fern has tears in her eyes. I pull her close, though she fights it.

Leticia, phone please. I'm calling my father. He'll have us picked up and lawyered up.

-Fern, we all agreed no calls.

--What if his phone's monitored?

---Wait till we're safe on the other side—the American side.

I nod my agreement and gaze off at the street that leads back to the city. A man in a white suit dismounts a Harley. With a lollipop in his mouth, he walks our way and produces a big pistol from inside his jacket. Backlit, it glares ugly in the harsh sunlight. Holy sh*t!

Duck!

-It's Carita!

We scatter for cover around the truck as shots rake the rear of the Silverado. Fern and I are under the truck. Holding on to one another, staying small, we crawl toward the front of the truck, away from direct fire. Bullets kick up around us, gravel spews. The double-wide radial tires explode into shredded rubber. The vehicle takes the brunt of the firepower, its back end crashing down to the asphalt. We join our friends crouched at the front.

Get ready to run!

Alvarado makes for his shotgun on a rack behind the front seat. Carita stalks closer, firing. It's a public active shooter situation, and pedestrians scream and hurry away. The five of us plus Antonio are coiled at the front end of the truck ready to spring. With the truck door as a shield, Alvarado swings out of the cab firing. Two shotgun blasts and a surprised hit man has to hide behind a car himself.

Go for the beach! Run!

It's a jailbreak. We race across the open parking lot, zigzagging for the sand. The sergeant and the killer exchange shots. Passing the taco stand, four hardcore Los Sucio bikers, unfazed, dine with family and show zero desire to be disturbed. I slow down and take a shot of my own. With a polite wave, I get the attention of the biker closest to me. He looks like an angry lion and has a patch over one eye.

Escusame.

-Scram!

Tonto de blanco asesinó a tus hermanos in El Rosario de Arriba.

Fool in white murdered your brothers. That gets their attention. I think. Not. None of them move. Did they not hear me? Patch sips his drink.

We'll check it out.

More shots fired between Carita and Alvarado shatter the air. I wonder how many rounds are in Alvarado's shotgun. And more disturbing, why are there no police sirens? No police rushing here at the sound of shots fired. I push it.

Date prisa, por favor! Robó la moto de tu club.

Donde?

I point to the street where Carita has parked the stolen Harley. More sips, no movement. You're kidding me. Finally, Patch rises with a nod of recognition and shoves me on my way. I have no idea whether they're jacking me, but I have to tell the sergeant to hold on. I wait for the next volley exchange and sprint for the truck when it stops. Alvarado shoos me off. I don't listen.

Help's on the way.

-Ha, I doubt it. I only have one more charge in the chamber. Go back when I say.

You'll cover me?

-I'm using you for bait. I want one clear shot at him.

Glad to be of use.

-Here he comes.

Carita counts on the sergeant being out of ammo. He breaks for a series of vehicles and doesn't draw fire. The Tootsie Pop is down to its chocolate core, and he's alive and having fun. He ducks behind a service van, welcoming the competition. We're maybe half a football field away. Alvarado is all in, and I must have a death wish to have come back. I can hear the Duke, *Gilly what were you thinking? Stay in your lane!*

What's my lane, Pop? I'm the pool guy's son. Scion of go-with-the-flow. I'm flowing. I mentally rehearse my route to draw out Carita. With gratitude, Alvarado pats my cheek. Carita trolls.

Hey, friend! Why help the gringos? You know who I am?

-I do. Remember my mother, Connie Alvarado?

Sorry for that. And the puppy. You don't need to die, too. Let me have them.

-They're at the beach. Go for it.

Oh. Trying to trick me. So you have more ammo. So sad. It's all going to end the same way.

The sergeant shifts position, eyes narrowing for focus, sweat beads on his furrowed forehead. It's on. He gives me the nod. *Uno, dos...* I bolt out. He jumps up to shoot Carita, who's poised to shoot me. It isn't necessary. Iron chains whip out on either side of Carita and viciously curl, snapping around his neck. They tighten. He fires a burst wildly into the air. Silence erupts, except for the gurgling from the hit man. The Tootsie Pop pops out. Alvarado stands, shotgun lowered. I turn in wonder. The Los Sucio bikers are on either side of the white-coated killer, tugging at their bike chains with a vengeance. Carita is helpless, struggling for breath, face red and eyes bulging. His pistol drops to the pavement from his lifeless fingers. With a toothy, gleeful grin, Patch tosses me a peace sign.

El collar Tijuana!

The Tijuana necklace.

It's an execution. Street justice. Justice for Alvarado, too. The good-as-gold cop salutes me, grateful for my help. My knees go jelly.

Numb, struck dumb, I don't have enough bandwidth to process this. I rock in place like the Mookie bobblehead hood ornament on the Montrose Pool Service truck. I didn't take ayahuasca, but I feel tripped out. It's a reverse adrenalin drain, the good kind of PTSD. (Is there a good kind?) I look toward the beach and see, as witnesses, Antonio and VJ at the edge of the parking lot. Behind them, Aeura, Leticia, and Fern wave. I'm about to take a humble brag victory twirl, when the angry wail of multiple police sirens changes that.

They're coming now that the shooting has stopped!? Can we trust the police? Alvarado answers the question.

Go! Get across! They're still after you!

15.

wednefday afternoon

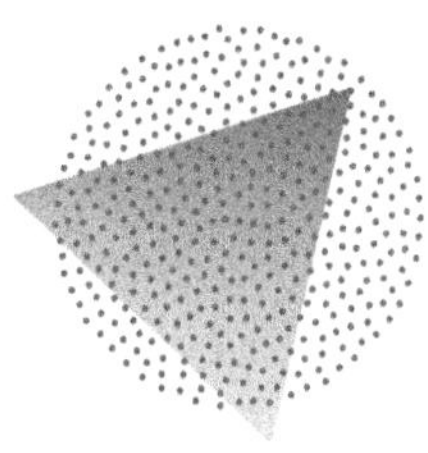

the ALMighty fun fcorched through any attempt by a random cloud to block it. It was late November and unseasonably warm. The Tribunal Federal de Justicia Administrativa in downtown Tijuana was an imposing modern edifice open for business. Marcia Steiner, the doyenne of Beverly Hills, in a lightweight beige Merino wool power suit and bag ensemble by Chanel, took the concrete steps two at a time in short heels, marching to the courthouse to retrieve her son Donald. She was flanked by two Color Guard Marines borrowed from the U.S.

Consulate. They held the door open for her, and she steamed inside while they waited at the entrance.

In less than half an hour, Marcia came back, marching her boy out of the courthouse and down the steps with the Marine escort. Flip Marks had also made bail, thanks to Donny's mom, and was accompanying them. His own disapproving father had wiped his hands of the situation, and Flip was on his own. Marcia, a universal mother above all else, took pity and took custody of Flip at Donny's insistent urging. On the street, a limo was waiting for them.

The Marines were on guard for any trouble, though none seemed forthcoming. They drove off without incident, returning to the safety of the consulate.

The Los Zetas assassination crew that had been ordered to take out the boys was nowhere to be seen.

***

Inside his Mexico City estate, Juan Carlos didn't see it coming. Though Juárez and Los Zetas hated the Tijuana cartel jefe, Rodrigo, they feared him more than they feared Juan Carlos, who'd gotten soft embracing the corporate world. The old double-cross ensued, and Juan Carlos's own security had been used to betray him. He'd been hung from the high, pinyon pine rafters of the mansion's great room and beaten with his golf clubs like a piñata. His traitorous body was riddled with bullets, too, for the cautionary tale photos that followed. The cartel CEO had tried to bridge two worlds and had drowned in mistakes, starting with El Chino, his handpicked Cabo capo.

Juan Carlos's rich turf would be absorbed by the other two criminal gangs, happy to be aligned with a winner like Rodrigo.

****

Rodrigo was with his loyal male assistant in his home office, savoring the good news. He had confirmation that the coup against him had been turned back. Juan Carlos was brutally erased, and his personal assassin, the dangerous psycho Carita, was also history. Rodrigo planned to celebrate at the bullring.

His assistant, a trusted nephew, reminded him that they still had the Tijuana police and federales on an APB manhunt for the fugitive Americans with extreme prejudice. Did El Jefe de Jefes want to rescind it? Rodrigo took a long look at the ocean vista from his twenty-four room Tijuana villa and told his assistant to cancel the order. Let them go free. All they can do is give testimony to further ruin Juan Carlos's name and take the pressure off the other cartels. The assistant agreed that it made sense. Any cover-up for their deaths from this point on would be on Rodrigo—and the heat with it. The young man who fancied himself an advisor was about to go off and make that cancel call, when Rodrigo's wife stormed into the office with gun in hand. She was crazed, out of her mind with anger, having learned that her young sister was dead. Rodrigo tried to reason with her. She didn't want any explanation. She wanted blood and plugged both her husband and the assistant, one in the head, one in the heart, without another word.

The "shoot to kill" order for Gilly and his friends remained in effect.

***

The Friendship Park strip mall was throbbing with local police and *federales*, questioning all witnesses about the shootout with the Americans. Despite a protest, Antonio had hurriedly been sent off in a cab by Alvarado, who saw no healthy reason for the Good Samaritan teen to be around. The sergeant had stayed at the scene and was cooperating. He'd avenged what Carita had taken from him and expected to be arrested. Whether he'd be murdered himself in custody was another question. Under the ranking lieutenant's grilling, Alvarado swore that he had no idea where the gringos had fled. The body of Carita was gone, too. It had been dragged away along the streets, chained behind a rumbling phalanx of Los Sucio Harleys. A report from an eyewitness at the taco stand alerted the cops. A number of young Americans were seen headed to the beach where the migrants where camped.

The lieutenant, who feared displeasing the local lords, took some SWAT team members and headed for the shore where the onlooker had seen them amassing.

16.

right now

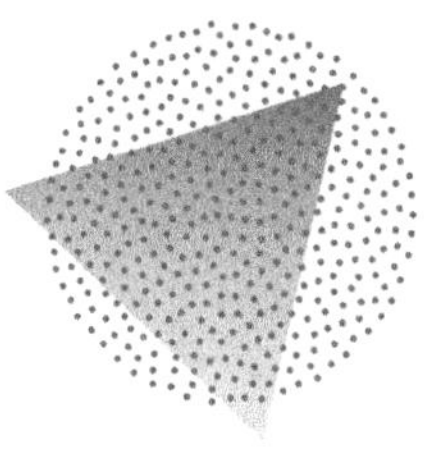

time and tide are not our friend. We have no choice, nowhere to hide. We cannot wait for the late afternoon's lowest tide. With the clothes on our backs, we're in the water up to our armpits, making our way to the U.S. of A., walking into the Pacific Ocean along the barrier wall. It's colder than I expected, and shivering adds to the urgency of our task. The undertow is strong and makes balance that much more difficult for each of us. With our right hands on the wall, our left hands are linked, one to another, in a chain. I'm first, followed by Fern, Leticia, VJ, and last, Aeura. Fern's hand is shaking. It reverberates through mine. She's always a rock, confident and courageous. Not this time. I sense mortal fear. She doesn't have to say it, but she does.

Don't let go of me, Gilly.

-I won't.

Gripping tight, we make our way, step by perilous step, like the unfortunate migrants we have seen for years on news clips. And, like many of them, we're fleeing for our lives from the criminal gangs. Seeing us go for the border crossing in the less-than-ideal conditions, a migrant mother and child are inspired to risk it, too. The young Latina and her son fight through a wave to catch up to us. The brown-skinned woman with raven hair can't be any older than us. She grabs hold of Aeura's wrist, and Aeura grabs hers back with assurance. We're all in this together. A towering wave cracks over the head of the jetty wall and splashes down on our faces. The salt water prickles, and I'm stalled, slipping, losing footing. I lean back against the cold concrete for a quick reboot and peek behind. Police gather on the shoreline. A bullhorn makes clear their intention.

Detengase!

Stop? As if! I pick up the pace, shouldering through the ocean's raw power. I pass the word down the line.

Keep coming!

-Ultimo aviso! Alto o disparo!!

Last warning. They're going to shoot.

Get down!

I lower into a crouch walk, with only my head above the water. I tug at Fern, who tugs at Leticia, and so on down our chain till all our bodies, including the migrant woman and child, are immersed.

Bullets blast, a volley riddling the barrier fence above us. It's terrifying. The migrant pair have thrown their fate in with ours, and I'm sorry that they're in harm's way. We hold our breath to duck under the waterline. I'm back in that black hole of a dream, underwater, trudging ahead in slo-mo. If only I could wake up in my bed. With each tortured stride, I feel the weight of many souls counting on me. The gunfire ceases. When I come up for air and stare ahead through the sea mist, the wall's dividing edge is in reach. I shake my left hand, and it vibrates along the lifeline as I count the heads that pop up, catching air. On the other side is home. The chain holds, and a surge of energy empowers the group.

Behind us, the police up their game and launch a Zodiac motorboat in pursuit of us. We can beat them. The closer we get to barrier's end, the more the current increases and the harder and more uncertain our steps become. It's the rip you must avoid or be pulled out to sea. The unnerving sound of the police boat's motor straining through the chop gets louder—all part of a horror movie soundtrack that plays in my head on repeat.

Wave!

An inside breaker crashes down and pins us flat against the wall. It hurts.

Keep coming!

We're so close. I don't notice the moment when the migrant mother loses her grip on her child. She breaks free of Aeura to swim for her boy. I do hear VJ's distress cry.

Aeura, no!

And I see Aeura, of all people, our weakest link. She casts off VJ's grip to go help the mother and child. Fern sees it, too, and squeezes my hand.

Keep going. You have to.

-Can't. Take them around, Fern. You got this!

Gilly!

I drop Fern's hand to save another. She's shattered. I don't look back. I swim for Aeura, duck diving a wave. Duke says that you only get so many chances to cheat death. He told me that without a liver, he'd reached the max. Have I already maxed out before I'm twenty-one? Pool guy's kid drowns. Good meme, bad optic. Ahead of me, Aeura and the mother and child are caught in the rip, pulled out in a building swell. If they fight it, it will exhaust them and it will win. I have to block the urge to swim directly toward them. I need to reach them on an angle, or I'll be caught in it, too. Parallel to shore is the safe way out of it. All I can think of as I stroke through the surf is that look on Fern's face. It may be the last I see of her and me, even if I survive.

My late mother always said that the tipping point for her and Pop's marriage was after a wild, all-night New Year's Eve beach party. When they got home, coming down, sobering up, she asked Duke the silly question: If she and his mother were drowning, who would he save first? He said his mother because his missus was the stronger swimmer. After that, Mom knew that it wasn't meant to be. I thought that was so damn unfair of her. She said it was a test that he'd failed. He could have lied, she explained. He should have lied. What can I say? Women have their own rules. Marlena tested VJ, flashing her lying red hair like a siren that lured him to his near death. To her credit, Leticia wouldn't fail VJ and gave him a makeup. Spirit soar, Marlena. It all began with you. And again, I'm atop a watery grave, hoping that I haven't overestimated my swimming strength.

Gilly!

Aeura sees me. I keep to the indirect course, drawing down deep with each watery reach. I turn my head for a peek. She's treading water with a crying child of about five hugging her around the neck. She's a better waterwoman than advertised, holding her own in the vicious elements, bouncing in a whitecap, not thrashing. The young mother near her is sinking fast. Exhausted, she gives up and goes under. Aeura cannot grab for her without losing the panicking kid. I have no choice. There is no time. Screw the angle. I swim right into the rip.

wedNeſdaY, Late afterNooN

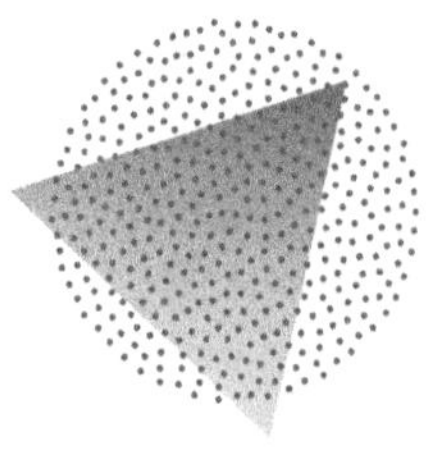

 than trudging out around the wall against the tide. They were jubilant, racing one another, splashing through the receding water on the US side of Friendship Park. They'd ducked behind the corner of the wall and were inside America, out of range of the Mexican police boat. The armed craft turned around at the demarcation. The trio were soaking wet and kissing the sand, the object of curiosity and scorn among the families of innocent parkgoers at their picnic tables at sunset. Surveillance cameras were everywhere. Two dispatched Border Patrol Jeeps were on their way. The trio shook out, steadied, and took stock.

Gilly?

-He's out there. Somewhere. After Aeura and... I should have helped.

--No, VJ!

-We all made it in one piece because we held together.

VJ climbed a dune for a better view of the sea. Leticia produced Donny's iPhone, wrapped in plastic from the takeout food.

It works. Sweet, 5G!

-Can I use it now?

I have a better idea. Let's go live. Worked once before.

It did a few years back, when they hacked into a cable TV business network to expose the murderer behind a stock IPO. Fern was their anchorwoman in that fake broadcast and was convincing enough to bring down the criminal kingpin. Leticia didn't forget. She slid into Donny's Instagram app and started an IG live broadcast. The cell phone's camera framed Fern like a talking head, with the approaching Border Patrol Jeeps in the background.

You're live, Fern. Identify yourself for the court of social media.

-I'm Fern Fifer from Beverly Hills at the southern border wall, sneaking back into the United States. I have no makeup on, and I have no ID. I'm not convinced which is more important. My friends and I are being chased by a Mexican cartel that falsely accused us of murder, and we need asylum ASAP. Can someone watching vouch that we're American citizens? Fern Fifer, Leticia Almora, VJ Ohara, Aeura Kim, and Gilly Montrose. Write it down, peeps, and share! Call your power people. We need help! Free the Five!

Leticia turned the camera on herself to add:

And call our parents to watch this. We are live. Free the Five!

She videos the Jeeps arriving to arrest them. Fern mock gestures their arrival for the camera like she's Vanna on *Wheel of Fortune.* VJs interrupts, pointing off with urgency.

I see him! They got Gilly! Free the Five!

***

In their Zodiac, the Mexican police had to stand down and watch, with their guns lowered, as we drifted into open water on the US side. Head bobbing in the water, eyes crusted to slits, muscles in fatigue, I was determined, if nothing else. I had hold of the migrant woman, and Aeura had her kid. Holding together, tied with a T-shirt I'd removed, we'd frog-kicked and sidestroked our way parallel to the shore to lose the undertow's rip. The surface current to our good fortune carried us along north, not south. A US Border Patrol boat was there to fish us out of the high surf and into their boat. The rescue was not met with a celebratory mood from the border agents who treated us like illegals, and foolish ones at that.

In front of me, Aeura, the mother, and her child were seated, and we were each put in zip cuffs. It would have made for a fine photo tableau, if someone could have snapped one. Exhausted all, bound wrists in our laps, Aeura's head rested on my shoulder, the young woman's head leaned on Aeura, and the child's head found comfort on his mother's chest. Aeura's breathing synched with mine, and the mother's and child's did, too. With a shared solar blanket over our heads, we were like one living organism—*living* being the operative word. With a declaration in mind, I started singing the Springsteen classic, drumming my bound hands on my thighs. Aeura harmonized, picking up the beat to "Born in the U.S.A."

Truth. We were born in the USA. It actually got a smile from the boomer border guard.

The patrol boat powered off for the homeland, and we kept singing.

18.

rigHt NOW

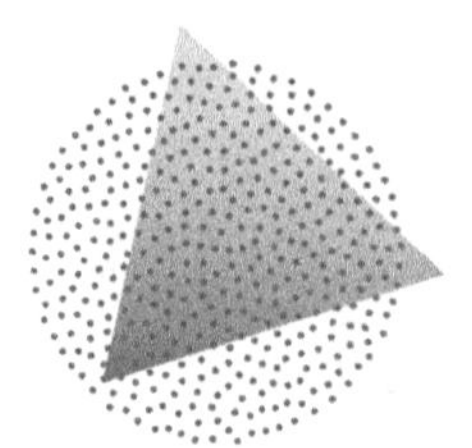

It's sweet to be reunited with everyone, even though it's in the migrant detention center outside Imperial Beach. Yes, it's a holding cage, but it's our cage—we five together—and no one's chasing us. Fern stands before me, all business, and repeats it in case I have water in my ears.

Gilly. You let go of me.

-I had to, Fern. I...had to.

Like the Duke, I don't lie. And, like a drowning man, I see my romantic life with Fern flash before my eyes. She's my ride or die, too amazing to lose like this. I know that I'll forever regret abandoning her. Everyone's watching.

Gilly doing Gilly. What's more surprising? That or that I can't help loving you?

She surprises me with a lips-seeking-missile of a kiss. Our friends—Aeura, Leticia, and VJ—actually applaud. My embarrassment and elation run neck and neck.

We all look so lame, like TV extras in numbered orange jumpsuits, waiting to be processed out of this holding zoo and moved. Without papers, we're treated like our young mother and boy.

Aeura introduces us to Estella and Rico. Estella is a natural beauty from El Salvador, a teacher in her village, looking for a better life, a safer life. She's grateful and shines, embracing me.

Estella should be hugging Aeura.

-Oh, we've hugged. Yours is due. Give into it.

Estella won't let go of me. Rico piles on. I see how much Fern is enjoying this. My happiness is hers. Go figure. Lightheaded, dehydrated, but clear as a bell, I realize that a lasting relationship is built day by day. Good day, bad day, the stats add up. How you made her happy, how you hurt her. Knowing what not to say and when not to say it. It can be learned. You can get better at a relationship, can't you? Follow the running tally. There's gotta be daily interest accrued, equity grown weekly that can sustain you through those bad times. Duke would say, *It's how you walk through the fire.* Of course he'd be quoting the LA poet Charles Bukowski, whom my mother warned me about. I'd add to that. It's how you do it together, what you share to survive that fire. My mother and father didn't make it through. And neither did Fern's, Aeura's, or Leticia's. We're "children of divorce," with only VJ experiencing the stability and trauma of two overbearing parents. What a bunch of broken, happy campers we are. Against the odds, we all still believe in love and—dare I say—marriage. Did I ask Fern the other day? An OMG, would be appropriate.

And seriously, why won't Estella and Rico let go of me?

A Department of Homeland Security guard unlocks our group cell and calls our numbers, leading us out. Uncertain, we five follow, escorted down a cement hallway that leads to a large, tented area.

Dad!

Fern bursts out, seeing her father. Dressed in his country club best, Philip Fifer is behind a barricade, standing with the other excited families. VJ's folks are here. Leticia and Aeura's moms are crying. Waving a cell phone and palming a cigarette is Abby Jo. We're kept apart by the government security. Everyone's talking at once. Everyone hears every word.

I got Duke on FaceTime!

-Mr. Fifer flew us all here.

--You're being released.

---...into our custody!

--You look sick.

-Are they feeding you?

--Fern's IG went viral!

---See you soon!

We're overwhelmed. The guards don't let us linger. They herd us to a double-door exit. Abby Jo is persistent and moves with us along the barricade, phone in my face.

Say hi to Duke with his new liver!

-Dad! Ya! Super ya!

I see him on the display screen in his hospital bed. He throws me a two-handed kiss.

--Glad it's not VJ's. Hey, you're famous again, kid. It's all over the news.

-What? What?

I don't get to hear the answer. We're out the doors to a waiting DHS van that VJ says is taking us to the federal building in San Diego for debriefing. Outside, the wind is whipping on the cloudiest day. A cheer erupts as a growing cluster of young protestors catches sight of us. They're behind a chain-link fence and holding signs of support for us. A local network news truck and camera crew capture the moment live. The demonstrators start a chant.

Free the Five! Free the Five! Free the Five!

Despite the guards' order, Fern, Aeura, Leticia, VJ, and I stop in place to acknowledge the unexpected fandom. The Stars and Stripes on the pole outside the detention center flaps in a metronomic backbeat, a Levon Helm drum riff, encore applause. The chant builds in rhythm, our chests swell, and like an Olympic team with hands clasped together, we raise them high over our heads in victory.

Oh yeah.

***

(In the movie version, I see us in the government van, passing cheering fans on the side of the road and under a freeway overpass with a banner hanging down, music swelling: Free the Five. In reality, the DHS van got a flat tire on the way and we waited at a Poway Chevron station in a dust storm for two hours, laughing and eating vending machine candy and chips, until five rental Kias took us separately to San Diego, avoiding the glare of the media. That was perfect, too.)

NINE MONTHS LATER

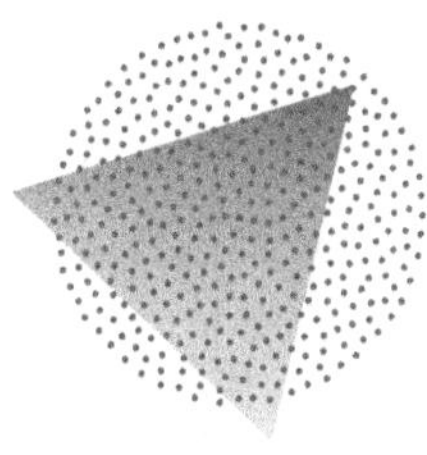

THE STATE DEPARTMENT TRIED TO KEEP A LID ON IT AS MUCH AS POSSIBLE. With Flip Marks's deposition, the truth came out that their appointed senior man in Baja, the late Consul Craig, was on the payroll of a Mexican cartel. The circumstances of his death made a cover-up impossible. VJ's testimony about the deadly organ-harvesting operation was corroborated by Diego Ortiz, in exchange for his immunity. The result: Heads rolled on both sides of the border. A US congressional investigation was still to come. The cartel power vacuum created by the deaths of the two top chiefs gave rise to new strongmen who had no interest in pursuing vengeance against us. The *federales*, exposed in their complicity, along with local police, were compelled to drop the charges against us.

And it got better. Flip was offered the Baja consulship for his heroic action and integrity. He declined it, further pissing off his father. Instead, he took a better position in Washington, D.C., with the Justice Department. Yes, he and Aeura are living together in Georgetown. She's working for a nonprofit focused on preventing violence toward women in conflict zones. Her emails to me are so upbeat that I've learned to stow away my silly jealousy and enjoy their happiness.

Antonio fell into it. He lost his job at the Todos Santos hospital and went back to Ensenada. Persistent, he hooked up with Maya, the band singer. He teased that, minus the tattoos, she looked just like the alluring Joy on *Beverly Hills, 90210*. Being around her, he started to help manage Guapo and booked the band at a Cabo spring music festival. It got them great exposure and a new tour bus for their first mainland tour. Antonio earned his seat at the front as manager, sound engineer, medic, roadie, and most important to him, Maya's main man.

Our friend and savior Sgt. Alvarado was promoted to a captainship with the Baja State Police and gifted with a new Chevy Silverado. His former partner—the lady cop who betrayed us—was relieved of duty and had her pension stripped. Bite that.

The single mother and child from El Salvador, Estella and Rico, were granted asylum based on the fact that she was a victim of sexual assault, and they settled in Orange County with relatives. We all follow each other on Facebook, IG, and TikTok. We five were not five anymore—our circle of friends and *compañeros de armas* had grown.

Not everything was sweet. Bunky Green died. In a medical miracle, he survived the Tijuana hospital. Fully recovered from being shot in the back, he enjoyed a resurgence of work and respect on his return. On a cross-country tour as the drummer with a revamp of the band America, he caught COVID-19 and died. It was so wrong, after everything he'd been through with us. At the memorial, Donny was beyond grateful that he had all that time on the lam with his dad. The pot-infused memorial at the Troubadour was classic rock-star–studded, and Bunky would have dug it. Donny was more than a year sober and made his mother proud. He got a managerial position at Hillcrest Country Club and had a bevy of Beverly Hills beauties vying for his manicured hand.

Leticia and VJ returned to their schools. VJ quit yoga and mindfulness and got back to junk-food–enabled late-night video-gaming, which for him was healthier. Leticia stopped taking birth control and micromanaging VJ.

Fern was all about me being me. She was only going to be in Paris for her classes and, if I didn't want to live with her in the City of Light, she understood. For sure, it was a Fern feat of reverse psychology. Feeling flattered at the freedom of choice, I fell for it. Paris became my new address.

Fern and I were together, making it work, day by day. She was deep into her architecture courses. I was learning French and studying prelaw at UCLA online. Go Bruins!

In our *très* hip Rive Gauche flat near Café de Flore, we were finalizing August plans for a long-awaited spa week in Saint-Malo, when our cell phones dinged at the same time. It was an urgent group text from Leticia. It had a geolocation map pin and an August date and time when we were expected to show up. Nothing more except the epigram:

Ask me no questions, I'll tell you no lies.

The map pin was dropped, longitude and latitude, in the Southern Hemisphere, in the Remarkables, a set of mountains south of Queenstown, South Island, New Zealand.

That was all it took.

Spa week scrapped, me besties. See you in NZ!

acknowledgments

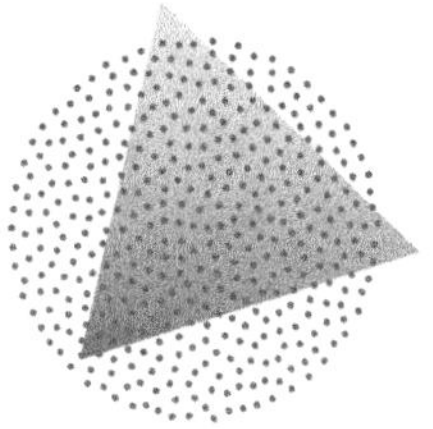

i am a lucky man to be surrounded by my wife Dee and sons, Johnnie and Jackson, daughter-in-law Stephanie, and grandson August John. They helped guide my days and nights in California, Ohio, and Massachusetts while I got to go along for a wild Baja ride with Gilly and company. Thank you, Mollins!

Also, thanks and gratitude to my publisher Virginia Underwood of Shadelandhouse Modern Press and her talented team, Carly Schnur and Shannon Wright, and to my readers.

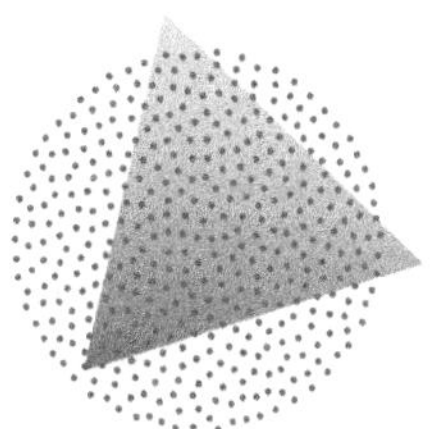

About the Author

Before Moving to Los Angeles, Larry Mollin was a playwright and the artistic director of Homemade Theatre, a seminal performance group of the 1970s in Toronto, Canada. Transitioning to Hollywood, he wrote and produced prime time TV for over 30 years, beginning with *CHiPs*. He is best known for his work on *Beverly Hills, 90210*, for which he wrote and produced 128 hours from 1993–1998—the zenith of the show's success. Mollin returned to the theater world in 2012 with a 1960s-themed trilogy of plays produced in New York City, London, and Martha's Vineyard.

Turning to long form, he created the *Max Dean Adventures*, a trio of novels about an aging detective with a rock-and-roll background. Mollin is also a published poet and songwriter, as well as the cohost of the internationally popular podcast *Beverly Hills 90210 Show*.

The *Pool Guy's Kid*, published in 2024, was Larry's first young adult novel and the first book in The Pool Guy's Kid series. It introduced Gilly Montrose and his friends in an action-packed adventure brimming with fun, danger and kissing. *Crushing Cabo*, book two in The Pool Guy's Kid series, with Gilly and company, delivers even more excitement and romance from a master of the young adult genre.

Learn more about Larry Mollin and his work at larrymollin.com and follow Larry on TikTok @mambochicken2 and on Instagram @mambochicken.